OUTFLANKED!

"They're flanking us," Major Thornburg said. "We can't keep riding or they will cut us off from the supply wagons. Start the retreat. Get the men back to the wagons where we can circle them and defend ourselves."

"They're comin' at us from both flanks, sir," Rankin said. He no longer needed to look through his binoculars. The enemy was coming so fast that they would ride over the Army position in a matter of minutes. "Open fire. We've got to hold 'em at bay till most of the boys reach the wagons."

Thornburg drew his pistol and cocked it but did not give the order.

"Sir, there, along the ridge. Indians. Give the order to fire on them," Rankin urged.

"I'm sorry, Mr. Rankin, but I cannot. It runs counter to my orders. If they fire on us, we may defend ourselves. Otherwise, we can't shoot at all."

"That order's gonna be our death," Rankin said. He pulled his rifle from its scabbard.

The Ute let out bloodcurdling cries and attacked the soldiers.

WHITE RIVER MASSACRE

KARL LASSITER

PINNACLE BOOKS
Kensington Publishing Corp.
http://www.kensingtonbooks.com

While based on actual events, this novel is a work of fiction.

First Printing: April 2002
10 9 8 7 6 5 4 3 2 1

Printed in the United States of America

For Gwynne.
Lots of years, lots of schemes. Someday the jackpot . . .

It seems to me evident that the greatest obstacle to civilizing the majority of these Indians [Ute] is their ownership of horses, which is proved by the fact that those who work have either few or no horses. An Indian who has a band of horses devotes all his time to them and to racing. Such a one will not work, nor will he sell any of this stock, but he is clamorous for goods and supplies, and, having influence by means of his possessions, he is an obstacle to progress.

Letter from Nathan Meeker to
Commissioner Edward Hayt,
April 1879

THE BEAR DANCE

March 15, 1878
A High Park on the Western Slopes
of the Rocky Mountains

The Tabeguache band of the Ute assembled in the high meadow for the first ritual dance celebrating spring. Cray Eachin shifted nervously from one foot to the other, wondering how the hell he had convinced himself that sneaking into the most important ceremony of the season was a good idea. Then he saw her.

Towa was about the most beautiful woman he had ever laid eyes on. She wasn't tall, but carried herself proudly, chin high and ebony eyes bright and alert. Her long black hair was pulled back and held in place above her eyes by a headband fashioned from a broad strip of ginger-colored bear fur. He knew it was bear fur because he had made it for her.

The young woman strode past where he stood in shadows hoping to catch a glimpse of her. An electric surge filled the air, more compelling than the steady beat of the Ute drums down near the bonfire. Their eyes locked, hers dark and his chocolate brown. In that instant a world of communication passed between them. She reached up and brushed her fingers along the bearskin band, smiled, then pointedly looked away and joined other maidens around the blazing fire a dozen yards away.

"She knows I gave it to her," Cray said to himself, smiling like a fool. The Ute were good hunters, and all the braves could boast of killing a bear, sometimes with only a knife. Cray had not been that courageous or skilled. For him it had been a matter of killing the bear before it killed him. It wasn't any great feat of pluck or hunting prowess that had brought the she-bear to his camp. The bear had been half starved, and had hunted for food after rousing from a warm, dry winter. The bear had started pawing through his supplies while he watched in futile rage. Cray had decided to let the bear have all the food she wanted, until the close-set, hate-filled ursine eyes had turned on him and chosen him as a better meal.

His first shot had been accurate—and had only infuriated the bear. His musket had spat out its .60-caliber ball to a target directly between the squinting eyes. The thick bone of the bear's skull had deflected the musket ball, even as it must have given the enraged creature one massive headache to avenge. Not having time to reload his rifle when the bear charged him, Cray had hightailed it up the slope toward his mine.

Cray swallowed hard as he remembered how he had started to run into the narrow, ineptly shored-up shaft, only to decide he didn't want the bear looming between him and escape. If he was going to be bottled up, he wanted a chance at fighting for his life that being trapped in a mine shaft did not offer. He had spun around, grabbed a long pry bar, and used it to lever up a large rock that had tumbled downhill during the winter, budging it slowly at first, and then with increasingly deadliness, into the bear.

He had crushed the hungry bear in less time than it would have taken him to reload his ancient musket.

The bearskin had cured nicely, and he had made jaunty ornaments out of the claws and teeth. But he had taken special care to make the headband attractive, combing and cleaning it a dozen times before he was satisfied. He had left it in front of Towa's father's tepee, praying to a God he didn't believe much in anymore that the lovely young girl would find it before Kanneatche discovered it. On that spring morning almost a week before, Cray had watched anxiously until Towa poked her head out and grabbed for the lovely headband. He had ducked away since her father hadn't liked him when they first met.

Truth was, none of the Tabeguache Ute much liked Cray because he was rooting around hunting for gold in mountains promised them in an 1868 treaty. But the lure of riches was strong enough for Cray to dare even their ire. After all, he had killed a bear. A few Indians weren't going to run him off when he was certain he would pull true color out of the mine.

And the lure of Towa's beauty was enough for him to face the wrath of her father, whose twin brother, Curicata, was chief of this band of Tabeguache Ute.

Now Cray stepped even farther back into the constantly twisting shadows cast by the bonfire as Kanneatche came strutting from his tepee, his old plug hat looking out of place amid the other braves in

their finery as they prepared for the dance. Cray
had asked about Kanneatche's curious headgear
and had been told, somewhat contemptuously by
another miner, how it had been given to him by a
printer in Denver when Kanneatche and Curicata
had visited the *Rocky Mountain News* offices. A large,
dangling white tag with the inscription "Superior
Cocktail Bitters" flapped as Kanneatche swaggered
about, as if he were the reason the Bear Dance was
being performed this night.

Cray knew the festivities hid his presence as well
as anything could. From the way Towa glanced sur-
reptitiously in his direction, feigning a lack of interest in anything but the progress of the Bear
Dance, the object of his affections was not likely to
say anything to her father. Kanneatche was something of a roué, and inclined to get drunk whenever he could, giving Cray added reason to give the
man a wide berth. Kanneatche might have five
wives, but that didn't mean he would look kindly
on his favorite daughter taking up with a white
man who wanted only one.

He took an involuntary step forward to follow
Towa as she and the other bear dancers moved
away from the fire to the dance area, set off by willow poles interwoven with horizontally twined tree
branches. Cray hurried around to the east side so
he could watch them enter the enclosure. His heart
hammered in his chest as he saw Towa vanish to
one side of the cleared area. He stared straight
across the meadow to the west side at the large
hole, symbolizing a bear's den. He remembered his
own fight with the she-bear, and had the sinking
feeling he had to do even more if he wanted to
win Towa's hand.

Cray jumped when six Ute drummers squatted

around the hole, lowered a huge drum, and began a rhythmic beat that seemed to penetrate to
the core of his soul. They did not use drumsticks,
but laid a curved, notched stick on the taut deerskin, then dragged a gleaming white bone rapidly
over the notches. The reverberation made the
very ground shiver and shake in sympathy. When
they started to sing, the dancers moved, the
women going to the south side and the men to
the north.

Cray swallowed hard as he moved closer to the
entry of the enclosure, his eyes on Towa alone. He
didn't even realize he was moving toward her as
the women all moved across the willow-ringed
dance area and began pointing to the men. Towa
smiled and reached out to him, drawing him forward even more.

The chanting began to rise in volume and the
tempo changed. The odd resonance of the sticks
on the hide drumhead sent Cray's blood racing. Or
was it Towa who excited him? The other men
formed a line, and he found himself advancing
with them to where the women waited. For the first
time he realized he had joined the dance, and self-
consciously looked around, wondering what he
ought to do. If he bolted and ran, everyone would
notice. But while he stood in the line with the
other men, no one took notice of him. The men
had eyes only for the women.

And Towa had eyes only for him.

Cray walked forward at the end of the line and
reached out for Towa, who took his hand. In time
with the music, they began the Bear Dance, two
fearless steps forward, three small ones in timid retreat. As the men advanced, the women ran away;
the dance reversed when the women boldly stepped

forth. Cray was not certain how long they danced like this, but his legs began to cramp. Somehow, being with Towa and not having anyone object to his presence overrode any physical discomfort.

Towa pulled her hand from his and stepped back so she could look past Cray. He glanced over his shoulder and saw a brave decked out in a bearskin come mincing into the enclosure. The bear-man tumbled and danced and reared up and then fell over.

Cray wasn't sure if it was from nervous release or simply because the antics amused him, but he laughed. The small buzz that had passed for conversation among the others died suddenly and all eyes fixed on him.

"No, I—" He had no idea what he had done, but he had drawn unwanted attention. He was sure they would throw him out—or worse. Kanneatche didn't like him, and might scalp him.

Cray swallowed hard when he saw the bear-man roll to his feet and come stalking over. The bearhead bobbed almost hypnotically and held Cray fixed to the spot. Somehow, he couldn't look away from the gaping mouth filled with sharp yellowed teeth, although the bear had long since died.

With a cry of alarm, Cray jumped back when the bear-man made clawing motions at him and reared up to growl ferociously. Laughter rippled through the lines of men and women, setting the bear-man off on a new hunt for others to paw at and menace.

"It's all right," Towa said softly. "The bear is angry when he comes out of hibernation."

The resonant drumming began and the dance resumed, this time with the bear-man joining in. Cray danced and danced until he was sure he could go no longer, then danced some more as the first light of dawn streaked over the mountains to the east. The Shining Mountains, the Ute called them, and he knew why. The pale light dribbled down like liquid silver and lent a magical aspect to the land.

Still the Bear Dance continued.

Cray found himself barely shuffling as Towa came toward him. When he had to advance on her, his legs almost refused to move. Muscles knotted from more than twelve hours of dancing, but he saw that the others kept at it with dogged determination. Or did until the man next to him stumbled and fell. Cray started to help, but a warning cry from Towa froze him in his tracks.

The bear-man rushed over and jumped about, growling and pawing at the exhausted dancer. When this did not rejuvenate the brave, the medicine man shuffled closer, carrying a notched stick he had taken from a drummer. As the drumbeat continued, the medicine man lightly whacked the fallen brave's legs in matching cadence, and he worked his way up to the man's head.

Still the fallen man did not regain his feet. The medicine man repeated his treatment, and this time energy flowed into the exhausted brave, who was now revived enough to join in the dance again. Seeing the attention the brave had received from the bear-man, the medicine man, and the rest of the dancers convinced Cray to force down his own weakness and continue the rhythmic step the best he could.

Almost in a daze, the sun high over his head after more hours of dance, Cray was not sure what happened when he stumbled. He tried to regain his balance, but a sharp push sent him reeling.

"Towa?" He wanted to ask why she was shoving him away like this. He had done everything the others had—more! He had not weakened so much that he needed the medicine man's healing touch.

She shook her head slightly, then reached to brush her fingers along the bearskin band around her forehead. How Cray wished those fingers touched his skin.

He let her shove him ever backward until he noticed the other women were doing the same to the men they had chosen as their partners. When he bumped into the enclosure wall on the north side, the drumming stopped. The women turned and silently left, but Towa paused at the entrance and smiled at him.

Then she was gone.

Cray stood alone, wondering what he should do now. The smell of meat roasting made his mouth water. The other men walked away, one by one, going to their tepees. Cray wasn't a member of the tribe and had no tepee. But Towa had smiled at him, and he had danced with her, and no one had objected.

Feeling full of himself, Cray left the willow enclosure, intending to go to Towa and declare his love for her. He had made his way from the sin and degradation of New Orleans, across dusty Texas and New Mexico Territory, working at a dozen different jobs, and had never seen a woman who could hold a candle to Towa. Emboldened, Cray hurried through the Tabeguache village, only to slow and eventually stop and stare.

Kanneatche stood outside his tepee, arms crossed over his broad chest and looking fierce. Towa knelt by a cooking fire, her eyes downcast and her shoulders slumped in defeat. Cray Eachin sidled away and silently retreated the long miles to his claim, damning himself for being such a coward and wishing he was not confirming the arrogant, drunken warrior's opinion of all *Maricat'z*.

A CHIEF RETURNS

April 2, 1878
Near San Juan

The assembled Uncompahgre and Tabeguache Ute heard the cries go up long before Chief Ouray rode into sight. The women crowded close together and the men stood with arms folded, waiting for their leader to tell them tales of the white man's strange, far-off dwellings. The times before when he had returned from Washington, D.C., Ouray had regaled them with stories of immense, peculiar buildings of white stone, dinners with amounts of food beyond comprehension, strange dress, and even stranger behavior. They exchanged glances when Ouray and his attendants rode proudly up the valley toward the large village.

Ouray drew rein, looked down at the assembled bands, and held back a smile. It was good to return home after such a tiring trip. He had fought the best he could—with words—and had threatened the *Maricat'z* with the force of a thousand warriors only when it had become necessary. He had enjoyed their rich food and large, soft beds, but it was good to be home.

"Chief," greeted his brother-in-law, Sapavanari. Ouray looked past his hulking in-law to where his lovely wife, Chipeta, stood, a broad grin on her face. He had only one wife; he wanted no more as long as he had Chipeta.

"My brother," Ouray greeted, slipping from the saddle. He landed lightly enough, but the pain that shot up through his legs told him too many winters had passed for him to ride as he had when he was a young brave. He should get the white man's chief to give him one of the fancy wagons, or even a carriage, although it was not very practical in such rugged terrain. But what did that matter? He was chief of the Ute and deserved easier transportation. Had not the great chief in Washington declared him to be *tawacz viem* over all the People?

"You look tired," Sapavanari said, eyeing him closely. Ouray always got the feeling that his brother-in-law was a sharp-toothed wolf and *he* was a rabbit timidly peering from its hole and hoping not to be eaten.

"I am well," Ouray said brusquely, pushing past Sapavanari and going to his wife. Chipeta smiled even more broadly and reached out to him eagerly. He took her hands in his. "It is good to be home."

"You will be even happier soon," Chipeta said boldly. Ouray had to laugh. His wife would be the death of him—not her brother. And what a delightful death it would be!

"Tell us everything you saw," urged a brave whom Ouray did not recognize immediately. "Tell us what happened with the *Maricat'z* and their lying tongues."

Ouray stared hard at the warrior and saw he was from a northern band of the *Nunt'z,* a Yampa brave eager for the old chief to make a mistake. Since the Treaty of 1868 there had been bad feelings between the Southern and Northern tribes.

"The *Maricat'z* are strange people, riding on *panakarpo,* their wood and glass carriages that roll along on steel rails faster than any pony can race. Everything they do is rushed. Let us smoke a pipe," Ouray said, pointedly chiding the Yampa brave for his rudeness.

Ouray and others crowding close went with him to his tepee, where he brought out his pipe and carefully tamped in tobacco given him by the leader of the *Maricat'z* he had met, Secretary Karl Schurz. Sinking to the ground and sitting cross-legged in spite of the stiffness in his legs, Ouray puffed a moment, then passed the pipe. As the medicine pipe made its circuit, Ouray considered the threats posed to the Tabeguache—north of the Southern Ute—by the restless Northern faction. The Yampa were less likely to cause unrest than the Nupartka, although Ouray had to reconsider this in light of the brave so aggressively questioning him. To the south of the Tabeguache were the Capote, Mouache, and Weeminuche, all unfailingly loyal to him.

What trouble brewed up north and how could he avoid it? Washington had placed a great burden on his shoulders, requiring him to keep the various bands united and peaceful.

Ouray took the pipe again, puffed, and heaved a deep sigh as he exhaled a cloud of blue-white smoke.

"The *Maricat'z* tobacco is good," he said, carefully choosing his words. "The supplies they send us are good, too." He puffed and passed the pipe for another round before he continued. "Perhaps they will send the blankets and food on *panakarpo* or overland on huge gray animals so tall I could stand on Sapavanari's shoulders and still not see over the top."

A titter went up at Ouray's outrageous claim. This pleased him. He had their attention now.

"The ears on what the *Maricat'z* call an elephant are larger than any blanket stolen from my rump by my *piwán* in the middle of a cold winter night." Ouray got another chuckle at this. The idea of his wife, Chipeta, stealing his blanket so his haunches would turn cold amused them. "They parade such strange creatures up and down their streets; then they put them into cages."

Silence fell at this.

"They will not put the *Nunt'z* into cages," Ouray declared, knowing the thoughts that ran through his people's minds. Such thoughts had already occurred to him.

"What of the agreements?" rudely demanded the Yampa brave. "They steal our land inch by inch, day by day. They dig for their filthy black rock."

"Coal mining was approved all along the mountains," Ouray said with some distaste. "But no other mining. They cannot dig for their gold or silver. The *tawacz viem* in Washington says only the rock that burns will be taken."

"It is *our* land!"

"The land of the Shining Mountains is ours and will remain ours," Ouray said forcefully. "No one will fight the *Maricat'z* and give their great chief reason to bring soldiers into our land. No one will pluck even one hair from their scalps, unless I say so."

"Even the arrogant new agent who makes his

home along the Smoking Earth River?" asked the Yampa.

Ouray had not known there was a new agent.

A NEW BROOM

May 1, 1878
White River Agency

"It is only a dream, but I can make it happen," Nathan Meeker said, staring out across the grassy meadowlands above the White River Agency with appreciation and great anticipation of the chore ahead of him. In a normal year, the grass would have been verdant and rippling with the ceaseless breeze, but now it was tinged in brown from lack of rain. Even the normally wide, fast-moving White River flowed sluggishly, the victim of poor snowfall in the winter and sparse spring runoff from the high mountains.

"What's that?" asked the guide. He spat, scratched himself, and wished the trip was over. This was the last time he ever hired on as scout for the Department of the Interior, no matter how good they paid. Listening to the old codger rattle on endlessly all the way over the Rockies from Greeley had been a chore he wasn't likely to repeat any time soon. Better to take the job Major Thornburg had offered over at Fort Fred Steele, though he wasn't much inclined to the rigid Army life. Better to wrestle warring Cheyenne and Arapaho stark naked and blindfolded. He spat again, wondering if there was any chaw left in his saddlebags.

"You look out and see only savage wilderness populated by heathens," Meeker said haughtily. "I see plowed fields and toiling red men engaged undauntedly in agriculture."

"You got better eyes 'n me," the guide said, squinting into the bright Colorado sun. He remembered that he didn't have any more chaw. Meeker had seen it, grabbed the small package, and thrown it into a stream. The guide wasn't above putting a little tobacco that had been water-soaked into his mouth—he had done far worse in his day—but the stream had been flowing rapidly and he had lost sight of the tinfoil pouch in the dark.

"Your eyesight may be better than mine," Meeker said grandly, "but my vision far exceeds yours."

"Your family comin' soon?"

"In a few months, after they settle accounts in Greeley," Meeker said, some bitterness coming into his tone. "The death of Mr. Greeley left us in poor financial condition."

"Heard tell he stiffed a lot of folks by up and dyin'. Debts all over the place and his family wants accounts settled. You one of them settlers in that godforsaken place that owed the banks for your land?"

"For land and seed," Meeker said. "Moreover, there are spurious claims that Mr. Greeley never held title to any of the settlement we proved for him."

"Cain't trust them Easterners," the guide said, wiping his lips after taking a deep drink from his canteen. It wasn't tobacco and it sure as hell wasn't whiskey, but it went down good. He didn't bother offering Meeker any. He had learned that the man had ideas of his own about what made for good drinking.

"I'm an Easterner," Meeker said coldly. "The Panic of '57 wiped out my investment in a store in southern Illinois."

"As long as you ain't one of them folks who does nuthin' but write about settlin', you're all right by me."

"I am the author of two books on farming," Meeker said, his dander rising. "Mr. Greeley was my mentor, and I not only wrote books but also owned and edited the *Greeley Tribune.*"

"Cain't say I heard of it," the guide said, wondering if he ought to keep needling Meeker. He knew most of the man's background, but had reached the point where Meeker's pompous behavior and holier-than-thou pronouncements had finally festered. "But then, I never paid much mind to the written word, 'specially words written by lyin' reporters out to scare the livin' daylights out of folks."

"Severalty," Meeker said.

"Beg pardon?" This brought the grizzled scout up short. "That some sort of cuss word? I thought I'd heard 'em all, but if it is, that's a new one on me."

"It is the policy I will follow in civilizing the native tribes. When I was given my appointment as Indian Agent by Secretary Schurz, we discussed the matter at length. The problem with the savages is that there is no private ownership of the land."

"The tribe owns the land, leastwise around White River," the guide said, taken aback by the sudden change in direction of the conversation. He had never gotten used to the way Meeker's mind flowed one way only. It might stray for a moment, but always snapped back into the same riverbed, torrentially flowing as it swept away all logic.

"That is precisely the problem. Individual ownership of the land is necessary for the individual Ute to work and prosper. Toil. Each Ute male should plow his own field on his own land and reap the rewards of his personal effort."

"They ain't farmers," the guide said. "Not that I much noticed. They hunt. Damned good at it, too. The only thing they might be better at's raising horses and racin' 'em. Don't go bettin' them on a race or they'll take you for every penny you got. I know. I've watched 'em for years."

"Do not swear, sir."

"Sorry," the guide said, wanting the trip to be over quickly. He had reached the end of his rope with Nathan Meeker. All he had intended was to pass along some friendly advice to the man, and it got Meeker all hot and bothered about the way he'd said it.

"There are other problems. Life is far too easy in this park, as they call it. Look at it!"

"Purty, ain't it? Course, it's usually a lot greener after the rains."

"A day's hunting brings in a week of food. That shall cease. Agriculture shall rule the White River Agency or I shall know the reason!"

By nightfall they reached the agency headquarters, and not an instant too soon for the guide.

"This is where we part company, Mr. Meeker," the guide said. "You want to make your mark on this here paper so's I can collect my fee back in Denver, I'll be travelin' on right away."

"It's almost dark. You are allowed to stay."

"That's real neighborly of you, but I got to go," the guide said, handing over the sheaf of sweat-stained papers he had carried since leaving Greeley. Meeker took them, scribbled his name, and thrust them back. "Much obliged," the guide said. He looked up to see the former agent coming from a cabin.

"Reverend Danforth?" said Meeker as he slipped from horseback and walked stiffly to where the man stood in the doorway. Sixty years of age was too old to be riding for days on end, Meeker decided, but somehow the excitement of relieving the former agent of his chore lent an almost preternatural energy to Meeker's step.

"Who might you be?" the reverend asked.

"Your replacement, sir. I am Nathan Meeker, come to bring order and prosperity to the White River Agency."

"Wasn't expecting you so soon," Danforth said. He looked up at the guide, licked his lips, and added, "I was on my way out to deal with some, uh, whiskey peddlers."

"What? On a reservation? Outrageous!" Meeker cried.

"Not on the reservation exactly, but along the fringes. It is deucedly hard keeping the settlers from dealing with the Ute, trading whiskey for elk meat and venison. I must give them a stern talking-to every time I hear of such trade."

Meeker looked up at the still-mounted guide, an expression of triumph on his face. "See?" he said. "When I educate the Ute properly and institute severalty, there will be no more trading of meat and hides for whiskey."

"Reckon not," agreed the guide. "All them Ute

warriors'll be busy plowing and planting and chasing away the crows tryin' to eat their seed grain."

"Are you too tuckered out from your trip, sir, or would you join me in finding these, uh, dealers in whiskey?" asked Danforth.

"It is a serious matter and one I must tend to if I am to be successful," Meeker said, thinking hard.

"Tell you what, Mr. Meeker," the guide said. "Why don't me and the reverend here go tend to rootin' out the liquor dealers for you? If I find 'em, I promise they won't be left with a single drop of corn squeezin'."

"Excellent," Meeker said, finding reason to approve of the rough-hewn agency guide for the first time since leaving Greeley.

"You get your gear unpacked," Danforth said to Meeker. "I, uh, I'll have mine out of here in a day or so and be on my way."

Meeker watched as Reverend Danforth and the guide rode off into the darkness to dissuade whiskey dealers from trading with the Ute. He sucked in a deep breath and looked around the cabin, desolate since three-legged stools and crude tables were all that had been built by the agency carpenters. But then they no doubt had better things to do other than furnishing luxuries for the agent's living quarters.

Meeker stepped outside and sucked in a deep breath as he looked out over the shadowy reaches of the valley around White River. The air was good here, but it would be better south of here in Powell's Valley. It would be well to shake up the Ute by moving the agency headquarters to show that new ways were going to be observed.

He certainly was not leaving behind sumptuous quarters. Meeker vowed to begin the move right away and build a decent dwelling for his darling wife Arvella and daughter Josephine before they arrived in July.

If he worked hard, he might even have the barbaric heathens out in their own fields tending summer crops. With this cheering thought, Nathan Meeker went back into the tiny cabin, laid out his bedroll, and was asleep in minutes, finally more exhausted by his tiring journey from Greeley than he was invigorated by the challenges before him.

GAINFUL EMPLOYMENT

June 14, 1878
White River Agency, Powell's Valley

"I don't know, Towa," Cray Eachin said, looking apprehensive. "It's a big step." He didn't add that it was away from what he wanted to do. Since making his way up from New Orleans after his folks and two brothers had died of cholera, he had worked at about every job possible, and not a single solitary one of them had offered him any hope for the future. Not until he reached the mountains above White River and found his claim.

It hadn't given up any gold yet, but it would. He felt it in his bones. And if digging around in the hard rock didn't yield gold, then there was always hope to find the black carbonates of lead that went along with silver. A decent silver strike would make him a fortune. Him and Towa.

He looked at the diminutive woman and saw the determination in her face. Her lips had thinned and her jaw was set harder than any of the rock he drilled and blasted in the mountainside. She had inherited a lot of traits from her father. One too many, Cray thought. When she got an idea into her head, nothing shook it free.

"We did the Bear Dance," she said heatedly, as if this explained everything.

"We did," he said, grinning like a fool. After the dance had been awkward, but he had finally returned to Kanneatche's tepee, resolved to have it out with Towa's father. The man hadn't been there, but the lovely woman had been. One thing had led to another, and he had spent the night with Towa. Somehow, in her mind that made them married, although Cray wouldn't feel easy about it until they stood up before a real preacher.

She took his powerful arm in both her hands and hugged him close. Resting her cheek against his rough woolen sleeve, she stood for a moment and let the silence do the arguing for her.

"I suppose it won't hurt to see what the new agent has in way of odd jobs," Cray said. "Don't reckon he'd pay well for them, but I have some spare time when I'm not working my claim."

"You cannot dig for gold on Ute land," Towa said. "My father does not like it. My uncle does not like it."

"Curicata might be the head fellow around here, but not even a Ute chief tells me what to do. Not when I strike it rich. We'll both be living high off the hog then, over in Denver or maybe back East. You'll love New Orleans. That place has pretty near anything you would ever want in the shops along Royal Street." He didn't mention the dens of depravity, the so-called coffeehouses where men bet on how many rats a terrier could kill in an hour, or the cribs in Pirate's Alley filled with soiled doves making lewd suggestions to anyone who walked past. Cray certainly did not tell her of the men who paid those women for their sexual favors.

"I have all I need," Towa said, squeezing harder on his brawny arm. She knew the right things to say to bring him down from his lofty ambitions. The Ute woman might say she had all she needed, implying *he* was just that, but he wanted to give her more. Living on hardtack and bear meat might be fine for a miner, but it wasn't enough for a man with a wife-to-be and the family to follow.

"A day or two, I could come down and tend the cattle," Cray said, eyeing the rude corrals where the agent penned a dozen head. "Don't see why he doesn't let them graze across the valley."

"He digs the earth," Towa said with some distaste. "He ruins fine hunting ground. He even tells the men they cannot race their horses because he wants to plow their track for a farm."

"That's the way it's done back East," Cray said, remembering the vast fields he had seen while traveling through Kansas and Missouri before heading back south to hunt for work in Texas.

"Then I do not want to go there," Towa said hotly. "I want my man to be a mighty hunter, not grubbing in the ground like that." She lifted her chin and indicated a few of the Ute who worked lethargically at the White River Agency.

"That one must be Mr. Meeker," Cray said, wanting to divert her outpouring of anger. The Ute weren't known as farmers, in spite of what Nathan Meeker proclaimed for one and all to hear. For his part, Cray would sooner have a plate of venison stew than bread baked from wheat raised on a small plot of land. A medium-size deer fed more people for a lot less work.

Towa tugged a little to get him moving. They went down the slope to where Meeker hammered stakes with fluttering blue ribbons into the ground. Cray wondered what the man was doing, and then figured it out. Meeker was laying out a road to run alongside several of the twenty-acre plots of land he had already fenced in with low rock walls.

"Good day, sir," Cray said in greeting, touching the brim of his floppy hat politely.

"And to you, sir," Meeker said somewhat coldly. He glared at Towa and the way she hung on Cray's arm. Cray shrugged her off, and Meeker's expression lightened a mite.

"This is a mighty impressive spread you've built in only a month or so," Cray said, trying to ease into asking for a handyman's job.

"I have done what I can to deal with Chief Douglass and get his band settled. Are you familiar with them?"

Cray shook his head, but from the corner of his eye he saw the slight sneer twisting Towa's lip. He wondered what Douglass had done to deserve her scorn. Douglass was principal chief of the Tabe-guache in the area and was, from all Meeker had heard, decent enough.

"An honest man, although lazy like so many of the heathens when it comes to actual work."

Cray blinked, wondering if Meeker intended to be insulting or if he even realized Towa understood every word he said. Most of the Ute spoke some English, and a few, like Chief Ouray, had been raised speaking Spanish, Navajo, and several other languages including English.

"I work a claim up in the hills. A gold mine," Cray said, trying to justify his hard work to the Indian Agent.

"Gold?" Meeker sniffed. "There's no gold here."

"Might be some silver then," Cray said.

"How can I aid you, sir?" Meeker said impatiently. He tapped his heavy hammer on the top of the stake, making certain it was securely driven into the soft, rich dirt. Because of the dry soil, it took extra work to drive the stake deeply enough for it to stand on its own.

"Seems like a man of your station ought to be doing other things and letting chores like laying out roads fall to someone else."

"Like you, sir?" Meeker looked from Cray to Towa, and then fixed his cold eyes on Cray. "I will not tolerate fornication on agency land. Nor will I provide sustenance for its vileness by employing—"

"Fornication?" asked Towa. She smiled for the first time, then tittered.

"She speaks real good English," Cray said. "And we're not, well, you know. We plan on getting married when we have enough money. You're not a preacher, are you? Since Reverend Danforth left, there's not really anyone in Powell's Valley to hold Sunday services."

"I did not take you for a religious man," Meeker said, looking at Cray with new eyes. "But she is a heathen, is she not?"

"We danced the Bear Dance," Towa said, any smile fading as her anger grew.

"How nice for you," Meeker said, dismissing her. To Cray he said, "It is not fitting that you marry into her tribe. That is miscegenation, something I frown upon."

Towa didn't understand, and Cray did only partially.

"A part-time job's all I'm asking for. I need to work my claim, but if you can pay for a carpenter,

I can do that. Or someone to lay out roads. I worked as an assistant on a survey team back in Louisiana for a few months."

"Louisiana?" asked Meeker, tilting his head to one side as he studied Cray more carefully. "Whereabouts?"

"New Orleans, sir."

"I walked to New Orleans from Illinois when I was younger." Meeker stiffened and his expression returned to its usual dyspeptic mien. "Are you a slacker or are you capable of giving a decent day's work for pay?"

"I can work with the best of them," Cray said.

"Perhaps I can find something for you to do then. There is so much work moving from the old headquarters and establishing new buildings here. There are fields to be laid out and paperwork to be done, assigning ownership. You see, we plan to give every Ute his own plot of land so the government no longer has to dispense food and goods to them."

"We are owed food by treaty," Towa said. "You would break the treaty?"

"I would employ the principle of severalty and turn each and every man in your heathen tribe into a productive citizen no longer dependent on Washington's largesse."

Cray didn't understand what Meeker meant, but he didn't like the sound of it. He started to step back, but Towa held him firmly. The sight of her hand resting so familiarly on his arm earned them a dark scowl from Nathan Meeker. The man tolerated no show of affection whatsoever in public.

"Do you have work or not?" Cray asked pointedly, hoping his rudeness would spark anger in the agent. The more he talked to Meeker, the less he wanted to work for the man.

"We have so much to do before my family arrives. The agency headquarters needs roofing, the roads ought to be better aligned to give a semblance of civilization—Mrs. Meeker insists on that. And many of the Ute are still out hunting and need to be contacted, telling them to return to receive their allotment of land. Reaching them is a chore."

"The summer hunt," Towa said.

"Yes, yes, the summer hunt. There will be no need for it when the farms begin producing. I am quite knowledgeable about agriculture, and will help every Ute who settles get his fields planted." Meeker stopped and fixed his cold eyes on Cray again. For a moment the ice melted, just a little. "You are from New Orleans?"

Cray nodded.

"There might be work for you later. Yes, there will be soon." The stiffness returned when Meeker glared at Cray and said forcefully, "No fornication!"

With that he returned to his job of driving stakes with blue ribbons on them into the dry ground. Obviously dismissed by the agent, Towa and Cray headed back to his mine. Along the way, Towa gripped his arm hard and asked, "What is fornication?"

From the way her eyes danced impishly she knew, but Cray said, "I can't explain it. I'll have to show you!"

DISCORD

July 1, 1878
Powell's Valley

Nathan Meeker stood openmouthed at such insolence. He started to speak, but the words refused to come out. The Ute chief laughed at him and made him even angrier and less articulate.

"You know nothing," Jack said arrogantly. "You cannot come here and tell us what to do!"

"I can," Meeker said, getting his wits back. "By order of the great father in Washington, I can. I have been appointed agent and given full authority."

"You are an old man. Where is your tribe?" Jack strutted around, thumbs hooked into a pair of bright red suspenders. He pulled them out and let them snap back against his broad, bare chest. Then he laughed. "I don't see a tribe. *I* have a tribe."

"That's the problem with you savages," Meeker snapped. "Anything more than your own family and you call it a tribe. Chief Douglass has many Ute following him, and he has agreed to settle here."

"Douglass? You mean Quinkent," Jack said, letting the other chief's Ute name roll off his tongue like bile. "He is old, too, so of course he would do what you tell him. All the fire has gone from his belly. All the power has leaked from his—" Jack grabbed his crotch and squeezed. He laughed at Meeker's indignation at such a crude gesture. The Ute chief began rocking back and forth in mock intercourse, and then made a gusty sound and seemed to go boneless, sinking to the ground in feigned exhaustion.

Meeker's lips thinned and he straightened, pulling back his shoulders. The Ute were heathens, and Jack was among the worst. Meeker wondered if the chief acted this way when he joined council with Ouray and other powerful chiefs of the Uncompahgre to the south. It would not surprise him since such rudeness often permeated the entire character of a man.

"This land is suitable for agriculture," Meeker said in measured tones. "See how I have divided the valley into arable tracts? You can grow wheat here. Corn, if you prefer." Meeker looked across the green-going-to-brown valley and admired the amount of work he had accomplished, even dealing with slackers among the Ute.

"The Ute grow corn," Jack admitted, getting up from the ground and pacing back and forth in front of Meeker like a cougar circling its prey. "But why so much? To feed the deer? But no, you cannot feed the deer because all your sawing and hammering drives them away. We must chase them into the mountains now to eat!"

"You don't need to hunt if you can grow crops," Meeker said, warming to his project. "The supplies from the government can be reduced and eventually eliminated if you are self-sufficient."

"You would take away what the great chief in Washington has promised to give us always?" Jack's good nature evaporated.

"I can do more than that," Meeker said angrily. "I can bring soldiers. Just like that!" He snapped his fingers. "If you don't come settle in the valley, near the agency headquarters, I will see that the soldiers fill the Ute's land from the north to the south!"

Jack backed away now, his demeanor more to Meeker's liking. Gone was his arrogance. Meeker had learned the Ute fear of the cavalry was potent enough to motivate them, although he had not had to threaten military incursion when dealing with Douglass. The old chief had been willing to go along with Meeker because he was wise enough to see the superiority of growing food to hunting a few days, then frittering away the rest of the month in pointless activity like raising horses and wanton fornication. The idea that most of the Ute had several wives appalled Meeker, but there was nothing he could do about that. For now.

"When can I expect your tribe to move into the valley?" Meeker asked, pressing his advantage.

Jack spat, spun, and stalked off. Meeker was startled at the flagrant contempt. He stamped his foot and started down a marked road toward a field where a half dozen of Douglass's tribe worked to get rocks out of the ground. A new twenty-acre farm would soon bloom there with a field of newly sprouted wheat. He sped up when he got closer and saw they were not toiling as he expected.

"Why aren't you working?" shouted Meeker, seeing the Ute had flopped to the ground in the shade of a tree rather than doing the job he had assigned them. He jumped over a low split-rail fence and rushed to them. The Ute looked up, as if they didn't understand—and Meeker realized they might not. While the chiefs and many of the tribes spoke adequate English, the ones most likely to work at the agency tended to speak only their own tongue.

Or they pretended to speak only Ute, Meeker told himself.

"Work, work! It's not time for a break. You cannot expect to be successful if you stop, you—" He choked back the insult that had almost come to his lips. How was he expected to accomplish anything important here if they refused to work? Greeley had been a success because everyone in the colony recognized the importance of hard work and proper preparation of the land for agriculture.

"What will my wife and daughter think when they come if they see you lazing about like this?" Meeker demanded, trying a different tack. He was not sure if the Ute could be shamed into working by threatening them with lowered status in the eyes of white women. The four men sat and stared at him, showing great interest in his tirade but not moving.

"They don't see the point," Cray Eachin said, coming up from the far side of the field. "None of them understand."

"Tell them! In their own tongue."

Cray nodded, brushed off his hands, and began a lengthy parley that made Meeker increasingly impatient.

"Well, what of it? Are they going to work?"

"Please, Mr. Meeker," Cray said. "It's not that easy. They are hard workers. This one's 'bout the best hunter in the tribe, but he doesn't see the point in moving rocks."

Meeker stared blankly at Cray and didn't know what to say.

"They aren't used to farming," Cray explained. "They're hunters. Some of the women raise corn, but not many. What they need, they trade for with hides and venison from their hunting. They range all the way out into the plains east of Denver, you know. Or they did before signing the treaty."

"They cannot live such an indulgent, indolent existence," Meeker said. "It's not God's will that any creature should carry on like that, and hasn't been since Adam and Eve were driven from the Garden."

"Some of them are Christians," Cray said, "but not many. None of these fellows are."

"That will change, along with the way they live. They shouldn't move about the land, endlessly dragging those tepees with them. They need solid cabins, houses that give them a permanent roof over their heads year-round. And the heads of their families."

"Surely is hard building a house big enough for some of them. Chief Douglass has five wives."

Meeker sputtered. "He doesn't," he said in shock. "You're lying. He's one of the good Ute."

"I don't lie," Cray said, bristling at the accusation. "You apologize right now."

"The chief isn't that kind of man to . . . to be a polygamist like the others!"

"Think what you like," Cray said. He barely held his anger in check. "It may not be for you or me, but the Ute braves often have more than one wife."

"Is that why you have taken up with that red-skinned harlot?"

Cray stepped forward, his fist cocked back.

Meeker stood his ground. His faith gave him courage in the face of such licentiousness.

"You take that back," Cray said. "Towa is a fine, upstanding woman."

"My wife will take her in hand when she arrives and teach her true morals."

Meeker blinked in surprise when Cray backed down suddenly. The young man lowered his ham-sized fist. He spoke rapidly to the four Ute, who jumped to their feet, clapped him on the back, and began laughing. With the four behind him, Cray set off across the field.

"Wait, where are you going? You can't take them with you! There's work to be done!"Meeker found himself alone in the middle of the field. He looked at the large rock the four had been trying to move. It wouldn't take that much to get it out of the middle of the field. He rubbed his hands together, then set to work. Meeker had much to do before his wife and daughter arrived in a few days.

WORK

July 23, 1878
Powell's Valley

Chief Douglass sat sunning his tired old bones in front of his *carniv,* eyes closed and thinking about times past and better times to come. In the hide *carniv* stirred two of his wives. Two others had gone to Middle Park, and the other visited her sisters in Ouray's village far to the south. His many children were away on hunts, and it was peaceful in what the *Maricat'z* called Powell's Valley.

"Quinkent," called a brave, trudging up to the tepee and disturbing Douglass's rest.

The old chief opened his eyes and looked to see who called to him by his *Nunt'z* name. It seemed that everyone used the white man's name for him these days. That suited him after Meeker had explained the importance of the name Douglass to the *Maricat'z* and how his new namesake was a great orator. They did him honor using such a fine name. Besides, the *Maricat'z* were unable to speak in the People's tongue without massacring every name.

"Why do you hurry so?" Douglass asked the

young brave whom he recognized as one who had lost his horse in a betting race two days earlier. Douglass did not want to settle such disputes right now. He had lost a considerable amount himself because of the race and choosing poorly who would win.

"I have to," the brave said, grinning crookedly. "I try to make everyone believe I am still on horseback."

They shared a chuckle at this small joke on the brave's part. Douglass offered a pipe and the brave accepted, as was fitting when a principal chief decided a smoke was in order. They puffed silently for a few minutes, wrapped in clouds of blue smoke and their own thoughts. When he considered enough time had passed for the anxious brave to have settled his thoughts, Douglass spoke.

"You have been to see the agent?"

"I have," the brave said, puffing slowly on the pipe. "He is strange."

Douglass considered this for a moment, then nodded solemnly. "He is older than I, and white and soft. Unlike other *Maricat'z,* he does not have a beard. Perhaps this is what makes him the way he is."

"His wife is older than he is!" blurted the brave. "She is an old crone, hardly fit to cook his food, yet she always tells him what to do."

"So it seems," Douglass said. "His daughter is four or five summers past marriage age and yet she has no man."

"She is uglier than a marmot," the brave said, laughing derisively. "What man would have her?"

"Even an ugly woman finds a husband," Douglass said, thinking about his fourth wife. She was hardly the best-looking among the Tabeguache, but had other talents he valued highly. Had she not given him two fine sons after many pleasurable attempts?

"They are strange and their ways are even stranger," the brave declared. "He wants to destroy our racetrack. And he wants us to stay in the park all winter. Nicaagat says—"

"Nicaagat is not your chief!" snapped Douglass. "The *Maricat'z* call him Jack for a reason. He is like their jack-in-the-box, always popping up and bobbing here and there. Never is he solid, consistent."

The other chief vexed Douglass constantly. The sub-chiefs were more likely to bow to Douglass's age and experience. Both Colorow and Canavish, whom the *Maricat'z* called Johnson for reasons Douglass never knew, paid him proper tribute and kept their small bands in line. But Nicaagat thought he was a big chief, as big as Ouray because he had been to Denver a few times.

More softly, Douglass asked, "What does Jack say?"

"He wants the *Maricat'z* agent gone from the valley. He wants him gone entirely before everyone moves north, following the winter game. There is no reason for Meeker to dig up the ground and move the rocks from one spot to another."

Douglass puffed a bit on the pipe, then packed in more tobacco. He held out the pipe to the brave.

"The tobacco comes from Meeker," Douglass said. "I speak often with the agent, who speaks for the great chief in Washington. We will receive many gifts if we stay."

"We have always gone to North Park," the brave said, frowning. "Would you have us stay while Nicaagat—Jack—and his people hunt elk and deer? What will we live on?"

"Meeker will give us food," Douglass said. He had developed quite a liking for the *Maricat'z* food, strange as it was. What appealed as much as the taste to him was the abundance. He patted his bulging belly. It was not as big as Colorow's, but it was well packed with *Maricat'z* food. And would continue to be all winter long.

The brave puffed a bit as he thought on this.

"Meeker has money," Douglass went on. This perked up the brave. "For those without rifles to hunt with or ponies to race, he has money to give away."

"I need a new horse," the brave said. Then he turned suspicious. "What does Meeker want for this money? Always he talks about 'work,' and I do not understand what he means."

Douglass waited several minutes before answering to properly couch his reply. In spite of spending so much time with the agent, he was unclear on all Meeker wanted and had to guess at what such words meant. It was not good to show any ignorance when he spoke, because a chief had to be certain in all things.

"He will give this money in exchange for picking up shovels and using the long knives on the end of sticks to cut the earth."

"Pah," spat the brave, starting to leave. "What is the point?"

"You do not have to do this 'work' very long," Douglass said, indicating the brave should sit again. "If you want rifles and ponies, it is little enough to trade."

"Why should we be like the *Maricat'z*?" The brave was still angry.

"The chief of the white men can be very generous. We do not ride out onto the plains to make

war with the Cheyenne or Arapaho or Sioux anymore. We do not have to when the agent will give
us what we used to take in war."

"I would ride against the Cheyenne," the brave
said proudly. "They killed my two brothers."

"Then 'work' for the agent, get his money to buy
rifles and ponies, and make war," Douglass said rea-
sonably.

"So much of our winter place is being destroyed," the brave said. "Meeker walks behind
horses and uses the big knives on the earth. Why
should we ever do such things?"

"We will receive many fine gifts."

"The land is being destroyed," the brave protested. "What elk will graze here? Where do our
horses pasture when there is nothing but turned
dirt as far as the eye can see? Receiving even the
finest presents does not change the way the ground
looks. Even using the powers given him by Sunawiv,
Canavish could not heal the earth."

Douglass began thinking along other lines for a
moment. Perhaps he ought to summon the sub-
chief to his *carniv* to heal the stiffness in his legs.
Canavish was blessed with healing powers by the
Great Spirit Sunawiv.

He looked up and saw that several other braves
of his tribe had gathered to listen.

"He is right," said a younger brave. "It is wrong
to kill the ground, stabbing it with knives and walking on it with shod horses."

Douglass started to speak, but a chill ran up his
spine. He stared up at the bright noonday sky,
squinted at the sun, and turned even colder. A
small piece of the sun, from which all power and
good flowed, had been eaten away by darkness. It

was an emphatic sign that the balance of the earth was being upset.

He stood on his arthritic legs, and knew there was no time to find Canavish and have him offer an appeal to Sunawiv, their great and beneficent god. Douglass walked slowly away from the now large group, all staring in fear at the sky as the sun turned darker by the minute. He climbed a hill near his tepee and thrust his arms skyward in supplication as he began his chant. He was chief, he was Quinkent of the Tabeguache, of the *Nunt'z*, and the god Sunawiv would listen to his prayers.

More and more of the sun disappeared, but Douglass knew no fear. He felt familiar power flow through him, dispelling all doubt in his own strength. The chant rose in pitch and carried across Powell's Valley, to echo off the distant mountains, the Shining Mountains, until the sun began to grow again and the darkness fled under the power of his potent prayer.

When the hot sun beat down unobscured by the dark ghost that had crossed the sky, Douglass lowered his arms and walked down the hill to where his tribe had gathered. Sweat beaded his brow and he felt as if he had run a hundred miles, from one end of Smoking Earth River to the other.

The braves and squaws parted as he went past his *carniv*. What he did now seemed as right to him as all he had done to pray to Sunawiv to bring back the sun from the devouring darkness. Without a word, Douglass kept walking down into the valley toward the spot where the agent wanted the "work" done. The men of his tribe followed, and began clearing the land at his insistence.

OPTIMISM

August 20, 1878
Powell's Valley

Nathan Meeker wiped the sweat from his wrinkled forehead, and then leaned wearily on the handle of his shovel. A smile came to his lips as he saw his wife, Arvella, beside the agency headquarters finishing the laundry, hanging it out in the bright, warm sunlight. She stood ramrod straight, shoulders back and her jaw set in determination as she worked. How he admired her. Arvella had had a rough life growing up in New England, and he had hardly provided her with an easier time, but she had always been there to give him support, even in the darkest hours. Not a belle physically, he reflected, but there was more to beauty than mere appearance. Arvella had strength of character and a shining soul that transcended the wrinkles and the additional six years of age she had on him. Meeker might have had doubts about his own path through life, but he had never doubted his wife.

She had stood by him when their store in Illinois went bankrupt, and she had gone willingly with him to Greeley to start the colony when Horace himself had urged them to go West. They had toiled to establish a farm, and then he had followed in his mentor's footsteps by becoming editor of the *Greeley Tribune*. Arvella had not faltered when Greeley had loaned $1,000 to keep the paper going, and then up and died in 1872. The great man's heirs had sued to recover the debt during the Panic of '73, forcing Meeker to sell his forty-acre plot and the newspaper at a tremendous loss. Not being able to pay back the debt had been worrisome for him. Not once had Arvella even hinted at leaving him during his financial setbacks. Always she had been the perfect helpmate.

Meeker put his back into shoveling dirt from the roadway in front of the agency headquarters to dig drainage ditches on either side. He had seen repeatedly during the summer how sudden mountain rains could wipe away a week's work, unless proper precautions were taken. And it was up to him to do that planning because no one else would—or could.

"Papa, they're not working again," came the high-pitched voice of his twenty-year-old daughter, Josephine. "I spoke sharply to them, but they pretended not to understand."

"Should I have words with Chief Douglass again?" he asked. Meeker felt the pressure of time to develop his small community here before the winter snows came. There had been no chance to plant this year. The first crops would go into the ground come spring—at the time of the barbaric Bear Dance, if he understood the way the Ute kept track of time—and the land had to be ready then. Only a hundred acres had been plowed, enough for five families.

He sucked in his breath and let it out slowly. Land

enough for four families other than Douglass's. The
chief had insisted on certain amenities, and had received his choice of the plots already cleared. Meeker
had thought about this, and finally decided it was a
good start toward motivating the Ute to work for
their own benefit. If Douglass was excited about turning the sod on land he owned, planting the seed and
harvesting a good crop for his own larder, his enthusiasm and success would infect the other heathens.

"The last time you did, the children didn't show
up for school for a week," his daughter said sternly.
Josephine pushed her dark, shoulder-length hair
back into its severe coiffure. In spite of the warm
afternoon, she wore her black dress and seemed
perfectly comfortable. Meeker marveled at the du-
rability of youth. He had hardly worked in the hot
sun and was sweating like a pig. "I want them to
attend classes longer each day," she went on.

"Chief Douglass claims the children are needed
to do chores around his camp." He leaned against
the shovel, wondering if he could persuade Arvella
to take over the children's schooling. Josephine did
not have the temperament for it, and Arvella already tended to the medical needs, being the clos-
est thing to a doctor within miles. Meeker did not
consider Johnson to be adequate at all. From everything he had seen about the sub-chief medicine
man, shaking rattles, chanting, and liberal—too liberal—applications of firewater were seldom sufficient to do more than get the patient drunk before
he died.

Josephine sniffed, and looked as if she had bitten
into a sour persimmon. She drew herself up even
straighter and stared directly at him, as if the Indians' reluctance to work was his fault. Meeker did
what he could to motivate them, but they were a

lot used to slipshod methods and a far too easy existence.

"I hardly think any of them do chores when they are released from school," she said. "Most real work is left to the tribal women. The men treat them like slaves, forcing them to do all the food preparation, cleaning, mending, and even moving their barbaric tepees as they flit aimlessly from place to place. All the men do is hunt and lie about the entire livelong day, smoking their loathsome pipes. And when it gets dark, they drink whiskey, get drunk, and carouse, making loud, obnoxious noises, then pass out, only to do it all again the next day. They are truly slothful creatures, the men."

"Secretary Schurz thinks highly of the Ute," Meeker said. "They are more peaceable than other tribes and have abided by the terms of their treaty."

Josephine sniffed again, smoothed her dark wool skirts, and looked even more displeased.

"That is hardly a resounding commendation, Papa. They haven't killed as many settlers as other tribes?"

"Douglass gets many of his tribe to come to our Sunday services. They will become Christians and learn to work for their sustenance. This is our job, our duty. And we are doing well, considering how poorly Reverend Danforth prepared our charges for their advancement to civilized ways."

"We are not ministers," Josephine said. "Their souls ought not be our problem, if Reverend Danforth was unable to get them to change their ways."

"It is all tied together, dear," Meeker said patiently. Sometimes, his daughter lost sight of the great work they did among the Ute and had to be reminded. "When they understand that individuals owning property is superior to the tribe controlling it, they will change. With that knowledge will come individual effort at farming and ranching. Who among the Ute wouldn't be proud to raise a hundred head of cattle when they might not kill a half-dozen deer in a season? With this excess meat and hide and grain will come trade for other items. And this will bring the Ute into closer contact with God. We don't have to proselytize. Severalty will accomplish that end for us."

"I'm not so sure," Josephine said. "The crop next year will be small because so little land has been cleared. And it has been quite dry this year also. How can we possibly prepare the soil when nothing will grow?"

"They fought us entering Powell's Valley to put the agency here, but we are here," Meeker said. "This was a wintering spot for the Southern bands." He smiled. Therein lay the genius of his move from farther north, where hunting was the sole activity. By putting the White River Agency near the Ute wintering grounds, he had the opportunity to work with them throughout the colder months, to teach them what they needed to know of agriculture and to get them ready for the challenges and victories of the new year. Any of the Uncompahgre Ute coming this far north would see how the White River bands lived on their own farms, in their own houses. Men like Chief Douglass would be better spokesmen than Meeker himself ever could be.

"I hope we have enough supplies for our own needs," Josephine said. "The winters here are more severe than in Greeley. They must be because the valley will funnel every storm down on top of us."

"You worry so," chided Meeker. "We will be fine. And we will succeed in bringing decent behavior to these heathens."

Josephine muttered something as she gathered her skirts, turned, and hurried back to her chores. Meeker doubted she would find any children left in the makeshift schoolroom behind the agency headquarters, but that was all right. For now.

He would wear the Ute down with the awesome power of civilization and show them how to better their pitiful lives. Whistling tunelessly, he set to digging the runoff ditches to protect the road all the way from the agency down to the edge of Chief Douglass's twenty-acre farm.

BLIZZARD

November 15, 1878
Deep in the Shining Mountains

"It's snowing harder than ever," Cray Eachin said as he peered out around the partially opened door, worried that Towa wanted to return to her village in this storm. "You can't go out in that and expect to survive."

"I have done it before. I am *Nunt'z*, used to weather," she teased. "In many snowstorms I have found my way home."

"What if your father moved the village farther south?" he asked. Cray was concerned she would try to leave his claim and find Kanneatche's tepee in a storm that built minute by minute. If he stepped out of his cabin snugly fetched up against the side of the mountain, the driving snow would blind him, turn him around, and kill him in jig time. Cray saw no reason the same fate would not befall Towa if she left now.

"We always move south," she said lightly. "We are not like that foolish Meeker and his family, who think they can ride out the winter in the park. That is hunting ground, not camp ground."

"If the winter has many storms as fierce as this, they might not make it until Christmas," Cray said. Mention of the holiday turned him morose. It was not the same celebrating Christmas with Towa, although he had explained it to her. She had nodded and said the right things, but he had no confidence she appreciated the depth of his feelings. He even considered making his way down into Powell's Valley and seeking out the Meekers. They were the only white people he knew of in the area, except for a large logging crew to the north cutting ties for railroads in the summer and firewood for the scattered settlements along the Grand River in the winter. He had spoken with one of the woodsmen about buying timbers to shore up his mine, but the logger had wanted too much and Cray had done what he could to supply his own.

"You value this Christmas as much as I do the Bear Dance," Towa said, sitting on the single chair in the one-room cabin. Cray had never needed much more furniture, and when Towa came to visit they had spent more time in the bed than they did sitting around talking. Now, the lack of furniture wore on him.

Even if they never sat on it, he could use it to fuel the cast-iron stove and keep the room a little warmer for Towa's sake. He stared at her and marveled at her vitality. She did not seem the least bit cold the way he did. The chill drove through his canvas pants and faded flannel shirt like a knife, but the whistle of wind through the poorly mud-caulked walls of the cabin bothered him the most.

"It's different," Cray said. "And it looks like you'll be staying here through the spring thaws. There's no way I'm letting you go into that storm."

Towa lightly popped to her feet and went to the

door he had just struggled to close. She opened it a crack, and was almost bowled over by a sudden gust of wind. Snow piled up on the floor almost two inches deep before Cray and Towa could force the door shut. He looped a couple of turns of rope around the latch to keep it from popping open, although he worried more that the flimsy latch assembly would pull out of the door—or the entire wall would come down in the fierce wind. If the snow drifted high enough, he would have to dig his way out because he had not bothered to put in any windows and the back wall of the cabin was the solid rock of the mountain.

They stood close to one another. Towa moved to put her arms around him and rest her cheek on his broad chest.

"You look after me," she said simply.

"I love you," he said. "I don't want you dying out there in the storm before we can get married."

"We *are* married," she insisted. "After I chose you at the Bear Dance, we were married."

"Not in the eyes of my people," he said.

"Sunawiv has given his approval," Towa said.

Cray wasn't going to argue with her over it. He knew there were other ways for a man and woman to marry on the frontier. If they lived together long enough, and if the traveling preacher took long enough between circuits, they would be considered married legally. But Cray wanted it to be more official than that. He knew he should have taken her over the mountains to Denver and found a preacher right after the dance, but Kanneatche had not taken kindly to the idea.

Cray wasn't even certain Kanneatche considered his daughter to be married since he thought so little about *Maricat'z*. The way Nathan Meeker had acted in setting up his Indian agency in Powell's Valley without Ute approval might be part of it, too. Kanneatche wasn't inclined to distinguish between one white man and another.

"You don't have any choice," Cray said. "You have to stay with me. All winter."

"No," Towa said. "Not all winter. The storm will blow over in a day or two. We can enjoy the time together." She grinned wickedly as she looked up into his face. "If you are man enough."

"You know I am," he said, never quite sure if she was criticizing or teasing. He held her close as much for the warmth of her body as to keep her from actually plunging out into the storm.

"Oh, Cray," she said.

They stood there for a few seconds, then drifted toward the bed since it was the only place they could both sit together. Cray kept his arm around her, appreciating her warmth and wondering how she was enduring the cold so easily. With the wind blowing and his heart hammering, Cray kissed Towa and, for a while, she became all there was in the world.

Later, huddled under the bear-hide robe from the she-bear he had crushed, they lay side by side talking.

"How long do you think the storm will blow?" he asked.

"Does it matter?"

"Of course it does," he said. "I need to get wood for the stove. And I have to get back to the mine. It doesn't matter what the weather's like outside. It's always the same in the mine."

"Cold and damp and you don't find what you seek," Towa said with some distaste.

"The gold's there. Or silver. I have this feeling this mine'll make me—us—rich."

"I am rich with you here. Come back to my village with me, Cray. When the storm blows over. You are strong and good with your rifle. You killed the bear, didn't you?" Towa ran her slender hand back and forth over the furry blanket over them.

"I, uh, I did," Cray said, hemming and hawing. He had not been entirely truthful with her about how he had come to kill the bear, and had embellished his skill with the musket. Just a little.

"Come live with my people. You speak the tongue of the *Nunt'z* well."

"Good enough to translate for Meeker," he said, remembering how insulting the Indian Agent had been and how he wasn't likely to go back to the White River Agency unless Meeker was replaced. Even then, Cray saw no reason to work on the peculiar project that obsessed Meeker and the government.

"You can hunt, you can talk to my people, so why not come live with us?" The logic seemed impeccable to Towa.

Cray hugged her close as a gust of wind threatened to rip off the cabin roof. Towa snuggled down, and soon was lost in exploring Cray under the bearskin rug. He tried to think about what she said. Going to live with Kanneatche anywhere nearby didn't strike Cray as too likely, but it was more likely than putting up with Nathan Meeker.

As his mind wandered, Cray knew he could never support Towa by hunting, even in the lush forests of the Shining Mountains.

"Silver," he muttered, and then forgot about grubbing into the hard rock as softer pursuits occupied him.

PLANTING

"We spend our own money on this ditch?" asked Chief Douglass, frowning. He stared at the section of land Nathan Meeker pointed out so eagerly.

"It will require about three thousand dollars to dig the irrigation ditches," Meeker said enthusiastically. "With the irrigation in place, planting can proceed and your crops will be the envy of everyone in Colorado. I have several men from Denver who can help with laying the pipe, but they need to be paid."

"Him?" Douglass looked at Frank Dresser and a half dozen with him busying themselves with small tasks around the agency headquarters. Two new buildings had been constructed by the men over the past few weeks, changing the look of the valley from wilderness to civilization.

"Mr. Dresser is a capable worker."

"I don't like him," Douglass said. "Get Cray. He speaks our tongue. I like Cray."

"That has never bothered you before," Meeker said, turning cautious. The Ute chief had never insisted on dealing with white men who spoke his language. Besides, Meeker had taken quite a dislike to Cray Eachin and his arrogant ways. More than Cray's attitude, he had a Ute harlot and presented a bad example for the other Indians. They should not consort with men outside their race any more than whites should intrude on the formation of Indian families, however disreputable those polygamous alliances might be. Meeker was certain the Ute would become more civilized as they learned the proper way of living.

The irrigation ditch would be a good start toward agricultural independence. But it would be expensive, both to purchase the pipe and to hire the men skilled in laying it.

"This is a vast amount of money," Douglass said. "Dresser and the others will do all the digging?"

"Of course not," Meeker said. "We all have to join in. There are supplies to buy, as well as hiring Dresser. He is officially an agency employee, he and the others who are carpenters and other skilled tradesmen."

"You want all to dig?"

"As many as possible, and we should begin quickly. We don't want to lose another growing season, as we did last year because of lack of arable land."

"Does she dig, too?" Douglass asked, indicating Meeker's daughter.

"Josie? You mean Miss Meeker? Of course she will not dig. Why should she?"

"She looks like a man. She should work like a man."

Meeker stared at the chief, wondering if he'd made a joke. From the mask that was Douglass's face, he could not tell.

"Get your men and we will start. We have the pipe and plenty of shovels and other tools. We can finish the first part of the construction within a week."

Douglass only grunted.

"Where are your men going?" Meeker asked. "There were thirty working yesterday. Today only fifteen showed up and we're almost finished." He brushed off his hands as he studied the irrigation project. Work had gone faster than he had hoped, but the miles of ditch could have crisscrossed the valley if Douglass's men had not slowly vanished. At the beginning of the digging, fifty men had lent their backs to the work. After ten days, only fifteen were present and they obviously did not have their hearts in the work.

"There," Douglass said, looking north.

A thunder of hooves sounded, giving Meeker pause. He touched the knife at his belt, then knew it would be a waste of time even drawing it to defend himself in the face of twenty mounted Ute warriors. As the hard-riding knot of horsemen drew closer, he saw Jack at the lead.

Meeker found it hard to believe Jack and Douglass belonged to the same tribe. Douglass was short, chunky, and sported a sparse mustache. He kept his dominance over his band by force of words, cleverness, and the experience brought by old age. But Jack! He was as tall and lithe as any Arapaho. He rode easily with an arrogance that set Meeker's teeth on edge. Jack was likely to shoot off his mouth without thinking, and had nothing but scorn for Douglass because he wanted to better himself by following the white man's ways.

Meeker had to show Jack that he was wrong following his traditional path and that Douglass was right. Only by settling down and forgoing the nomadic life would it be possible for the Ute to survive side by side with the white settlements springing up all through western Colorado.

"*Maiquas,* Quinkent," Jack said, greeting Douglass by his Ute name.

"Nicaagat," Douglass said, nodding slightly in the younger chief's direction. For a moment neither spoke. Then Jack spoke rapidly in his own tongue. Meeker wished he knew what was being said because Douglass grew increasingly agitated. If Cray Eachin had not been such a stiff-necked, immoral fool, he could have translated and possibly headed off a confrontation with the firebrand Jack.

"Chief," Meeker said, cutting into the rapid exchange between the men. Both glared at him for such rudeness. Meeker ignored it. "I am glad you are bringing your men up from your south wintering lands to join our project. We—"

"You deface the land," Jack said. "I have many of Quinkent's braves in my hunting party. We go to North Park to find deer and elk. He should come with us, if he wants to eat."

"He will grow plenty of food," Meeker said tightly. "You can join in the bountiful harvest if you stop your hunt and help us finish the irrigation ditches."

"You will be left behind. Five hundred—more!—*Nunt'z* will be at Steamboat Springs for the hunt," Jack said. "It will be better than ever before. All along the Yampa River we will hunt! We will feast and you will starve, Quinkent. You and the fools staying with you so you can scrabble about in the dirt like moles."

"The great father in Washington has blessed this project," Meeker said. "Many gifts will come to those who live here and work in the fields."

"Take their pitiful gifts," Jack said to Douglass, his tone insolent. *"I* will take *them!"* He laughed, wheeled his pony around, and rode off, whooping at the top of his lungs. The rest of his band followed, trampling a field Meeker had already plowed. The neat rows would have to be furrowed again if Meeker wanted the seed grain to be evenly sown.

"You have a decision to make, Chief Douglass," Meeker said.

Douglass grunted and walked away, all the Ute who had been working on the ditch going with him. They went some distance away and, in the shade of a tree, sat and smoked a pipe. Meeker wanted to go to them and explain all over how they would prosper and Jack would fail, but Frank Dresser called him to look at saw blades recently arrived from Denver. Half were rusted and useless.

Over the next month, Douglass and his braves worked sporadically, sometimes taking several days at a time off from their toil, but Meeker finally congratulated them when the first rush of water from the irrigation project raced through pipes and out into the fields to give thirsty crops a good drink.

DISCONTENT

"Don't fret so, Nathan," Arvella Meeker said, her voice gravelly although she tried to soothe him. "That Mr. Dresser seems like a responsible young man. He will be back soon. In fact, all your employees seem dependable enough, including Shadrick Price, though his wife has a tendency to overlook work that ought to be done."

Both Nathan Meeker and his wife looked across the table at Josephine when she sniffed indignantly.

"What?" the young woman asked. "Is it my fault I don't share your exalted opinion of Mr. Dresser?"

"Why not? He is a hard worker and a God-fearing soul," Mrs. Meeker said. She stared hard at her daughter. "What more is there? You know something, Josie. Tell us."

"He is a crude man and makes unwanted overtures," Josephine said in her clipped, precise words.

"You misunderstand him, my dear," said Meeker, spooning more of his wife's stew from the large wood bowl in the center of the table. "We are on the frontier. Men say things differently here, in ways you might misinterpret."

"Is the White River Agency so different from Greeley? I think not. People were polite there," Josephine said. "None of the single men ever said a word to me."

A silence fell as Meeker considered what his daughter was saying. He ate slowly, sopped up some of the juice from the stew with day-old bread, and finally swallowed it. A lump formed in the pit of his stomach.

"I'll speak with Mr. Dresser about his manners in your presence," Meeker said. "When he gets back from tracking down all the Ute who went north to hunt."

"I rather like it this way," Josephine said. "The whole valley is so peaceful without the Indians racing their ponies and hurrahing each other's settlements."

"I've done what I can to prevent the settlers around the agency from selling them rifles or whiskey," Meeker said. "I'm not certain how effective I am, but from the dirty looks I get from all the sutlers, I must be having some effect. I have written several stern letters to the Army commanders detailing the infractions, and if necessary, I will not hesitate to call them down on the necks of those fiends selling firewater to the Ute."

"It is a crime the way they take hides and meat from the Ute and trade them faulty rifles, bad ammunition, and whiskey that will surely be their deaths," said Mrs. Meeker. "I am surprised Reverend Danforth did not do more to stop this illicit trade while he was agent."

"I find much to respect about the good reverend's stay here," Meeker said, "but he was far too peaceable a man to accomplish anything by simply suggesting. I have had to threaten repeatedly."

Josephine and her mother exchanged glances; then Mrs. Meeker said, "You haven't been writing more letters to that Major Thornburg, have you? You must write one a week."

"I have. And to Washington, detailing the travails we have to put up with here. It seems all I do is write letters cajoling and threatening," Meeker said. He felt some small satisfaction in the number of letters and reports he sent out, although the responses had been less enthusiastic, especially from the military commander at Fort Fred Steele up in Wyoming Territory. He wished there were forts nearer, but the Ute had been peaceful for so long that the Department of War felt its strained resources were better deployed farther afield.

It was almost easier getting a response from the governor of Colorado than it was a response from the cavalry. Meeker frowned as he continued eating, wondering what he had said that had turned Governor Frederick Pitkin against him so decisively. Meeker shrugged off such political posturing as evidenced by the governor. Meeker knew he was right and that was that.

"Nathan," his wife said sharply. "Do you hear someone riding up?"

Meeker cocked his head to one side and listened hard. His hearing had not been the best of late, but he heard what Arvella already had. He hurried to the door and looked out.

"It's Dresser! There are several Ute with him. And about time. There's work to be done in the fields, and it's getting late in the planting season." Meeker stepped out into the afternoon sun and squinted as Frank Dresser and Chief Douglass drew rein and dismounted while the three others kept riding, heading back to their tepees down in the valley near the river.

"Welcome back," Meeker said. He wondered at the way Dresser glanced in Douglass's direction before speaking. "Where are the workers? On their way?"

"Well, sir, it's like this," Dresser began nervously. "They ain't comin' back. Not right away, at least. They're on one hell of a hunting spree up north."

"Don't swear," Meeker said mechanically. "What do you mean they aren't returning?"

"This is 'bout the best hunting any of 'em's ever seen," Dresser said. "They've already shot a couple hundred antelope, eighteen buffalo, and . . ." Dresser ran dry of words like a stream denied spring runoff.

"And what?"

"He lies," Douglass said angrily.

"Your people haven't been hunting?" asked Meeker, wondering what was wrong. "I don't understand."

"They're settin' fire to the timber up there to scare the game from hiding. There's huge fires eatin' up all the trees along the Yampa River," Dresser said in a rush before Douglass could object.

"He lies," Douglass said angrily. "My people do not burn the forest to flush game. They are mighty hunters and have no reason to resort to such methods of hunting. It is the *Maricat'z*—the white man—who burns the forests."

"Why would they do that?" Dresser shot back angrily. "They're up there cuttin' ties for the railroads. The last thing in the world they'd do is set fire to the very trees that give them their living."

"Whoa, hold on," Meeker said, hoping to quiet

the argument. "The forest fire is of great concern, of course, but it has nothing to do with getting the men back to work at the agency."

"They think you steal their money," Douglass said. "Nicaagat believes this," he added almost contritely, as if apologizing for his fellow chief.

"Jack can believe what he likes. The money from Washington has been held up. That happens all the time, as you know. I had to dip into the reserves for more irrigation pipe. That's why I couldn't give your people their full gifts this month."

"They're powerful mad, Mr. Meeker," Dresser said. "That's why they're burnin' up ever'thing this side of the Rockies."

"They do not do this," Douglass said, turning and squarely facing the agency employee. Meeker saw the set to Douglass's body and the muscles under the red skin begin to tense. For all the weight he had put on in his old age, Douglass remained a powerful warrior. And one about ready to throttle Frank Dresser.

"Please, Mr. Dresser. This is not the time for recriminations."

"What?"

"Don't keep repeating what you've said," Meeker said, changing his argument. "What will it take to get the Ute back onto the reservation so we can continue planting, tilling, and extending the irrigation system?"

"You should not stop my tribe from leaving the reservation," Douglass said, still casting hot looks at Dresser.

"Let 'em go and they'll git all likkered up, sure as the sun comes up, Mr. Meeker," Dresser said. "They want firewater and to get ammo and weapons so they can make war on us. They ain't so peaceful, not like Douglass here makes them out to be. Look at what Jack's doing. He set fire to most of northern Colorado!''

"Liar!" raged Douglass, who spun and grabbed for Dresser. Meeker acted fast, interposing himself between the two men.

"I'll speak to you later, Mr. Dresser. Go inside and get some lunch." Meeker backed off, pushing Douglass away from the agency employee. Only when Dresser was inside and out of earshot did Meeker turn back to Chief Douglass.

"I know these are trying times for you. It is hard to abandon a way of life that has served you well for so many years, but you are the one who is doing right. Not Jack. You must learn to live as we live, on farms, raising crops and cattle."

"We did not set the fires. The Ute would never do that." Douglass crossed his arms and looked so pugnacious Meeker wondered if the old chief might not try to strangle him, too. He stepped back a pace to put some distance between them.

"I am sure Mr. Dresser is mistaken since you are so sure of this," Meeker said. "But surely it is possible one of your tribe started the fire accidentally."

"No. It was the white man's doing."

"When might I expect the men of your band back to work in the fields?" Meeker said, single-mindedly returning to the issue that worried him the most. If a considerable amount of work was not done soon, the early Colorado winter would rob them of any chance of a good harvest.

"When we can trade for rifles and ammunition with white storekeepers. When we get the gifts promised us by the great father in Washington."

Meeker nodded. "We'll work on those things," he said, wondering how hard it would be to get the Army to cut off all arms and ammunition sales to the settlers. They would squeal like stuck pigs, of course, but it would keep them from reselling their weapons to the Ute. As to the matter of the whiskey, Meeker knew the best way of fighting its sale was to stop its production.

There were any number of church groups who would listen to his pleas for temperance and willingly crusade against the vile liquor. He might even send Josephine out to speak with the congregations scattered all over northern Colorado. Reverend Danforth had been inexcusably lax in his opposition to liquor sales to the heathens. It was time for an agent to do more than collect his salary.

Nathan Meeker was the man to do that, he and his devoted family.

A NEW MINE

July 30, 1879
Above Powell's Valley

Cray Eachin sat with his head in his hands. All his work digging and blasting into the obdurate rock had amounted to nothing. His shaft had run better than fifty yards straight into the mountainside, and he had found only traces of quartz. No gold. No silver. Nothing but the dross that tailed down the side of the hill from the mine like some insane mouth drooling pebbles.

"Damn it!" He shoved to his feet and looked up the slope, wondering if the elusive color he sought might be found higher up the mountain. The streams still ran strong from the winter snowpack, although this year was turning out like the prior with few thunderstorms and little of the rain they brought. He could set up a sluice and rocker to hunt for gold in the cold-running water until the stream petered out later in the summer.

He went to his pitiful cabin, where he and Towa had spent so many wonderful hours, and grabbed what belongings he could, stuffing them into a burlap sack. He could tear apart the walls and come back for the wood planks if he had to, but he preferred to use new wood wherever he started working a new claim.

Cray stopped to stare into the yawning pit that had devoured so much of his strength over the past eight months. He had been so sure this was the spot that would make him rich. Deep in his belly he had felt it. Now it was time to move on and find somewhere else, somewhere better, that would put him in a position to take Towa away from her father's tepee and to Denver, where they could live in luxury.

Tossing the burlap sack over his shoulder, Cray started trudging along a game trail, winding deeper into the hills. He studied the stony layers jutting from the inside of the massive mountains for any trace of glittering gold, but saw nothing but drossy rock as he hiked. As he walked, he worried that he had not told Towa he was giving up on the other mine site. What would she think if she came to the mine and found that he was gone? All his belongings would be missing, and she might think he had been carried off.

Cray laughed at that. Who would kidnap him or steal his pitiful belongings? Nathan Meeker?

The Ute had been peaceful for so long, war was a thing of the past for them. The braves still postured and beat their chests, but took out their aggression through horse races and harmless wrestling contests, in spite of what Jack said about the white men being their enemies and going on the warpath against them. Cooler heads like Douglass and Ouray kept the lid on that boiling pot, and Cray had never felt the least bit threatened.

Except by Towa's father, Kanneatche. He repressed a shudder at the way the man glared at him every time he went to the Ute camp. Cray knew it was a little cowardly on his part, but he had stopped going openly and now waited for Towa to come to his cabin.

The memory of her being snowed in for almost a week the prior winter was one of Cray's finest. For a spell, he had worried about the wood running out—and the food! They had both been more than a little hungry by the time he pried open the door and dug to the top of the snowdrift to get out. It had taken him almost a day after that to find a snow hare for them to eat, but it had been the tastiest meal he could remember eating. It had been all the better because Towa had fixed it for them, turning scrawny meat into something that would have been the talk of Denver gourmets.

Cray stopped to rest and sat on a large boulder. He spread out what food he had brought with him, wondering how long it would last. Hunting was a chore for him, but the game was plentiful enough. Still, he preferred to spend as much time as possible prospecting and mining for gold. He picked up an airtight of peaches, then froze.

He felt eyes on him. Cray put down the can and reached for his musket, wondering if he had bothered to load it after he had cleaned it a few days earlier.

"I want food," came the plaintive words.

Cray turned slowly and saw a portly Ute a dozen paces off. For all the man's bulk, he had approached Cray as silently as a hunting cougar.

"Do I know you?" Cray asked. The man looked familiar, but Cray could not place him. "At the Bear Dance last year?"

"You are the *Maricat'z* Kanneatche curses," the Ute said.

"I'm the one," Cray admitted. He saw no reason to deny it. But he still couldn't recognize the man. From the gear the Indian carried, he was well off, a respected member of a Nupartka band to the north of the Tabeguache.

"I am Chief Colorow."

Cray almost laughed. He had heard of Colorow. Everyone had. The man was quite a talker, when he got started, and something of a buffoon. The stories of him going from one white settler to the next, begging food at every stop, were almost legendary. What he couldn't get by simple begging, he usually got by veiled threats of trouble from his tribe. Cray had never heard of anyone being attacked by Colorow's band; Ouray and the other chiefs would never permit it.

"I don't have much, but what I have you can share," Cray said, seeing no reason to move from hearing pleas for food for the man's bulging belly to hearing outright threats. Besides, the earliest memories were of his ma feeding anyone unfortunate enough to come along begging for food. She had always told him he might be in trouble some day and need another's charity. Cray had avoided having to take handouts, but the memory of the hungry faces and the flash of hope that even a sandwich gave lingered over all the years and miles from New Orleans. In a way, this might be his ma's legacy to him more than the agonizing memories from the last days before she had died of cholera.

With an agility that seemed out of place in Colorow's bulky frame, the chief scampered up to the rock beside Cray and hunkered down. He licked his lips as he studied what Cray had spread out.

"This is all I have to last me," Cray said, not wanting Colorow to take advantage of him.

"We can trade," Colorow said. *"Maricat'z* should not dig into our rock. Sunawiv does not like it, and scraping at the earth brings bad luck."

"Your god is great and can surely accommodate one poor man struggling to find a way to live so he can give a lovely Ute maiden a better life."

Colorow considered this for a moment, then nodded sagely.

"This is true. What does Kanneatche know? He is a braggart and a drunk. Not like Colorow. I am a mighty warrior."

"I have heard the yarns," Cray said, grinning. The more Colorow ate, the bigger his exploits. Cray passed over a can of peaches. Colorow grabbed it and expertly used his knife to cut open the top before noisily slurping at the contents.

Cray had hoped to save some of the fruit for himself. He contented himself with gnawing a hunk of bread Towa had baked for him a week ago and cutting off a hunk of venison jerky. The salty meat made his mouth water. He drank deeply from his canteen, but as he put it down he saw Colorow had finished the peaches and was helping himself to the remaining bread.

"Whoa, not so fast," Cray said, grabbing the chief's thick wrist to stop him. "We can share it. Leave some for me."

"You are a fine, strong buck," Colorow said. "You can run for days without food or water. I am old and weak. Starving."

Colorow was anything but on the verge of starvation. From the look of his bouncing belly, he had missed fewer meals than Cray over the past week or two.

"We share," Cray repeated. He separated the bread and gave Colorow a big hunk, turning the piece around so the chief could not see the blue fuzz growing on it. He doubted it would have mattered much to Colorow from the way he wolfed it down, then started munching away contentedly at the jerky.

"Why are you up here alone? Do you seek a place to listen to your god?" Cray asked. It was unusual to see a Ute on foot, much less a chief. And alone? On a hunt they went in pairs and threes to better flush game and carry it out to where they could dress it out. It never paid to dress out deer or antelope near the spot where it was killed because other animals would avoid that spot. Better to keep a good hunting area pristine.

"My pony broke a leg," Colorow said around a mouthful of jerky. He took a drink from Cray's canteen, making the white man worry about finding a stream soon. He had lost track of the one he had intended to use to pan for gold. At this altitude in the hot sun, he got thirsty mighty fast. The salty jerky wasn't helping much either.

Colorow launched into a long story of how he had won the horse in a fierce battle with the Arapaho, how he'd fought well, and a dozen other matters.

"Too bad about your horse," Cray said when he could work a word in edgewise. "As a chief you must ride only the finest horse. A stallion that could win all the races." Cray saw that buttering up the chief was having its effect. Colorow nodded often as he shoveled in the food.

"I rode that horse into battle many times against the Cheyenne. I killed a hundred of them in one day! No one is a better fighter."

"Your reputation is well known," Cray said, finishing what crumbs Colorow had left him. He leaned back and stared up into the mountains. Somewhere up there was a mine waiting to be dug through the mother lode that would make him as rich as Horace Tabor at the Little Pittsburgh Mine near Leadville. Word of that strike had spread like wildfire, and was part of the reason Cray had come to the mountains above Powell's Valley to hunt for gold or silver. If a man who had done nothing more than run a general store could become fabulously rich, so could Cray Eachin.

"All I know of you is what Kanneatche tells me," Colorow said. "But he is wrong. You are a good man. You give me food."

"Thanks," Cray said, grinning crookedly. Then his smile died. "We both have troubles, though. You lost your horse. I gave up my mine."

"No gold?" Colorow asked shrewdly.

Cray shook his head, then turned and stared up into the higher slopes. "Up there somewhere is a real strike."

"You have my permission to root about like a marmot," Colorow said grandly. "Anywhere you want, you may dig."

"Thank you," Cray said solemnly. "Would you do me another favor?"

This caused Colorow to ease back and reach for his medicine bag, as if Cray was going to rob him.

"Would you tell Towa I've left my old claim and that my good friend, the mighty Chief Colorow, has given me permission to look for gold on these slopes?"

Colorow nodded once, then got to his feet. Without another word, the chief jumped lightly to the game trail below and walked off, head high.

Cray had to laugh. Colorow was something of a

clown but in spite of eating most of the food Cray had brought, he was likable.

"How can I miss now?" Cray asked himself as he gathered what was left of his larder and stuffed it back into his burlap bag. "Chief Colorow has given me permission to dig a new mine."

By sundown Cray Eachin had found another spot that his gut told him held enough gold to make him as rich as Croesus.

THE FIRST DEATH

July 28, 1879
Middle Park

John Turner rubbed his hands on his new store-bought trousers and wondered what trouble was going to come down on his head. He reached for his Winchester rifle and picked it up, then put it down again when he saw fighting wasn't going to get him anywhere but into a plot in the cemetery. Stepping forward so he stood at the top step of his front porch, Turner watched the Ute ride up. From the dust cloud they kicked up as they came down the Rollins highway toward his stage station, there might be twenty or thirty. Turner had no quarrel with the Ute before, but now he was getting antsy.

The fires in the forests to the west still left greasy dark smoke hanging in the still air. Lack of rain had turned the entire region drier than usual, and he needed all the water from the nearby stream for his teams. With the Rollins Road finished and connected to the Berthoud Road leading across the Continental Divide, traffic had increased tenfold, and would keep growing as more settlers came into western Colorado, needing supplies, mail, and gewgaws from Denver. More stagecoaches, more thirsty teams, and even thirstier drivers and passengers.

There wasn't enough water to go around for Indians who should have been south at the White River Agency and not up here shooting anything that moved and setting fire to the forests.

Turner looked down at his rifle again and decided to leave it leaning against the station wall. He might kill one or two of the red devils before they got him, but that would be ashes on his tongue since he would be dead. Better to bluff his way through and hope they were not a war party, as rumors made out many of the Ute roaming North Park.

"Welcome to Junction Ranch," he called to the lead rider. Turner had seen enough Ute come by to recognize the leader as a chief or someone danged close to it. The trouble was that the Indians had so many chiefs because they had so many small tribal groups, and it was difficult to deal with them. Each chief wanted his "gift," until there was nothing left in the stage station coffer.

The rider at the front of the twenty braves lifted his rifle in acknowledgment. Turner saw that this wasn't a chief after all, but still someone important. Perhaps the son of a chief.

"We want gifts," the warrior called out rudely, without so much as a "howdy."

"You can't even get water," Turner said, trying to hide his fear. They didn't look as much like hunters as a war party. He had not believed any of the hotheads over at Hot Sulphur Springs. Turner began to worry that Frank Addison might have been right the other night, drunk or not. The Ute were on the warpath.

"Go to the agent and ask there," Turner said, edging toward his rifle and some shelter if the Ute opened fire on him. They milled around, their horses pawing at the dry dirt in front of the station. More than one held a rifle in what seemed to him a menacing fashion, pointing in his direction but never firing.

"The agents steal from us."

"Who are you?" Turner demanded.

"I am Tabernash. As a chief's oldest son, I demand gifts!"

"Well, Tabernash, why don't you go on down into my east pasture? You can let your horses graze there." Turner's eyes darted from the Indians to his rifle and back. It was a bad gamble going for his rifle, and he knew it. "There might be some water in the stream there, but it might be a tad on the muddy side."

"We want gifts."

"I'll see what I can do, but I have to ask in Hot Sulphur Springs. I don't have anything for you here."

Tabernash sneered, then motioned to his band. One said something Turner didn't hear, but from the laughter that passed through the warriors, Turner knew it was not complimentary. That made him even angrier. Not only did they try to steal from him, they insulted him!

Turner watched the Ute band gallop off in the direction of the pasture. He heaved a sigh of relief for his own safety, then realized he had opened a real can of worms. He didn't want Tabernash and the rest of the Indians camped on his property. Turner grabbed his rifle and ran for the barn. He was glad the Ute had never checked the barn because there were two teams of horses stabled here. If he lost them, the stage line's solvency would be put into jeopardy and passengers would be stranded at Junction Ranch.

At the mercy of the Ute camped on his pasture.

Turner saddled his horse and mounted. He hesitated for a moment, wondering if he could retract his invitation to Tabernash. Deciding that this was something better handled by Sheriff Marsh Bessey, Turner galloped down the road toward Hot Sulphur Springs.

"You just hold your tongue now, John," Sheriff Bessey warned. He looked behind him at the small posse.

"You got to arrest them for trespass, Sheriff," demanded Frank Addison. The young hothead rode with two six-guns shoved into his belt and a brand-new Winchester in a saddle scabbard. "No matter what Turner said about lettin' them graze and drink the water, you gotta run them off. If you don't, they'll kill us all in our beds while we sleep."

"So don't sleep, Frank," muttered the sheriff. Louder, the lawman said, "I'll talk to this Tabernash and see if he won't listen to reason. It's bad enough havin' them racin' around and killin' the game."

"They set fire to the forest, Sheriff," insisted Addison.

"There's two thoughts on that, Frank," Bessey said. "Can't rightly see how it paid the Ute to set fire to the forest."

"Them loggers sure as hell wouldn't burn down the source of their money," grumbled Addison.

"They might if they got likkered up and let their

campfire get away from them. I couldn't rightly tell, but the fire might have started that way."

"It was them Injuns," insisted Addison.

"Please, Sheriff," pleaded Turner. "The forest is burned and there's nothing to be done to bring it back. But the Ute are on my property, pasture I need for my teams. I don't want them cropping what grass decided to grow this droughty year, and I sure as hell don't want them thinking on stealing my horses."

"Calm down, John. You, too, Frank. Let me go talk some sense into them." Sheriff Bessey put his spurs to his horse's flanks and trotted toward the Ute camp. The tops of the tepees were visible long before the braves around them were.

"They're not in their camp," Turner said. "Where are they? They wouldn't leave their tepees like this."

"Might be the lily-livered cowards knowed we was comin' and lit out like a scalded dog," Addison said, resting his hands on the butts of his two six-shooters. "We would have given them what-for, you can count on that."

"Quiet, Frank," Sheriff Bessey said. He dismounted and poked his head into one tepee after another. "They might be out hunting. They sure as hell didn't abandon all their gear."

"They were belligerent, Sheriff," said Turner. "I can't see them hightailing it, even if they knew we were coming."

"Hey, Sheriff, I spotted 'em," shouted another member of the posse who had gone scouting to the north. "They're racing horses along the stream."

Sheriff Bessey chewed at his mustache, wondering what to do. He could burn the camp, but that would only incite the Ute. But he wasn't likely to get a better chance to run them off.

"Sheriff, they spotted me. They're on their way."

"Everyone keep your heads. Don't go spoutin' off. Let me talk to them." He stared pointedly at Turner, who fidgeted.

"Why are you in our camp?" shouted the leading Ute.

"That's Tabernash," Turner said. "He's in charge."

"John," Bessey said in exasperation, "I figured that out myself." He hitched up his gunbelt and stepped forward to parley with the Indians.

"He's gonna shoot the sheriff!" cried Frank Addison. The young man whipped out both his six-shooters and began spraying lead in the direction of the Ute.

The Ute milled about in confusion, then returned fire that scattered the posse. Turner dived into a low ravine, where he crouched beside Sheriff Bessey.

"They were going to shoot you, Sheriff," Turner said, in shock from the sudden exchange of bullets.

"I didn't see that. Addison shot first."

"But Tabernash! He was pointing his rifle at you."

"That's the way they are," Bessey said. "They don't shoot everything they aim at, but that don't make no never mind now."

Turner heard sporadic gunfire, but it all came from the posse. The deeper bark of Indian rifles was missing. He poked his head up and looked around in time to see two Ute draping Tabernash's body over his pony's back. They quickly mounted and led the horse away from the small camp—and the still-deadly fire from the posse.

"They've left," Turner said, his voice almost as shaky as his legs. He looked down and saw he still clutched his rifle. He tried to remember how he had gotten into the ravine with Bessey, and couldn't. He didn't even know if he had fired the rifle. Turner touched the barrel. It was cold. He had seized up with fear and had not fired.

"You kept your head, John. You were the one with the most to lose and you didn't panic. Thank you," Sheriff Bessey said. "Wish I could say the same for that damned fool Addison."

"I . . ." Turner was still too shaken up to be coherent.

Sheriff Bessey stood and waved his arm over his head.

"Stop firing. They've left. Don't shoot anymore, damn it! That means you in particular, Frank Addison!" Sheriff Bessey turned his six-gun in the man's direction.

"He shot Tabernash," Turner said. "Tabernash is a chief's son. He told me when he came up to the station."

"Damnation, this is going to get nasty," Sheriff Bessey said. "Gather round, everybody. Come on over." Bessey glared at Addison, then turned to the others in his posse. "I want you to spread the word about what's happened. Get out to the settlements and let any rancher or farmer you come across know to be on the alert."

"We kin go after 'em, Sheriff," Addison said. "Why warn everyone when we kin run 'em into the ground?"

"You and me, Frank, are going back to Hot Sulphur Springs and let everyone in town know what happened here."

"He was gonna gun you down, Sheriff!" protested Addison.

Turner saw the guilty look and knew Addison was having second thoughts about shooting Tabernash. Like letting the Ute camp on his pasture, this was water over the dam.

"Mount up," Sheriff Bessey shouted. "Get your butts into the saddle, and let everyone know what came uncorked here."

Turner stood as the sheriff and the others rode in different directions. He wasn't sure what he ought to do. He had responsibilities to the stage line and needed to feed the teams in the barn. But he couldn't let it rest, not like this. Turner had been scared and wasn't sure what had really happened, but it looked to him as if Addison had gotten buck fever and shot down Tabernash without cause.

If it looked that way to someone who wanted to get rid of the Ute, what did it look like to the Indians?

Turner shuddered, then felt resolve stiffen his spine. He had to do something about it, other than turning every ranch house into a fortress with rifles sprouting like cactus spines out of every window. The sheriff had ridden off, taking the road back to Hot Sulphur Springs, but he had not noticed the Ute were also riding in that direction.

Tracking them was as easy as pie, even for Turner.

What he saw when he overtook them made John Turner stop dead in his tracks, gawk a moment, then wheel around and ride like the wind back to Junction Ranch.

BURIAL AND DEATH

July 28, 1879
Near Hot Sulphur Springs

"We must bury Tabernash now," said Saponishe. "They will come hunting for us and we cannot be burdened with him while we take his body into the Shining Mountains for proper burial among his family and other warriors."

"Who liked him enough to do that for him?" asked another brave. "Leave him for the *Maricat'z.*"

"No!" Saponishe saw that he was the most fit to lead the band. They had not chosen him and he was not the son of a chief, but leadership fell naturally to his broad shoulders. Even without a vision from Sunawiv, he saw clearly what had to be done.

"Why do you care? He hated you."

Saponishe sneered and said, "All the more reason to bury him here. With all the honor we can."

Saponishe looked around for the first time and realized they were riding toward the *Maricat'z* town of Hot Sulphur Springs. When they had escaped the ambush at Junction Ranch, the direction of their retreat had been secondary to simply surviving the guns aimed at them. Since the posse was not hot on their heels, they could take time to observe the proper burial rituals.

"Those two horses will do," Saponishe said, taking charge when no one else looked as if he would. "You, you, dig a grave."

"Here?" asked a surprised brave. "But the ground is too rocky. We cannot bury him deep enough to keep the coyotes from digging Tabernash up."

Saponishe shrugged this off. Let the coyotes gag on Tabernash's vile flesh. He would tell Tabernash's father that his son had been sent to the next world with all the proper accoutrements—those that were available to a war party. Saponishe gestured again, and got the braves scratching in the dirt to make a shallow grave for the body. He rode to where Tabernash's corpse lay on the ground, dismounted, and stared at the chief's son. Saponishe kept from spitting. There had been no love for this arrogant warrior.

Saponishe rolled the body into the trifling grave and motioned for the others to cover the corpse with the few handfuls of dirt they had scrabbled out. He turned, grabbed the reins of Tabernash's horse, lifted his rifle, and pulled the trigger. The horse tried to rear, realized it was dead, and collapsed with a gusty neigh beside the grave. Saponishe grabbed the reins of another horse, led the frightened animal to the other side of the grave, and fought to keep it from lashing out with its front hooves. The horse smelled the blood already spilled and instinctively recognized its own fate.

Another accurate shot to the side of the head killed the second horse. It fell a ways off, amid a cloud of dust. Saponishe snapped orders for the braves—*his* warriors—to drag the horse closer to

Tabernash's grave so there would be a horse on either side.

"Ride fast, ride well, may your hunt be good," Saponishe said, tossing off the words as quickly as he could. He had cared nothing for Tabernash when he was alive, and cared even less now that the arrogant son of a whore was dead. As Saponishe turned from the grave, he saw a man on a rise behind them, astride his horse and staring. He lifted his rifle and sighted in on John Turner, then lowered his weapon. It was a difficult shot, a long shot, and Saponishe had no animosity toward the owner of the Junction Ranch. If anything, he had given Saponishe the chance to show his mettle by removing Tabernash. Let another Ute war party lift the *Maricat'z* station manager's scalp.

Saponishe raised his rifle and vented an ear-piercing shriek, followed by an ululating cry like a coyote.

"We ride to avenge Tabernash," Saponishe cried. The other Ute were hesitant. He had to convince them. "The *Maricat'z* killed our chief's son. They would have killed all of us if I had not led us to safety. We must look into our hearts to see if this retreat was out of cowardice or the desire to live to avenge Tabernash. I say we avenge Tabernash's murder!"

This fired up the others. Saponishe saw several were skeptical of his desire to wreak vengeance for the dead man. It was no secret Saponishe and Tabernash had been more adversaries than allies. But Tabernash had been Ute.

Whooping and hollering, Saponishe rode off, hoping the rest of the band would follow. They did.

* * *

"That is Elliot," a brave whispered to Saponishe.

Saponishe stared at his companion and wondered why he was whispering. They were two hundred yards from where the white settler sawed at the logs he had felled. Even if he had the ears of a cougar and the eyes of an eagle, Elliot would not hear or see them.

"He is the enemy," Saponishe said.

"He gives us food."

"The man has been warned by the courier from the sheriff's posse. We saw it."

"Elliot argued with him. He is one with us," argued the brave. "We can get food from him if we ask."

"No," Saponishe said angrily. A war chief could not allow his decisions to be debated. He would not argue with mere warriors when there was a battle to be won.

He lifted his rifle, watched as dust and leaves fluttered about on the wind between him and his victim, adjusted for windage, then pulled the trigger. For a moment, Saponishe thought he had missed. The range was great, he was a good shot, but it took so long for the bullet to get to his target. Too long.

Then Abraham Elliot threw up his arms, half turned, and collapsed over the log he had been sawing.

"You killed him!"

Saponishe started to boast of the shot when he saw Elliot's son Tom rush to his father. He lifted his rifle for a second shot, but he had no chance. The young man looked around frantically, ducked down behind the large log his father had been sawing, and vanished before Saponishe could squeeze off another killing slug.

"We should stop him," the brave said. "He will spread the warning."

"Let him go," Saponishe said, seeing in such a hue and cry the stuff of legends. His only regret was his name would not be part of the warning yet. But the *Maricat'z* would learn to fear Saponishe.

"They do nothing to protect their horses," Saponishe marveled. He studied the ranch for any sign of a trap, but saw nothing that even hinted at men lying in ambush. The corral with the dozen head of horses was unguarded.

"The cowboys all went to Hot Sulphur Springs," a scout told Saponishe. "They left their spare mounts."

"Why did they go into town?" Saponishe asked the question aloud, but he knew the answer. Sheriff Bessey had formed a new posse, a bigger one, to come after Saponishe. The bigger the pursuit, the greater Saponishe's reputation.

"They fear us," crowed another warrior.

"They will fear us more," Saponishe said. He raised his rifle high, then slowly lowered it in the direction of the corral. With a war whoop, he put his heels to his pony's flanks and galloped downhill to steal some horses.

Saponishe slowed as he neared the ranch house, alert for any sign of a trap. By now the alarm had been spread throughout the *Maricat'z* community. Every settler would know how the sheriff had tried to ambush the Ute and what reaction this had provoked. Saponishe reined back, let his horse rear, then settled the animal so he could look more carefully at the house.

He jumped from horseback and dashed up the

steps to the front door. Saponishe kicked open the door and swung into the room, his rifle leveled and ready to shoot anyone who moved. The house was empty. He howled like a wolf, then rampaged through the house taking whatever he could. After a quick trip through, he was disappointed in not finding a new rifle or ammunition, but he had taken much cloth and glittering jewelry as booty.

Outside, Saponishe saw that the others had opened the corral and were claiming the horses as their own plunder. Saponishe slung the rude sack he had made of a tablecloth over his shoulder and got back on his horse.

"Check the barn," he ordered. "Then set it on fire!"

The warriors responded quickly now, eager to do what their war chief asked. Booty was a better spur than guilt or fear. Saponishe rode about, hunting for any curious *Maricat'z* head poking up out of a burrow. The ranch had been deserted. In a way he was pleased that there had been a quick, easy victory to bolster his band's enthusiasm for war. A prolonged fight might have soured them on their chances of winning.

"Saponishe! Down the road!"

He trotted to where the sharp-eyed lookout had spotted the cloud of dust moving over the hills.

"A *Maricat'z* posse comes for us!" the lookout shouted. Saponishe opened his throat with another inhuman animal-like cry and then galloped off, his bag of stolen wealth banging into his back as he rode. The wind whipped back the lank black hair from his forehead and caressed his face like a new lover. Saponishe felt alive and vital for the first time. It had been too many moons since the Ute had raided the Cheyenne and Arapaho. Who cared about fighting the Navajo to the south? They were a pitiful, broken people.

They were not Ute.

"They're chasing us, Saponishe. What do we do?"

"Ride for home," he said. "We can reach our land, and they will never touch us!"

REFUGE

July 30, 1879
White River Agency

"We've almost got 'em, men," Sheriff Marsh Bessey shouted to his flagging posse. "We can't let the murdering bastards get away when we're this close."

"Please, Sheriff, give us a rest. We been in the saddle for hours after them redskins."

Bessey knew he pushed the men hard. They were all volunteers from around Grand County, but they had been eager when they were deputized back in Hot Sulphur Springs after hearing of Abe Elliot's death. The man's son, Tom, had been well-nigh incoherent as he babbled out how his pa had been cut down while sawing wood, but it had taken Bessey less than an hour of examining the ground to find where the Ute had stood when they fired from ambush. He even had the spent brass cartridge riding in his shirt pocket as proof.

But the Ute had stolen horses and had the advantage of swapping off to their stolen mounts when their ponies tired. The sheriff and his deputies had to keep pushing onward with their exhausted horses.

"I'm not letting killers and horse thieves get away scot-free," Sheriff Bessey grated out between clenched teeth. "If I have to run them down on foot all by myself, I swear by God that I will do it!"

Some of his fierce determination spread through the posse. The men muttered, pulled down their hats a little more on their foreheads, and worked to get their horses moving a tad faster. It wasn't much, but it heartened Bessey. The Ute had been peaceable for a long time—as far back as he could remember. He had come to North Park after the Treaty of '68 had been signed by Ouray, so did not know firsthand the fights that had raged from one end of the Colorado Rockies to the other. If anything, his job as sheriff had been too quiet over the last few years.

Drunk settlers were a problem only on Saturday nights. He had more trouble with ranchers claiming they had been swindled by sharp-dealing store owners, but they usually settled their differences without gunplay or forcing him to have an occupant or two in his Hot Sulphur Springs jailhouse.

But lately, the friction between the settlers and the Ute hunters had grown to the flash point. The fires that had ravaged so much of the forest had been caused by careless white loggers. Again. He was as sure of that as he could be of anything, but convincing any of his neighbors—his white neighbors—that the Ute had not started the fires had been impossible. The problem, as Bessey saw it, was too many people.

Or maybe the problem was white folks moving into traditional Ute hunting grounds. Along with the cries of silver being found along the California

Gulch bringing in miners by the score, new settlers were crowding out traditional Ute villages.

He wiped sweat off his face with his dusty bandanna and then headed down the middle of Powell's Valley. It was as dry here as in North Park, the once-raging river now meandering along the valley floor more mud than water.

"They're stopping to rest, Sheriff," an outrider called. "I can see 'em ahead of us, maybe a mile off."

"Whoa, stop for a second and let's work this out," Sheriff Bessey said. "We want to arrest them, not gun them down." He didn't add that he feared many of his inexperienced posse might be killed in any protracted fight with a bunch of Indians who thought they were on the warpath. Bessey looked squarely at the one he wished had been gunned down a lot earlier. Frank Addison had lost none of his arrogance since shooting the brave back at Junction Ranch. If anything, his bragging had increased until he was making himself out to be something of a hero.

"What do you want to wait for, Bessey?" demanded Addison. "We get out our six-guns and ride down on 'em, shootin' as we go."

"I want them to stand trial, Frank," Sheriff Bessey said carefully. "Wouldn't you like to see the men responsible for killing Abe on a gallows, nooses around their red necks?"

"I'd be willing to act as executioner. For nuthin'! The county wouldn't even have to pay me for that chore!"

Bessey let the posse calm down so he could talk some sense to them. When they gathered around, he began.

"They are in the valley, near a stand of cottonwoods. I don't think they are expecting us to drop in on them. We'll split into two groups. You, you, and you, circle way round and come up on them from downriver to cut off their escape. The rest of us will ride on up—not shooting unless we have to—and catch them."

"Catch them red-handed," said Addison with a chuckle. "They have the stolen horses with them. That's more proof who we're dealin' with."

"Listen hard, Frank. Keep your six-guns in your belt until we get close. And I don't want you gunning them down if they try to surrender. You shoot a man with his hands in the air and I swear I'll see *you* on the gallows."

"They ain't men, Sheriff. They're only Ute."

Bessey glared at him and considered buffaloing the man. All he had to do was whip out his six-shooter, reach over, and smash the barrel into Addison's thick head. He resisted the impulse, though he might regret it later.

"Get riding, you three. I'll give you a half hour to circle and get between them and the agency headquarters."

"Where's that, Sheriff?" asked a deputy.

"Somewhere along the river. Never met the new agent, but Reverend Danforth didn't think much of him. Told me so on his way back to Denver last year." Danforth had told the sheriff far more than that, but Bessey wasn't inclined to believe much of it since the good reverend was in his cups. As usual.

"We don't need to wait that long," Addison said anxiously. "If we wait around sittin' on our thumbs, them Injuns'll get away. They're sneaky bastards. Look what they did to Elliot."

"You stay put, Frank," Sheriff Bessey said coldly.

"I'm sick and tired of chasing them across half of Colorado and want this to end."

"Hey, Sheriff, there's somebody joinin' them. Comin' up in a damned buggy."

Bessey hurried to get a better look. His keen-eyed scout had spotted the buggy long before he could have. Alongside the carriage rode two Ute.

"They're gettin' reinforcements. We got to go now, Sheriff. We'll be outgunned if'n we don't!" With that Frank Addison raked his spurs along his horse's flanks and lit out at a dead gallop.

"After him, men," Bessey ordered tiredly. Any hope of cutting off the Ute's escape was gone now since the trio of deputies wouldn't be in position for quite a spell yet. The sheriff wished he had given in to his impulse to lay an iron barrel alongside Addison's empty head.

Galloping the best he could on his exhausted horse, Sheriff Bessey arrived at the Ute camp expecting to find himself in the midst of a desperate gunfight. Instead, an old man dressed in work clothes stood by the Ute who had been identified as having led the horse thieves—and who Bessey thought was Elliot's killer.

"What's going on?" the white man demanded. "Why are you waving those guns around so?"

"I'm Sheriff Bessey and I'm here to arrest these horse thieves. And that one," he said, pointing directly at Saponishe, "is suspected of not only being the leader, but also of murdering a settler outside Hot Sulphur Springs."

"I'm Nathan Meeker, agent for the White River Agency. This is an incredible charge you levy against these men, sir. Can you prove it?"

"The horses all carry the Rolling J brand. The

rancher will testify he hasn't sold any horses to the Ute in over a year."

"We find them!" protested Saponishe. Bessey saw the evil grin on the warrior's face and wanted to smash his mouth in. He almost gave Frank Addison free rein in doing what he wanted, but held back. The law had to be served.

"So you don't have a sales receipt?" Bessey asked.

Saponishe looked blank.

"They don't think in those terms, Sheriff," said Meeker. The old man made tiny fluttering motions with his hands, then settled his hat squarely on his head as if this decided the matter. "I must believe Saponishe when he says he found the horses roaming freely. Is it a crime to capture mustangs?"

"They've got brands," Sheriff Bessey said.

"Is there reward for their return?" asked the Indian who had ridden with Meeker. The sheriff looked him over and saw he was a chief. He wondered which one. The Ute had so many he couldn't keep them straight.

"I reckon they'd return another fellow's property if they found it because that's the right thing to do," Bessey said.

"Then accept them with thanks for doing such a fine job," Meeker said.

"I'm arresting that one for shooting Abe Elliot in the back." Bessey pointed to Saponishe, who stiffened and reached for his rifle for the first time.

"You cannot," said the Ute chief.

"I can and I will. A man's dead, shot in the back from ambush."

"Betcha it was fine, long shot," Saponishe said, his evil grin causing Bessey's blood to boil. He knew he had the culprit and drew his pistol.

"You're under arrest."

"Chief Johnson is right and you are wrong, Sheriff. You have no authority on agency land. This is technically and legally Ute land. A sovereign nation under treaty with the United States Government."

"You're going to let a murderer walk free among you?" asked Bessey, fuming even more. "He killed a man for no reason. He—"

"Might be this dead *Maricat'z* murdered Tabernash," Saponishe said.

"What's all that?" asked Meeker, obviously perplexed. Chief Johnson shot a cold look at Saponishe, but the young brave refused to take the hint.

Bessey wished he could tie Addison and Saponishe together at the neck and let them fight it out.

"I don't believe in an eye for an eye," Bessey said. "That's why I'm taking Saponishe in for the murder of Abraham Elliot." He looked up and saw his three deputies had finally ridden into position and were coming up on the camp from the south.

"Don't," warned Chief Johnson. "This one is Ute on Ute land."

"I—" started Bessey.

"A word in private, sir," the agent said. Nathan Meeker came forward and guided the sheriff a few paces away. "This is a difficult matter, I know, Sheriff. But the law is quite plain. You have no authority on the Ute reservation."

"Why are you siding with a killer?"

"I have doubts about that, but consider the larger issues," Meeker said. "These men have agreed to work diligently on plowing and irrigating. I fear I must move my agricultural area to a spot with more water. The drought is taking its toll on what crops have been planted already. Chief Johnson has guaranteed that Saponishe and the others with him will be present every day for the next month, while we move the White River Agency farther south into Middle Park. It would create tremendous discord should I turn over Saponishe to you, after I have worked so long to get Johnson's cooperation to make this shift away from Powell's Valley, which he considers his summer home. He has shown himself to be very reluctant to go along with my program in other details, you see."

"Saponishe killed a man," Bessey said, beginning to wonder if the Ute agent was deaf.

"And Chief Johnson has guaranteed Saponishe will not leave the reservation again after we move farther south."

"Is that some kind of a threat?" Bessey bristled at the intimation that the Ute could deal better with a killer than the district judge when he made his circuit to Hot Sulphur Springs in a few weeks.

"There are other delicate matters I am on the verge of resolving. Chief Jack has been a constant annoyance to me and is openly inciting his band to war against the settlers. Chief Johnson and Chief Douglass assure me they can control him, even without going to Ouray for help. If you give Jack an excuse, he might start a war that will spread throughout the region."

"You're saying to let a guilty man go unpunished and Jack won't declare war? That's extortion."

"Hardly, hardly. It is a *solution* to both our problems. I keep willing workers on the reservation where my policies will take hold and bring the Ute into the stream of white settlements. If they work here, they cannot ride with Chief Jack and cause mischief."

"It sounds like all you want is to turn them into your pet Injuns," Sheriff Bessey said. The agent bristled at this, but the sheriff did not care.

"They can be transformed into productive human beings, sir," Meeker said stiffly. "Severalty will accomplish miracles of changing the heathens into citizens capable of mingling with polite society anywhere in the United States!"

"Bullshit," Bessey said.

This provoked an even stronger response from the agent. "Get off the reservation this instant, sir. Get off or I shall have Chief Douglass fetch his men and escort you off."

"I'll do it," Saponishe said, grinning from ear to ear.

"I want the stolen horses," Bessey said, trying to figure how to win some small victory in the middle of a crunching defeat.

"Very well," said Meeker. "Saponishe, cut out the horses carrying the brand the sheriff is hunting." For some reason Sheriff Bessey could not fathom, taking the horses seemed to please Meeker unduly. It was almost as if he wanted the Indians on foot and unable to ride off the reservation.

Sheriff Bessey wanted to tell Saponishe he would come to a bitter end, but held his tongue. Throwing out insults only stoked the fire of hatred burning in the young buck's belly.

As he rode away surrounded by his posse, leading seven of the stolen horses, Marsh Bessey wondered if he had done the right thing. Shooting it out now might save lives later. The worst of it was that Nathan Meeker was right about the law. Once the Ute had reached sovereign territory, they were safe.

For the moment.

WARNINGS

John Turner had spooked him something fierce with his stories of how the Ute had shot two horses, buried them alongside their fallen chief, and then had ridden on, maybe killing Abe Elliot. This bothered him a lot since he and Abe had been friends for all the years Charlie Beck had carried the mail along this road. Charlie might have been better friends with Turner and some of the folks up in Hayden, but Abe Elliot had been a fine, upstanding family man. From the way Turner told it, there had been no call for anyone to gun Elliot down. Abe hadn't even carried a gun with him when he went to saw some wood.

Charlie kept his old horse moving along at a steady pace, reluctant as it was. The day was hot, but the mail had to be delivered. Somehow, a nice, cool drink in Hayden—whiskey or water didn't much matter to him right now—would be just the thing.

Charlie dragged back hard on the reins, and his heart raced when he saw a Ute step into the road

from behind a nearby boulder. His eyes went wide
when he saw the yellow and black streaks on the
man's face.

Ute war paint.

"Where are you going?" the Indian asked.

"Over to Hayden. Goin' to Peck's store to fetch
some medicine for Mrs. Smart. She's taken sick.
And the mail. I got mail to deliver, too. Cain't forget the mail." Charlie's brain froze and his mouth
ran away with itself. He babbled uncontrollably. It
had been years since he had seen a Ute all decked
out in war paint and carrying a rifle, knife tucked
into the beaded belt and a heavy pistol shoved in
just above the knife's sheath.

"I know you, Charlie. Go on." The Ute waved
him along the road, as if he were a toll-taker.

Charlie Beck wasted no time in getting his tired
old horse trotting along at the best speed it could
muster. The Ute had not only worn war paint, but
had had his hair woven into double braids festooned with bright beads, one for every kill he'd
made—or so Charlie had been told. He recognized
the warrior as one he had talked to often as he
rode the mail route and sometimes had given tobacco or other gifts to. Never before had he seen
him in war regalia.

Looking back over his shoulder more than once
as he rode into the twilight, Charlie imagined the
Ute taking aim and opening fire on him. He
wished his horse could make better time to Hayden, but it wasn't in the old bones.

When he came to the outskirts of the small settlement, Charlie heaved a sigh. Even the horse took
on a new life now that a currying, grain, and some
water awaited it in the town livery. But Charlie was
determined to deliver the mail first, then pass

along what he had seen on the road to whoever would listen.

A Ute in war paint. He shuddered. John Turner might not have been spinning much of a tall tale at all.

Charlie stopped dead in the middle of the street when he saw the corrals at the end of town filled to overflowing with horses. He wasn't good at estimating herds, but there had to be a couple hundred.

"Five hundred head," came the quiet answer to his unspoken question.

"Mr. Thompson. You startled me." Charlie climbed down from the horse and pulled off the mailbags. "How'd there come to be so many horses in Mr. Peck's corral?"

"Peck runs a general store and trading post. He's been doing some mighty fine horse trading, I'd say," James Thompson said. The grim note in his voice warned Charlie of something really bad going on.

"Mr. Thompson, I know you was agent to the Ute a few years back 'fore you started your ranch. You ever seen any of 'em decked out in war paint? I mean recently?" He hurried through his recitation of what had happened on the road into town.

Thompson turned even more dour.

"This is bad, Charlie, the worst I've ever heard in a score of years. An old Ute friend warned me today to move my family up high into North Park because there's going to be trouble. I don't rightly know what's going on down at the White River Agency, but it's got the Ute stirred up. They don't cotton much to the new agent and his ways, and the young hotheads are talking crazy."

"Are you going? Up north?" Charlie asked.

James Thompson was no coward to run at mere rumor. If he intended to move his family, even for a few weeks, then there was substance behind the warning.

"Yes," Thompson said softly, looking at the five hundred horses in the corral. "The Ute traded Peck those horses for more Winchester rifles and ammunition than a dozen men could carry. There's bound to be *big* trouble."

James Thompson tipped his hat and left Charlie to deliver his mail—and get the hell over the mountains to Denver where it might be safer.

LOST PASTURE

"I don't know, Mr. Meeker," drawled Frank Dresser. "Movin' the agency south like you done caused all sorts of hard feelings. Even Chief Douglass didn't much like havin' to pull up stakes on his family and leave Powell's Valley."

"There's nothing we can do about it. The land there cannot be tilled and properly irrigated. It is far too dry this year for our irrigation system to work. All we got out of the pipe was mud, because that's all that was going in from the river."

"We put a powerful lot of money into it."

"It is money set aside for the benefit of the Ute," Meeker said. "I can spend it as I see fit, to improve their lot. There was no way of telling the river would dry up like it has this year. I think everyone can see that the move has been beneficial because there is better drainage and more water from run-off."

"We put a powerful lot of work into Powell's Valley to just up and abandon the land we already plowed," Dresser complained. "What are you gonna do about Chief Douglass's land? He took a patch down by the river and wants it cultivated 'fore anyone else's."

"He will understand if we tend to other matters first," Meeker said. "I'll give him extra rations of sugar and coffee. That always appeases him whenever he is feeling a bit off his feed."

"Papa is right," Josephine Meeker said firmly. "Questioning his decision as you just did was quite rude. Apologize this instant." The young woman looked severely at Dresser, who glowered back at her. He started to say something that would offend her sensibilities, then subsided.

"Reckon I was wrong. You want us to fence in that section of land?" Dresser pointed to a spot marked in red on the map. The boundaries of the new reservation were penciled in, but various plots allotted to the chiefs and sub-chiefs had been singled out.

"Why else would I have marked it thusly?" Meeker asked, as if speaking to a simpleton.

"That's Chief Johnson's pasture. He's got upward of a hundred and fifty horses grazing on that acreage already." Dresser screwed up his face as he worked out the dimensions of the plot marked on the map. "You'll be fencin' in danged near eighty acres of land he considers his. And it is, since you gave it to him for his part in helpin' get the rest of the Ute down here so fast."

"The land belongs to the tribe. Chief Johnson will have to learn that my decision is final in such matters."

Dresser started to say something, then looked confused.

"What is it, sir? Spit it out," Josephine said tartly.

"I thought you wanted all them Indians to believe the land was theirs to do with as they saw fit. Now you're sayin' it really belongs to the tribe, like they said 'fore you showed up. Either it belongs to Johnson or it belongs to the tribe. Why take Johnson's land if he ain't never gonna be able to use it the way he wants?"

"You cannot understand such legalities," Meeker told him. "You do as you're told and get the rest of the men working to fence and plow that eighty-acre plot right away."

"That's gonna be somethin' of a problem, too," Dresser said. "All that's left to work are the carpenters and other skilled workers from around the agency."

"What of the Ute?" asked Josephine. She glared openly at Dresser now. "You had dozens of them tilling the fields and working on the irrigation project back in Powell's Valley."

"It's like this, Miss Meeker," Dresser said. "After the sheriff chased Saponishe and the rest of his hotheads back onto the reservation, they promised they would work. The sheriff was hardly out of sight when they all lit out. Word is, Saponishe wants to declare war on us and a lot of the Ute belonging to Douglass's band are joining up. They're somewhere up north raisin' a ruckus."

"I have heard these rumors. That's all they are," Meeker said. "Chief Douglass can control his people. It is Chief Jack that I worry about. He is the firebrand."

"A drunken fool," muttered Josephine.

"Dear, please. Jack does not partake of inebriants like many of them do. Take that Kanneatche, for example. I am not sure I have ever seen him sober, but his brother Curicata is a fine, upstanding example of what can be done with the heathens."

"Sir, I heard tell that Curicata has left the agency 'fore the move and has gone north to join Jack. Other chiefs are all palaverin', too. Colorow is champin' at the bit to go on the warpath."

"That fat beggar," scoffed Josephine, "could not figure out which end of a rifle to point at an enemy. If this is the quality of the fighters Chief Jack is welcoming, there will be no war."

"Beggin' your pardon, Miss Meeker, but Colorow is quite the fighter."

"Only in his own mind," the young woman sniffed. "Papa, tell him to get to work. I believe he is arguing only to get out of earning his day's wages. We need to work twice as hard to prove this land, since we are starting over so late in the year."

"Yes, yes, you're right, Josephine." Meeker took Dresser by the arm and steered him out the door of the agency headquarters building, moved log by log from the north and hastily rebuilt on a tract of land overlooking the park. "Get however many workers you can find down to the field and begin plowing."

"Chief Johnson's land?" Dresser sucked in a deep breath and let it fly free in a heavy gust of resignation. "If you say so, Mr. Meeker. You're the Ute's agent." Dresser walked away, shoulders slumped in defeat.

"What a disgusting man," Josephine said primly after Dresser was out of earshot. "I cannot understand why you tolerate such impertinence from him."

"Mr. Dresser is an adequate worker, if motivated," Meeker said. He looked at his daughter and saw her gimlet stare fixed on him. "What is it, my dear?"

"He had a good point. Why plow up Johnson's

land if we are currying his favor? That seems a waste of effort, considering how little of it is ever expended in this terrible place."

"You don't understand my greater plan for the Ute, Josie," Meeker said. "Johnson is cooperating right now because he feels he holds the whip hand. He purposely let Saponishe and his warriors stray because he thought I wouldn't do anything about it, being involved in moving the agency as I was."

"So you are showing him he is wrong, that you are in charge? This is a silly way to go about it, Papa."

"It's more than that," Meeker said, his eyes fixing on a distant mountain peak and an even more distant future. "He is the worst of the Indians, raising his horses and racing and betting. I want to relieve him of the burden of pasturing his horses."

"You cannot stop the Ute from riding," Josephine said. "They have done it for centuries, and it is in their blood."

"I must do something about those horses," Meeker said earnestly. "It is key to my success with them. They must be convinced agriculture will supply their needs, not trading horses and gambling away their precious, hard-earned money." Meeker sniffed in derision. "Who really cares for money won gambling? It is fairy gold. Touch it and it goes away. The only real wealth is in the soil. A man is rich who can watch his crops grow and then harvest them."

"You've been writing letters again, haven't you, Papa?" asked Josephine.

"Of course I have, several times, as it were. I believe Commissioner Hayt agrees with my position on separating the Ute from their horses. At least he has said nothing about it countering official Bureau of Indian Affairs policy. Q.E.D., stripping Johnson of his pasture and ultimately of his horses is an accepted element of the general Indian settlement program. Besides, such plowing will make him more eager to raise crops when he sees the majesty of it. In Powell's Valley, he had not begun cultivation and therefore retained the old Ute ways. It is time to move him forward and show him new ways of living."

Josephine looked dubious but said nothing. She left her father gazing into the distance and imagining nothing but farms in Middle Park for as far as the eye could see.

"What are we supposed to do about them horses, Frank? They're runnin' wild and are gonna trample every row we plow."

Dresser scratched his head, thinking on it. The horses belonged to Johnson, no question about it. That meant Dresser had found the right place to begin fencing and plowing. Four men were already hard at work digging postholes. The only others he could find who hadn't quit on the spot when he told them what Meeker wanted were Summers and his string-bean buddy, Glencannon. Neither of them knew spit about farming or plowing, but they knew even less about putting up fence posts.

"Don't reckon it's possible to keep them chased off long enough to do good plowing," said Dresser.

"Frank, those horses'll be all over the field, kicking up their hooves and destroyin' everything we done," complained Glencannon. "You got to do somethin' 'bout them 'fore we commence to plowin'."

"Summers, go chase 'em off," Dresser ordered.

"Take off your shirt, wave it around, and yell like you've been scalded. That'll run the horses off so we can get to work."

"I suppose," Summers said, obviously unsure of himself. He stripped off his sweaty shirt and waved it tentatively over his head. A breeze came along, evaporating the sweat from his body, cooling him. More comfortable now, he got into the spirit of it and yelled like a madman, running and jumping and snapping his shirt like a whip to frighten the horses.

"See?" Dresser said to Glencannon. "That's workin' out just fine. Now you get to plowin'. I'll go to the far side of the field and set up markers for you so you can cut a straight furrow."

Dresser hiked to the edge where Nathan Meeker wanted the field plowed, turned, and sighted back across the pasture with its mixture of lush grasses. Destroying such pretty grassland seemed a pity, but it was necessary to keep Johnson in line and to persuade him to give up his remuda. Dresser planted a stake where Summers could see it, and had started pacing off the distance to the end of the next furrow when he heard a gunshot.

For a second, Dresser froze, fearing he was the target. He checked himself and didn't find any bullet holes. Then he swung around and fanatically searched for the gunman. He saw Chief Johnson riding across the pasture waving his rifle above his head.

"What'd you go and shoot at me for?" yelled Summers.

"Dog!" screamed Johnson. "You dig my pasture so my horses will starve." This time he fired more accurately and kicked up a clod of dirt at Summers's feet.

"Run for it!" shouted Dresser. Then he took his own advice, hoping Glencannon and the men digging postholes heard his command. If they didn't, that was their bad luck.

Frank Dresser didn't stop running until he had covered the four miles back to the agency headquarters.

COMPROMISES

August 10, 1879
Middle Park

"You cannot plow my land. You gave it to me. It is mine!" Chief Johnson clenched his hands so hard Nathan Meeker thought he would shake himself to death. Right now, that would have suited the agent. Johnson was not being the least bit politic about his demands. Meeker felt this gave him even more bargaining power to get the chief to agree to the tilling. When mention was made of firing on agency employees the day before, Meeker knew Johnson would have no choice but to agree to removal of his horses.

"Calm yourself, Chief," Meeker said. "You will have plenty of land to graze your horses, but not this land. We need to plow eighty acres to start our planting. It is already late in the season, but we might get a quick crop in if we can irrigate properly."

"My horses will starve," Johnson said, looking more furious than ever. For the first time, Meeker feared the Ute chief might attack him. He took a half step back, hating himself for showing such weakness in the face of adversity, but wanting to get away from the raving Indian. He had misjudged how angry Johnson would be over losing the pasturage.

"What is needed right now is to prove the land," Meeker said.

"No. You lied! You told me I could have the land for my horses if I helped you move from Powell's Valley. Now you take it and don't give me any gifts."

"Is that it? What can I give you?"

"I am no whore to be bought. You steal my land." Johnson whirled around and stalked off, leaving Meeker to wonder how safe he might be standing exposed in the middle of what had been Johnson's pasture. Dresser and Glencannon plowed along one edge of the field, looking apprehensive as they toiled. Meeker was not pleased with Dresser or any of the other white men who had been at the White River Agency. Many had left, claiming the entire area was a powder keg ready to explode.

Except for Chief Johnson, Meeker saw no trouble. And then he did. Riding along a road toward the pasture came Chief Jack and a half-dozen braves. Meeker almost bolted and ran. He had heard all the stories rolling from one end of the park to the other about how Jack was on the warpath. But he rode calmly enough now, or so it seemed to Meeker. And the man didn't wear any war paint.

"Jack!" Meeker called in greeting. His heart hammered in his chest, but he forced himself to remain outwardly calm. He kept telling himself he was the agent in charge and that his wards had to obey him. If they didn't, he could make good on his numerous threats to call in the cavalry. That always cowed the Ute, although Meeker was less than pleased with the response he got from the military as he detailed all that had gone wrong on the White River Agency. By the time Jack dismounted, Meeker about believed he was in control of the situation.

"Meeker," Jack said in greeting. There was no warmth in his tone.

"It is good to see you. What brings you around? Are you thinking of joining in?"

"There is much trouble here," Jack said, looking around the partially plowed field. "Why do you dig up the land promised to Canavish?"

"This is special land, right for growing crops and convenient to water for irrigation." Meeker paused when he saw Chief Douglass riding up from another direction. Douglass's appearance made Jack and the braves with him edgy. Meeker wondered at the power struggle that must be going on within the Ute nation. If he were clever, he could turn it to his own advantage and get the lot of them working at his agency.

"Welcome, Chief Douglass." Meeker felt a flood of relief having the old Ute here. Douglass could more than hold his own against the unreliable Jack, and had shown he was willing to go along with whatever Meeker asked of him. He had willingly moved without even asking why, although Meeker had promised much to the old chief to insure his cooperation during the move from the drier land to the north.

"This is wrong," Douglass said without preamble. Meeker puffed out his chest. Douglass and Jack agreeing? They were ganging up on him. Then he saw that Jack was as taken aback by the accusation as he was. Jack had not expected Douglass to side with Johnson.

"It is in the best interest of the Tabeguache,"

Meeker said. He started to wind up and deliver a nice speech that had been running through his head, but he hesitated when he saw the dark cloud settling on Douglass's countenance. The old chief was not going to accept anything he said about the future of the Ute depending on their cooperation now.

"You cannot take that which belongs to Johnson," Douglass said sternly.

"If we pay him . . ."

"He must have more than land to turn over such fine pasture," Jack said. Meeker felt as if he were being set upon from all directions. He started to wave Dresser over to join him to provide some support, physical if not moral, but Jack continued relentlessly. "You must dig Johnson a well."

"We can do that," Meeker said. "After all, the reason we moved into Middle Park was for the water here that we lacked up in Powell's Valley."

"More," Douglass said, coming at him with a new and different demand. "If I am to stay here, I must have an iron stove."

"I—" Meeker wasn't allowed to respond. Jack cut him off.

"What good is an iron stove to Quinkent if he has no place to put it? He needs a cabin. A new one, a big one. Down by the river so his *piwán* does not have to carry water far to his *carniv.*"

"In exchange for plowing Johnson's land?" Meeker asked. "You want me to dig Johnson a well and give Douglass a new cabin with an iron stove?" Meeker had heard of double-dealing before, but this was incredible.

"Is this not your way?" responded Douglass. "If he truly owned this land, then he should receive something of value for it."

"That is only fair, but a cabin for you? And a stove? These are expensive, both in time to build and in material. We have to get the fields plowed and the land apportioned and—"

"He should have other land of his own," Douglass went on relentlessly. "You take this land. Canavish is no farmer. You give him other land. Up along the side of the park where the grass grows knee-high. That would be good for grazing horses. And digging a well."

"I'm sure it would," Meeker said, confused by the barrage of demands from the two chiefs in support of Johnson and to increase Douglass's prestige among the Ute. The latter did not bother Meeker too much since he needed Douglass's cooperation to keep the heathens in line. It still surprised him how Jack kept upping the ante for the other two chiefs and had yet to make a demand on his own behalf.

"Then it is settled. You plow here. You give Canavish a well. And Quinkent will get all you said," Jack declared. He crossed his arms across his broad chest and glowered at Meeker. The hostile expressions on the faces of the braves with Jack told the agent not to argue. He would have to implement his no-horses policy in other ways to avoid a future head-on collision with Douglass and Jack.

"What you ask for your friends is fair enough," Meeker said to Douglass, backing down rapidly. "It will take a little time to build the cabin, but there is a spare stove from the old agency headquarters we can give you right away."

"The well," insisted Douglass.

"As soon as we finish plowing this eighty-acre plot, I'll have Dresser and a couple others get to work digging Chief Johnson's well."

Jack nodded brusquely, then said, "I would bring my people into Middle Park. Do you object?"

Meeker saw that the request was directed more to Douglass than to him, but he answered anyway. "That would be fine, Jack. When we give out the land to Chief Douglass's braves, we can survey a patch for you on the other side of the park and you can begin clearing, plowing, and planting soon."

"My band will come soon," Jack said. Again he directed his words to Douglass, but the old chief only grunted assent.

Meeker worried for a moment that the two chiefs would press for more, but both Jack and Douglass were satisfied with their day's extortion. Douglass rode off without so much as a look back, while Jack spoke rapidly in the Ute tongue with his cadre of bodyguards. The other warriors argued, but Jack prevailed. He glared at Meeker, then let out a whoop and raced off, the braves trailing behind.

Meeker worried that Jack and his warriors had run into trouble up in North Park and sought refuge on the White River Agency until the tumult died down, but that was all right with him. He could keep his eye on Jack and persuade him to pick a plot of land for his own farm. Once the wild-eyed brave saw the greatness of raising his own food rather than hunting it, he would become, like Douglass, one of Meeker's great supporters in his drive for severalty.

Whistling, Meeker started across the field to where Dresser and the others worked.

"I'm going back to the agency for a few hours," Meeker said. "I need to send a report to the commissioner on what just transpired."

"You want us to keep a' plowin'?" asked Dresser,

obviously uneasy at having two Ute chiefs meet so near him. Meeker could not blame him. Dresser had been shot at before and probably thought it would happen again.

"Of course. I have come to an agreement with both Jack and Douglass. The plowing must continue with all speed! I need another eighty acres ready for planting as soon as you can do the plowing."

Meeker mounted his horse and rode back to the makeshift agency headquarters. Seeing the ramshackle building, he promised himself to get the cabin rebuilt into what it had been in Powell's Valley before the move. With events moving so quickly here, he needed suitable quarters for his family and the agency.

Progress was being made, he decided. The Ute were finally coming around and agreeing with him on government policies. Even Jack.

LEAVE. NOW!

August 18, 1879
Above Powell's Valley

Cray Eachin wiped sweat from his forehead, licked his lips nervously, and then bit down hard on the blasting cap. He hated this part of mining, and had never gotten comfortable handling dynamite or blasting caps. More than one miner of his acquaintance told stories of having dynamite freeze on them during the winter and then boiling it in water until it was hot enough to explode. Cray believed them, having seen dynamite warmers that looked like candle dippers for sale in general stores up and down the western slopes of the Rockies. But everyone agreed that the blasting caps were the most dangerous.

He wished he had enough money to buy a crimper to fasten the cap to the fuse. If anything went wrong while using the gadget, he'd only blow off a hand and not his head.

Cray bit down hard and fast to get it done. When the cap didn't explode and the fuse was securely crimped, he heaved a sigh of relief. He stuffed a few sticks of dynamite into the holes he had drilled, added the cap with the fuse, then tamped in rock and mud to hold it all together. His new mine was proving more difficult to sink than his earlier ones because it drove into harder rock.

"A little work now, a lot of fortune later," he muttered as he unrolled the spool of black miner's fuse until he had several feet stretched out. The waxy black fuse burned at precisely one foot per minute, giving Cray enough time to get back downhill to his crude cabin and take cover. He remembered all too well the time he had blasted with less dynamite than he used now and had hit a gas pocket. He had thought the world was coming to an end and would never stop raining down rock and dust.

That shaft had been nothing but dross, like the rest. But this one would make him rich. He knew it deep in his gut that his luck was changing for the better.

Cray struck a match and applied it to the end of the fuse. It sputtered a moment, then took off on its slow trek toward the blasting cap and the dynamite. He walked fast, trying to appear calm as he went in spite of wanting to run like the devil was after him.

"You take cover!" he shouted to Towa. The woman looked at him and shook her head, as if wondering what the fuss was over. "It's gonna blow in a couple minutes!" He had not been counting the time. An eternity crept by, though he knew he still had three or four minutes left before the explosion.

"You should stop this foolishness," Towa said. "We can go back together. My father is drunk all the time and would never know what we do."

"Towa, stop it," he said sharply. "You can stay

here. You don't have to go back to Kanneatche."
Cray thought the man beat Towa, but she would
never fess up to it. If he found out Kanneatche had
so much as laid a finger on his daughter . . .

"I want to be with my own people," she said,
color coming to her cheeks. He recognized the anger mounting and wondered at it. He couldn't live
with the Ute. When he got enough money to find
a preacher and get properly married, he and Towa
could live anywhere they wanted and to hell with
what people thought.

"Is there anything you can get there you can't
here with me?" he asked. Cray swallowed hard
when he saw her expression. He knew the Ute had
looser morals than he did, but he had thought
Towa had been as faithful to him as he had to her.
The look she gave him now made him wonder
about that. "Is there someone else?"

"We are married under Ute law," she said. "But
you do not live like a Ute. I am caught between
my people and yours. Where do I belong?"

"With me," he said earnestly. Then he staggered
forward and caught her in his arms as the dynamite
went off with a ground-shaking thunder. They
stumbled and went down in a heap, Cray on top
of her. This felt so right—until he saw her dark expression. Towa struggled out from under him.

"You do nothing but make little rocks from big.
It is not right," she said.

"It's making us rich. You and me. Whatever you
want, I'll be able to buy for you," he said.

Dust settled and made him cough. Towa turned
her head and looked at the ground to keep the
debris from making her sneeze.

Cray was ready to argue his point some more
when he heard horses approaching. He looked

around frantically, wondering where he had left his old musket. Wherever it was, he wasn't likely to find it before the four Ute rode up.

Cray wiped dust off his face and tried to look pleased at seeing Chief Colorow again. The fat Indian had come by at odd intervals, never staying long but always begging what food he could. Cray had grown increasingly nervous because of the way the man looked at the mining paraphernalia.

"You blow up our sacred mountains," Colorow said angrily. "You stop it now."

"This is all the blasting I'm going to do for a spell," Cray said, wishing he had a six-gun to strap to his hip. Most miners had only a rifle, but Cray saw the Ute as claim-jumpers of the worst kind. They technically owned the land where he dug for gold and silver and could chase him off if they put their mind to it.

"You leave now. You and all the others who dig our earth," Colorow said.

"You told me I could dig in your land after I fed you. Are you running off the settlers, too?" Cray asked hotly. "Or just the miners because this is where the real riches are?"

"We do not like this . . . mining," Colorow said.

"I can give you gifts, Chief Colorow," Cray said, thinking the corpulent Ute only wanted to extort a bit more from him, even after all the food he had given him over the past few weeks.

"I get plenty gifts from the *Maricat'z*," Colorow boasted. "I sign up at two agencies for gifts. They give me sugar and coffee and dried fruit. I eat better than you!"

Cray had to smile at that. From the way Colorow's belly bounced as he rode, it was obvious the blowhard chief ate better than most folks in these parts.

The smile faded when Cray realized how Colorow was acting. Before, he had been insistent. Now he was aggressive. It might be because he rode with other warriors, or it might be because Colorow saw Towa was in camp and wanted to impress her. Or maybe he wanted her for his own squaw. She was mighty pretty.

"I'm staying." Cray spoke flatly so there wouldn't be any confusion as to his meaning.

"You hunt and kill our game. You blow up our earth looking for golden rock. You will go."

"If I have to get the cavalry here, I will," threatened Cray.

"We know of your cavalry and do not fear them, not even the black-white soldiers."

Cray wondered what Colorow meant, but wasn't going to ask.

"You'll fear them a lot more if you try to chase me off this claim," Cray said. He glanced toward Towa, wondering whose side she would take. He could not tell from her expression.

"There is no gold or silver here," Colorow said. "Only the black rock that burns. Go. Leave. Stop causing trouble."

"You're the ones causing trouble," Cray said. He braced himself as Colorow swung about, his hand going for a knife sheathed at his hip. The chief considered for a moment, then took his hand away from the knife and motioned to Towa.

"You. Come with us. I will take you back to Kanneatche, your father. Where you belong!"

"Towa, no!" Cray said, stepping forward. She jerked free and looked at him.

"I will go with Colorow," she said, "so there will be no trouble."

Cray stepped back and saw that the braves with the chief had their rifles leveled on him. He almost wished they would put him out of his misery, but if they killed him, he would never see Towa again. He watched, disconsolate, as the Ute rode off in the direction of the valley.

A tear of frustration crept down Cray's cheek, and he angrily wiped it away, then noticed his fingers came away smudged with black soot.

"Coal," he muttered. "The black rock that burns." He turned and looked up the hill to where dust still settled.

No gold. No silver. Coal.

PURSUIT

August 22, 1879
Middle Park

Sheriff Bessey looked left and right to be sure everyone still rode with him. Three men in his posse. In most other cases, this would have been enough, but now it felt as if he were riding away from Hot Sulphur Springs stark naked into a raging fire. He hitched up his gun belt and rested his hand on the slick wooden grips of his Colt. In his saddlebags rode three boxes of ammunition for the six-shooter and two more for the Winchester rifle rubbing against his right leg as he rode. He had made certain the men with him were similarly armed.

He still felt naked as he rode down into the grassy sweep of Middle Park hunting for the men who had burned down Jim Thompson's house. Luckily, Thompson had taken the warnings he had received about the Ute seriously and had gone north to Steamboat Springs with his family to wait out the fracas brewing. Bessey wished he could leave Grand County himself and go stick his head in the sand back in West Texas.

But he couldn't. He had taken an oath to uphold the law, and enough witnesses had told him that Chinaman and Bennett, both Tabeguache Ute, were responsible.

Bessey wished the owner of the general store in Hayden would use more sense when it came to trading with the Indians, but Peck had a mind of his own. In a way, Bessey couldn't blame him too much. If the Ute wanted to trade so many fine horses for a few cases of rusty rifles and old ammo, the profit would keep Peck going for a year or two.

Long enough to sneak off, outwait the fight coming lickety-split down the pike, and then return to sell his goods to the victors, whoever they might be. Bessey didn't like it, but he couldn't fault Peck that much for wanting to make a profit.

"You sure them two Ute are the ones what burned Mr. Thompson's house, Sheriff?" asked R.D. Coxe. "I ain't ridin' into this hornet's nest without being damned sure."

"Enough folks said so," Sheriff Bessey said.

"Nobody at Peck's store would say a word. It was like the Sabbath, only for gossip. Ain't natural them bein' so quiet, with Peck not wantin' to tell all he knows—and more."

"None of this is natural," Bessey said. The fires throughout Grand County had been fierce. For every one barely snuffed out, two more started in the tinder-dry forests. He was certain the first had been the result of careless railroad tie-cutters. Since that fire got blamed on the Ute, though, every one after had also been laid at the Indians' doorstep. It did no good pointing out that heat lightning had started two others. Then there had been some suspiciously near mining camps. These, the sheriff had decided, *these* were set deliberately by the Ute in retaliation.

"Chinaman and Bennett did it, and they can't run off to the reservation and escape justice for their crimes," Bessey said, even as he had second thoughts about going after the two criminals with such a small posse, even if the agent cooperated. Letting Saponishe get away with murder had been a thorn in his side that had festered and threatened to devour his entire body and mind. As legal as it was for the Ute to return to their reservation and be held accountable only under tribal law, he wanted Saponishe—and Bennett and Chinaman— to stand trial in a white man's court and not be let off scot-free.

"What if that snooty Indian agent objects to us draggin' 'em back to Hot Sulphur Springs?" asked Coxe.

"We'll cross that bridge when we get to it. I already sent a copy of the arrest warrant ahead to Agent Meeker so he can't say he doesn't know what we want when we show up." Bessey looked across the grassy expanse that was the new White River Agency and saw the sluggishly flowing river snaking its way down through the mountain park. He estimated they were at the eastern side of reservation land. With a kick to the flanks of his horse, he started riding directly westward, toward the river.

"Sheriff, look there. Ute!" Coxe stood in his stirrups and pointed. "Looks to be a brave, his squaw, and a little girl."

"You speak their lingo, don't you?" Bessey asked.

"A little," Coxe said. "Enough to get myself into trouble."

They rode closer, Bessey and Coxe in the lead and the other two deputies hanging back. They drew rein a few yards from the brave, who smiled brightly and held up his hand.

"How!" he called.

Bessey studied the brave closely, noting how he wore a straw hat, which many of the Ute had taken to wearing, and was decked out in his Sunday best. But there was something more that sent a cold chill up the sheriff's spine. On a travois slung behind one of the brave's ponies were stacked hides. Another travois carried about everything he owned in the world.

"Ask him where he's going," Bessey said.

Coxe and the Ute chattered cheerfully for a couple minutes.

"Seems like him and his family're moving off the reservation," Coxe said. "I suspect he's going to trade everything he's got for some gewgaws for his wife and girl and then get himself a powerful lot of rifles."

Sheriff Bessey looked carefully, but did not see that the brave was armed now.

"Get him moving on his way," Bessey said.

"I asked if he knew Chinaman or Bennett, but he denied it."

"He probably doesn't. He has the look of someone in Douglass's band, not Jack's." Bessey waited impatiently as Coxe finished with the brave and got him and his family moving on their way north toward Peck's store, or another with a proprietor willing to exchange hides for guns.

At least the brave didn't look like he was going to buy firewater. Bessey wasn't certain if that was good or not, since the Ute could buy an extra box of ammo with money that might otherwise be spent on whiskey. Firewater spelled short-term trouble, but a well-provisioned warrior could kick up a fuss for months.

The posse slowly wended its way toward the river. Sheriff Bessey saw another Ute, clad only in a shirt, busily washing his clothing in the muddy river.

"Go around him," Bessey told his men. "No reason to get him all stirred up."

"His horse has taken a fancy to us," Coxe said. The horse jerked free of its tether and came trotting over. Bessey frowned, then motioned for Coxe to get the animal back to its owner. Coxe grabbed the horse's halter and swung it around, returning it to the half-naked man. The two talked for a few minutes; then Coxe returned where Bessey waited impatiently.

"Well, what'd he have to say?" the sheriff asked.

"There's a whale of a lot of activity all through the agency," Coxe said. "He says he doesn't know what's going on, but I think he's lying."

"Did you ask how much farther it is to the agency headquarters?"

"He said a mile," Coxe replied. "That means there's no telling how far it is. To a Ute anything less than five miles is only a mile."

It proved to be three miles to the new White River Agency headquarters, every mile increasingly tense for the posse. Fires burned high in the mountains, an especially large one along Gore Ridge. None of the Ute took notice of the fires, as if they knew there was no danger. Sheriff Bessey did not share that sense of security as he rode toward the building with the feeling of hundreds of eyes on him. Large camps of tepees lined either side of the river, but there were a few log cabins mixed alongside to show these might well be permanent villages.

"I got to admit, Meeker's done himself proud," Coxe said. "The valley's not even a mile wide here, but this is the best spot for a farm I ever did see."

"He surely did spend their money on the best equipment," Sheriff Bessey said, shielding his eyes as he peered into sheds beside the headquarters building. He looked up to the bluffs on either side of the valley and made out the small, slowly moving dots of grazing cattle. Everything seemed quiet on the reservation.

"Sheriff," Meeker said in greeting, his tall, angular form unfolding from beneath a wagon he worked to repair. "You showed up quicker than I thought."

"I reckon that gives you some idea how important this is, Mr. Meeker," Bessey said, dismounting.

"What do they want, Father?" asked an old Ute, waddling out from the agency cabin.

Sheriff Bessey blinked at this form of address. The Ute had called Meeker by an honorific usually reserved for only the most respected members of the tribe.

"Do you know Chief Douglass?" Meeker asked Bessey, pointing to the Ute.

"He speaks danged good English," Coxe said. "Better English than I do his tongue."

This pleased Meeker more than anything they could have said about his accomplishments in agriculture and how the entire valley looked to be a model of farming efficiency.

"Douglass has been principal chief for ten years and has negotiated much of the benefits for his tribe," Meeker said.

"Where does Jack fit in?" asked the sheriff.

"Jack is a secondary chief, in a way I do not quite understand," Meeker admitted. "He is respected by many of the younger warriors, but the days of fighting the Arapaho are over, thanks to Chief Douglass and the warriors of his generation."

"So the Ute scattered around the valley will obey Douglass?" asked Bessey.

"What's your business?" asked the old chief. He pulled himself up to his full five-foot-seven-inch height and tried to look fierce. The extreme bowing of his legs kept him from achieving his goal.

"The sheriff contacted me earlier about two men in Jack's band," said Meeker. "I hope you can help him find them."

"Bennett and Chinaman," said Bessey. "They're wanted for arson."

"They are not on the reservation," Douglass said quickly. Too quickly. "Therefore, I cannot give them to you for this crime."

"Mr. Meeker, tell the chief what the law says." Sheriff Bessey watched Douglass's reaction carefully, but the Ute had on his poker face.

"You must turn them over, Chief. It is your duty to send away any Ute violating the law. Sheriff Bessey has a legal warrant for the arrest of these two men."

For several minutes the silence hung like a lead weight because Douglass did not speak. When he did, his face was so contorted in anger that Bessey stepped back a pace and put his hand on the butt of his six-shooter.

"They will not be turned over for *Maricat'z* justice," Douglass said decisively. "You have no use for them, Meeker, so you turn them over, unlike how you defended Saponishe."

"Saponishe left without doing the work he was supposed to," Meeker said, turning testy. "But this is not why I want these two handed over to the law.

They burned a man's house. That is not to be tolerated."

Sheriff Bessey frowned. It sounded to him as if Meeker was saying murder was fine but putting a torch to a man's house was a terrible crime. He held his tongue, though, watching the agent and the old chief.

Douglass glared at Bessey and the others in his posse, then went to the corral behind the headquarters, mounted, and rode off without so much as a look back.

"He's a man who knows his own mind," Meeker said. "I am sorry your trip did not turn out better, Sheriff. As it is almost four o'clock, would you and your men join us for dinner before departing?"

"That your wife?" Sheriff Bessey asked, indicating a young woman bustling about inside the agency headquarters.

"That's Mrs. Price. My wife's over there."

"She—" Bessey bit back the comment he almost let slip about how much older Mrs. Meeker was than her gray-haired husband. She looked old enough to be his mother. "She must be a good cook. The smell is enticing."

"Break bread with us; then you can be on your way," Meeker said.

Bessey and Coxe exchanged glances, then looked at the other two men in the posse. The sheriff shared their desire to be away from the center of so many camped Ute warriors since it didn't look as if their mission to arrest the two arsonists was going to be successful. Meeker worked on the farms, oblivious to the tension all around him. If Chief Douglass was any indication, the slightest misstep on any white man's part would cause the entire reservation to explode in war.

The sheriff and his posse ate quickly. He wondered if he ought to warn Meeker to get the womenfolk off the reservation and to Hot Sulphur Springs or Hayden until things settled down, but he kept quiet.

"Thanks for such a fine meal, ma'am," the sheriff said as he and the three deputies mounted to retrace their path off the reservation. Bessey felt relief at the notion he was leaving with his scalp still in place; the meal the old woman had cooked hadn't been good enough for him and his men to stay one second longer than decorum dictated.

"Sorry I couldn't help more, Sheriff," Meeker said, "but I have to believe Chief Douglass when he said the two men you seek aren't here. I'll ask after them."

"There any friction between Douglass and Jack?"

"There always is," Meeker said, "but Chief Douglass is firmly in charge of his people. The band that follows Jack is small." Meeker paused a moment, thought over what he had to say, then shook his head vigorously. "No, no, it would do no good to find Jack and ask him to turn over these two criminals. Douglass has already spoken for the entire tribe."

"That's what I thought," Sheriff Bessey said. "Much obliged for your hospitality, Mr. Meeker. Mrs. Meeker." The lawman tipped his hat in the old woman's direction, then got his horse trotting back north away from the peaceful valley where the undercurrents threatened to drag everyone to their death.

REPORTS

August 22, 1879
Middle Park

"Are you about finished?" asked Arvella Meeker. "You've been working on that report for hours and hours."

"I need to finish it as soon as possible," Meeker said to his wife. "The annual report to the Indian Bureau is an important part of my job. It keeps Washington abreast of all I am doing, and the problems I face daily."

"You aren't chiding them again about not sending more supplies, are you?" The hatchet-faced woman scowled. "The major up at Fort Steele is sick of you warning of trouble on the reservation."

"It's Thornburg's job to back up any action I take, and I find him deficient because of his attitude. Look how annoying that sheriff from Hot Sulphur Springs is, and all because of Ute leaving the agency to cause mischief."

"Burning down a man's home is hardly what I would call mischief," Arvella said acidly.

"Part of the problem, and I am detailing this in the report to Commissioner Hayt again, is that the

Indians are allowed to keep their horses. This gives them far too much mobility. Consider how easily Jack's men race off from the reservation to start fires, shoot at settlers, then ride back where they are safe."

"Douglass protects them," Arvella said. "I don't care what the law says about this being a sovereign nation. Without Douglass's help they would not loiter about the agency."

"Now, dear, Chief Douglass is cooperating with us. Considering how obdurate Johnson has become, not that it matters in his case, we need Douglass's support."

"He only takes what you give him. He does nothing to keep that awful Jack under control."

"It's not Douglass's fault," Meeker said. "The horse gives the Ute the ability to range far. I am proposing to the commissioner that we take away all their horses, except plow horses, of course. And what Ute would ride one of them?" Meeker laughed at the image of a proud Ute warrior astride a lumbering Suffolk or Percheron.

"The heathens will never agree to that," Arvella said.

"Chief Douglass has great sway over them. Look at how he has kept his band peaceably at work on their farms. Together, we can convince them to give up their horses. If only Johnson would agree to give up his herd, things would go much smoother."

"Johnson, pah," sniffed Arvella. "He races horses, breeds horses, trades horses, lives with them, I do declare!"

"The only Ute who will work on the farms are the ones without horses," Meeker said. "Johnson actually gives horses to some of the younger braves to keep them from working in the fields. That is the sort of behavior I fight and must find a way to stop."

"He sends them out to find more pastures for his herd," Arvella said. "You should never have taken his land to plow for farmland. This forced Johnson to hunt for grazing areas farther from the agency. Now he is beyond your authority and still has his herd."

"I had such hopes that he wanted to quit his life of savagery when we first came to White River, too," said Meeker with a sigh. "I held Johnson up as a shining example of what could be done to civilize the Ute, but he has proven to be a great disappointment. We must make an example of him and show how his heathen ways will not be tolerated any longer."

He turned back to his report to the commissioner, writing in his precise hand how he had ordered more land to be plowed into fields fit for crops to take away yet more pasture from Johnson.

SCARED AWAY

August 22, 1879
On Johnson's Land

"They will take all our land," Tim said to his older brother, Tatit'z.

"How do you know? Did you hear the agent say this?" Tatit'z was more cautious when dealing with the *Maricat'z* since they changed their minds often. Even when they spoke of one thing, they sometimes did another. Had not brother's father Canavish been told to leave his grazing pastures so the *Maricat'z* could plow up the earth to plant their seeds? The land given Canavish had been better for pasturing, and a well had been dug to provide water even in the midst of the drought. This had been good, and Canavish had found it easier raising even more horses.

Instead of being happy at this good fortune, Agent Meeker had complained about it. But Tatit'z found it hard to think even Meeker would plow up another meadow given to their father. Once, Canavish had benefitted. Twice, he would be furious.

"We can ask Quinkent. He speaks often with the agent," said Tim.

"I wish Father were here," Tatit'z said. Canavish had taken a dozen head of horses north to trade with members of Chief Nicaagat's band. Nicaagat had been trading with the *Maricat'z* for rifles, and Canavish thought he could trade his horses for rifles to use hunting later in the year.

"Quinkent will know," Tim insisted.

Tatit'z nodded. Together the two agitated youngsters crossed their father's pastureland, skirting the agency buildings and heading for Quinkent's cabin on the north bank of the White River as it wound around and headed east in the center of the park. The old chief sat in front of his fine new cabin, smoking a pipe and staring across the valley being transformed from rolling, grassy meadow into farmland by the tireless *Maricat'z* plows.

Tatit'z and Tim waited politely for the chief to notice them. It was not the place of the younger brave to speak unless spoken to.

"Sit," Quinkent finally said. The two hastily sat and waited for him to ask their reasons for coming. Quinkent did after another ten minutes had passed. Tatit'z almost burst apart with his questions.

"Chief Quinkent, you know the agent. Has he told his men to plow my father's land again?"

Quinkent frowned and puffed a bit more on his pipe. Then he said, "I have spoken often to Father Meeker about the way he gives and then takes away land. In spite of being so eloquent, even in the *Maricat'z* tongue, I do not sway him."

"They call you Douglass, after a black-skinned slave," Tim declared.

"Douglass is a mighty orator," Quinkent said, his ire rising.

"What can we do to keep the *Maricat'z* from stealing our father's land again? Canavish is not expected to return until tomorrow."

"Rumors, gossip, they spread like wildfire," Quinkent said. "Meeker is not so foolish as to take away your father's land. Canavish is a well-respected member of the Tabeguache Ute, a sub-chief, a medicine man, and a warrior of great ability. If Meeker steals from such a man, he steals from all Ute."

Tatit'z and Tim exchanged glances, then sat silently as Quinkent puffed at his pipe. When he said no more, Tatit'z nudged his brother and they silently left the chief to his thoughts.

"What should we do?" asked Tim.

"I have a rifle I traded for," Tatit'z said. "You heard what Quinkent said. Any theft from our father is the same as stealing from all of us. We have to defend our property or we will be considered less than men."

"Our father would approve," Tim said, warming to the argument. "He would protect his horses, his land, all that has been given him. Since he is gone, we must do it."

The two boys hurried to their father's *carniv,* and Tatit'z found the rifle he had gotten from one of Nicaagat's braves. They went higher up the slope and found a spot looking down into the pasture where they feared the *Maricat'z* would begin their plowing.

For an hour they sat, saying nothing. The race-track Canavish had built at the far end of the meadow had given them many victories. Tatit'z had won a pair of fine horses racing there and had given one to his brother.

"There, look, look!" cried Tim, jumping to his

feet. "They are coming to cut the earth of our father's pasture."

Tatit'z sucked in his breath. What Tim said was true. Three *Maricat'z* struggled to move their heavy plow up the road from the agency headquarters. Two worked with their balky gray mules while the other, a man named Price, dragged the rest of the equipment to the edge of the pasture. They hitched up the team, and the two husbanders went to the far side of the pasture to line up the plow.

"We must stop them! They are stealing our father's land!"

Tatit'z nodded as he raised his rifle and sighted along its smooth metal barrel. Sunlight caught the bright silver bead on the front sight. He positioned it properly in the notched rear sight, gently squeezed, and loosed a round.

The reaction to the single shot was far out of proportion to the effort. The mules squealed like pigs and raced off, dragging the plow behind them. The man at the plow fell forward, then jumped to his feet and ran in the opposite direction, kicking up a dust cloud under his pounding boots. The other two men dashed away, running as fast as any of Canavish's horses ever had along the racetrack.

For a moment, the boys stood and stared, not believing they had successfully defended their father's land with a single shot. Then they laughed and slapped each other on the back.

"Let's go tell Quinkent what we've done," Tatit'z said.

Before they reached Chief Quinkent, Tatit'z and Tim had told dozens of other Ute of their victory over the three *Maricat'z* land thieves.

LIES AND THREATS

August 22, 1879
White River Agency Headquarters

Nathan Meeker fumed, then began pacing like a caged animal. He clasped his hands behind his back to keep from wringing them as he walked to and fro in front of the agency headquarters building. When he saw Douglass making his way up the road from his cabin, riding his horse slowly as if nothing had happened, Meeker became even more enraged.

"Father Meeker," greeted Douglass, dismounting from his horse. His bowlegs were perfect for riding the animal, conforming themselves to the horse's bulging flanks. On the ground away from the horse that was so much a part of him, he appeared ludicrous.

"It has happened for the last time," said Meeker. "I will not have my men shot at, killed!"

"What are you saying?" Douglass frowned. He pointed to a nearby bench and took out his pipe. He recoiled when Meeker angrily swept it from his hands with a furious swat.

"Mr. Dresser was shot at before. That might have

been a mistake, although I am sure Johnson meant to hit him. I will overlook the intent because Mr. Dresser was not injured. But now Mr. Price has been shot at."

"Are you saying he has been killed?" asked Douglass, growing mad, too. Canavish's two boys had told him what had happened. The story was old by the time they reached him, but they had not claimed to shoot any *Maricat'z.*

"By God, I will have the cavalry into this lawless hellhole to restore order. I cannot have my men killed from ambush. That is cowardly. The lot of you heathen savages are cowards, shooting and kill ing from hiding."

Douglass glanced at his fallen pipe, but made no move to pick it up.

"No one was killed," he said.

"So! You know who shot at Mr. Price! Who was it? One of Jack's vile killers? Or was it Johnson himself? I demand that he be brought to justice immediately."

"They tried to steal Johnson's land," Douglass said. "That could not be permitted."

"I gave those men orders where to plow and what to do. Johnson has too many horses and that land is needed for crops. I dug him a well. What does he do with it? Put in pipe to irrigate the land? No! He waters his horses. His herd is immense. This cannot be allowed to stand."

"You would call the soldiers?" Douglass turned impassive, in spite of the heat he felt building over this. Tatit'z and Tim were honest youngsters and would never have lied about killing one of the agent's men. If anything, it would have increased the boys' esteem in the eyes of many in Jack's band if they *had* killed Price. As it was, their description of how the *Maricat'z* had turned into rabbits scurrying for their burrows had caused much amusement and laughter.

"I will, sir, I will. A man has been killed!"

Douglass said nothing. He knew Meeker lied to him.

"That land will be plowed and irrigated for crops. I swear no amount of deaths by you savages will stop me from accomplishing it!"

"What are you saying?"

"All you heathens will cultivate the land or I'll move you farther south! You *will* stop raising horses and *will* work in the fields."

"No." Douglass spoke firmly and simply.

Meeker's eyes went wide with surprise. "You deny my authority? You murder my workers and then you defy me! This is not to be, sir!"

Douglass watched as Meeker turned redder in the face. The chief turned, carefully stepped on the pipe the agent had knocked from his hand, and put his full weight on it.

The crack as it broke sounded like the peal of doom.

VIOLENCE

August 26, 1879
White River Agency

Nathan Meeker sat heavily, wishing he had some lemonade to quench his thirst. The day was hot and he had been outside in the burning Colorado sun since dawn. But he felt a definite glow of pride in what was being accomplished. Frank Dresser and Glencannon plowed at the eighty-acre plot up on the western slopes, and would finish within a day or two. The unfortunate incident in which Price had been shot at was not forgotten, but seemed to have been swept under the rug.

Shadrick Price and his wife were leery about continuing their employment at the agency, but Meeker was sure he could convince them to stay. Price had a tendency to look at the dark side of events. A few days of rest and reflection would permit him to have a better perspective on matters and how the agency was helping the heathens at the reservation.

Meeker sighed and got to his feet. Bringing civilization to the savages was difficult but not impossible. He had reached Douglass and had the old chief firmly on his side. Even Chief Jack was coming around more and more. Meeker scowled at the last meeting, when Jack had insisted on getting more than his share of coffee and sugar, but Meeker had been firm and given him only what was his due.

"Soon enough, they'll be independent and growing crops," Meeker said with some confidence.

"You!" The shout brought Meeker around.

"Good day, Chief Johnson. What brings you here?" Meeker hoped the Indian would tell him how Tatit'z had been punished for shooting at Price.

"You plow my racetrack! You do this all the time. In Powell's Valley. Here in Middle Park. You give me land, then you take it away."

"You have your land, Chief," Meeker said, wondering when Johnson would understand how important it was to have the best land tilled for agriculture. "I even put down a well for you."

"You steal my pastures. You steal my racetrack. What good is a well if I cannot graze or race my horses?"

"Ah, yes, your horses," Meeker said. "I have been meaning to tell you to move them farther south in the park. There is less need for horses when you have fields full of waving grain." Meeker wanted to tell Johnson how he considered the horses to be the single most important obstacle to be overcome in civilizing the Ute. "You won't need to ride to North Park any longer. You can stay and farm."

"I need horses. I trade horses. I *race* horses."

"Yes, of course you do. Rather, you *have been* racing. I do not approve of gambling and consider this an inappropriate use of your skills."

Johnson glared at Meeker but did not answer.

"You see, Chief Johnson, you spend too much of your time with the horses. Your children do also, when they could be learning to read and write."

"You teach them your religion." Johnson was accusing, but Meeker took it as a compliment.

"My daughter is doing a fine job educating the children, but yours do not attend Sunday services."

"I want my sons to raise horses, to race horses. You cannot take my land for your weeds."

"Weeds?" Meeker laughed. "More than weeds will grow. The weeds will need to be pulled or hoed, of course, and this is a splendid job for children to teach them responsibility. I—"

"Thief!" screamed Johnson. He swung a meaty fist and connected squarely with the side of Meeker's jaw, sending the agent reeling. Before Meeker could regain his balance, Johnson swarmed over him, pummeling him repeatedly.

"Stop! You're hurting me," groaned Meeker, feebly struggling. The first blow had stunned him, but Johnson was too strong to oppose even if it hadn't. Meeker tried to shove his attacker away, but this only opened his body to a flurry of relentless punches that robbed him of breath and made him moan in growing pain.

"Get away from him!" Shadrick Price rushed from the headquarters building and grabbed Johnson by the arm, swinging him around.

Meeker blinked to clear his vision, and saw Price block a punch Johnson launched at him. The Ute chief stepped back, his face a mask of unadulterated fury.

"You steal my land. You want to steal my horses. You won't! Old Meeker cannot do this terrible thing." Johnson shoved Price back against the wall of agency headquarters, then stormed off.

"Enough is enough," Meeker said, getting to his feet painfully. Every breath sent a lance of pain through his body, making him worry that Johnson had broken one of his ribs. His ears rang and his jaw was beginning to swell.

"Are you all right, Mr. Meeker?"

"I'll be better after I send a stern letter to Major Thornburg and get a company of soldiers here to arrest Johnson! I'll show him that he can't attack me for no reason! I'll show all the Ute. There are laws!"

Limping on a twisted ankle, faint from pain in his side and his face looking like a side of beef, Nathan Meeker went inside to begin yet another letter of complaint. He vowed that this one would not be ignored as had the one concerning whiskey sales to the Indians.

PETERING OUT

Cray Eachin sat cross-legged on the ground, painstakingly going through every rock blown from the mouth of his new mine. He grew increasingly angry as he tossed the chunks over his shoulder onto a pile that was far too large.

"Coal, nothing but damned coal," he grumbled. "It'll keep me warm, but surely won't light up my pocket with gold or silver."

"You find nothing but the rock that burns?" asked Towa, coming from their cabin. She had a deerskin bag slung over her shoulder. She sat on her heels nearby, watching as he pawed through the coal. His hands were black from touching the black mineral, but his mood was blacker yet.

"Not a single, damned gold flake or smear of silver anywhere to be seen. I don't know what to do, Towa," he said. "Where do I find pay dirt?" Cray looked up, rubbed his nose, and then jerked his hand away as if he had burned himself. He knew his slightest touch would leave a dark streak—like the one on Towa's cheek where he had touched her this morning.

"You will keep digging," she said in a curiously flat tone.

"That's what I always do," he said. Cray got to his feet and stretched. All he did was blast, drag the shattered stone from the shaft, and go through it for any trace of lead carbonate that might signal a silver strike or the bright gleam of gold.

"Yes," she said in the same tone. Towa stood and looked at the ground, as if wanting to say something more but not knowing how to find the right words.

"What's wrong? Are we out of beans again?"

"Plenty of cans," Towa said. She paused, then said, "I am going to the reservation."

"To see Kanneatche?" The name burned Cray's tongue. He had never gotten along with his father-in-law and never much cared except for moments like this. He could not begrudge his wife the chance to see her family, but every time Towa went, she returned a little more confused because of the lies her father told her about white men—and about Cray.

"I will see him," she said. "Good-bye, Cray."

"Wait!" Cray jumped over the knee-high pile of coal and took her by the arm. He left a sooty hand-print, but somehow this seemed less important than finding out what he was missing. Towa had said one thing, but he had a feeling in his gut she'd meant something else.

"Yes," she said, turning and looking at him with her big, dark eyes.

"What's going on?"

"I return to my father's tepee."

"When'll you be back?" Cray read the answer in

Towa's face before she shrugged and turned from him. "Wait a minute. You're not just going for a visit, are you?"

"No. I leave you now. Good-bye, Cray."

"You're walking out on me? You can't! We're married. The Bear Dance last year. You've lived with me. I know common-law marrying isn't the same as a church wedding, but it's not my fault there's no circuit preacher who could marry us all legal-like. I promise as soon as I get a strike, we'll go to Denver and—"

"Good-bye," she said more firmly now. Her chin thrust out and fire came into her eyes. "You have been a good husband, but I seek another now."

"Why are you leaving?" Cray's mind refused to focus, and felt as if it had been dipped in molasses. Everything moved in a curious slowness that confused him even more.

"You do nothing but dig. I want husband who hunts. One who provides." Towa shrugged. "Perhaps I even settle for husband who farms like Meeker says."

"It's because you're all alone up here. I mean, except for me. You miss your brothers and sisters, the others in your tribe. That's it, isn't it? You don't have to go, not permanently. Visit for a spell. Then you can—"

"Good-bye." Towa stepped back faster than he could grab her again. The fire in her dark eyes told him not to stop her.

"You're going to take another husband, aren't you? You don't think I'm good enough. I thought better of you. I thought you loved me. You *chose* me!"

"I did. Now I no longer choose you. It is the way of the People." Towa backed off another few steps, settled her leather bag over her shoulder, and walked away with long, confident strides.

"No!" Cray shouted. "You can't go to another man. That'd make you a whore! You're my wife."

"I unmarry you. It is *Nunt'z* way. Do not follow or my father and brothers will kill you."

"Do you mean your family, or do you have a new man? A new *husband?*"

Towa ignored him, lengthened her stride, and vanished downslope into a ravine within minutes, leaving Cray behind. He stared after her, shocked at her sudden departure.

Or had it been so sudden? He had seen how unhappy Towa was living here away from her tribe, but being unhappy was a way of life. It was hard work prospecting for gold, and he worked damned hard. Cray had never slacked off a day in his life, and had worked even harder after marrying Towa.

"I should have found a preacher," he said, hunting for the reason she had left him. "That would have shown her I was really serious."

Cray found himself running downhill at a breakneck pace, yelling Towa's name. He slid to a halt in the bottom of the gravelly ravine.

"Towa!" His shout echoed down the canyon and out into Powell's Valley beyond. There was no response. Cray started after her, but like his mine, his determination petered out, and he came to a halt a dozen yards off.

"Towa," he said, trying not to cry. "I love you." Cray looked back up the slope to his mine and the huge piles of coal he had brought from the bowels of the earth. Not a speck of silver or gold had he found. Only coal. Black, sooty coal.

He trudged back up the hill to his cabin and

looked inside. Towa had stripped the place of her belongings and half his larder.

"Take it," he said bitterly. "If that's all you ever wanted from me, good riddance." Cray began shoving his sparse belongings into a burlap bag. There was nothing keeping him here. He would never get rich pawing about in the filthy dirt, but there wasn't anything else he knew.

Unless he wanted to swallow his pride. Cray started back downhill, but did not head for Kanneatche's tepee, where Towa would live. Instead he went to the White River Agency headquarters to offer his services to Nathan Meeker again. He didn't like the agent, but working for him would bring in a small salary.

And keep him close to Towa until she came to her senses and realized that she loved him as much as he did her.

JACK AND
THE MAJOR

September 26, 1879
Along Bear River at Elkhead Creek

"It's a damned wild-goose chase," Major T.T. Thornburg said. He looked around the peaceful mountains for any sign of trouble in Coffee Creek Canyon. "Look at this place, Rankin. Do you see Ute poking their rifles out from behind every bush, ready to start a war?"

"Sir," said Joseph Rankin, "we saw enough sign of trouble farther north."

"I spoke with Sheriff Bessey in Hot Sulphur Springs while you were scouting," Thornburg said. "He assured me the trouble lay only with a few malcontents. Every reservation has them. In spite of what that alarmist Meeker says, there is no uprising. It is a shame that a house was burned to the ground, but considering how many fires there have been this year, the two Ute responsible might have caused it by accident."

"I don't think so, sir," the scout said. His head

swiveled around, taking in every detail of the terrain. Rankin grew increasingly wary of the route.

"We're all on edge," Thornburg said. "I wish someone had broken Meeker's writing hand instead of a few ribs. If he maintained better discipline on his reservation, there wouldn't be any reason to bring us all the way out of the fort. A wild-goose chase. That's all this is."

"I talked with some of the settlers around Hot Sulphur Springs," Rankin said, "and they don't agree with their sheriff about the Ute. Enough of them have friends in the tribe who're warnin' them to hightail it north, away from where the pot's gonna boil over."

"Some pot, some boiling," Major Thornburg grumbled. "The only boiling I see is being done by *me*. I have real troubles at the fort to tend to, but Meeker built a fire under the Secretary of War, who put a bug in General Sheridan's ear about this. That's the only reason we've been on the trail for the past week. Politics, not reality." Thornburg snorted contemptuously and rode along, muttering to himself about inept bureaucrats, weak-spined generals in Chicago unable to stand up to them—and Indian Agent Nathan Meeker.

How could any land this peaceful-looking be on the verge of rebellion, as Meeker had described it? The agent had done nothing but complain about the Ute and how lazy they were. Now he changed his tune and sang about them being dangerous.

"They're the peaceful Indians," Thornburg said to Rankin. The scout looked sideways at his commander. "Ouray has been to Washington enough that he gets invited to big parties. Tribute flows like a river into the Ute hands. When was the last time we heard of a skirmish between them and the Cheyenne or Arapaho or Sioux? It's been years."

"Yes, sir," Rankin said, still alert.

"Years, and yet we are ordered to bring two entire companies of cavalry, two of infantry, and all necessary support to the White River Agency." Thornburg craned his neck around to see the squad struggling on the backtrail with the thirty-three-wagon supply train. "Four companies—a hundred forty men!—tied up when we should be dealing with weightier problems in Wyoming, not Colorado."

"Sir, Ute." Rankin drew rein and pointed ahead. "Can't rightly tell how many, but there might be a considerable number of them."

"And why not? This is their hunting land," scoffed Thornburg. "With the drought driving them out of the parks and onto higher ground, they might have to range this far to find antelope and elk."

"We've seen our share of game," Rankin admitted. Thornburg had ordered hunters to bag a few deer to supply fresh meat, but Joe Rankin had convinced him not to reveal their position that way. Now he was not so certain that the meat wouldn't have been a decent addition to their dried rations and wouldn't have kept the men more alert.

The Ute had spotted them before they had found the Ute.

"This looks like a decent spot, at the junction of the two rivers. Make camp here," Thornburg ordered the head of his infantry, Captain Payne. "I'll ride out with Mr. Rankin to see what they want."

"Sir, we don't have to. They're already here." Rankin touched his carbine, but Thornburg motioned for him to leave it in his saddle sheath.

"We might put this matter to rest without going all the way to the agency. How much farther is it anyway, Mr. Rankin?"

"Sixty-seventy miles, sir," the scout answered, less interested in distances than he was the Indians. "I don't like the look of this."

"Nonsense. The Ute are peaceful." Thornburg straightened his uniform jacket and waited for the party of ten Ute to ride up to where he stood stiffly at attention.

"Maiquas," Thornburg called, holding up his hand in the traditional greeting.

The leader of the Ute rode a few yards ahead of the others, his dark eyes darting all around as he sized up the Army column.

"Maiquas," Jack returned. "You chief of these soldier fellows?"

"I'm Major Thornburg, from Fort Steele in Wyoming Territory."

"You come long way to hunt. You kill our deer?"

"No, not at all. Who might you be? A mighty chief, I am sure."

"Nicaagat," Jack said.

Rankin moved closer to his commander and whispered, "That one's named Jack. A mean son of a buck, sir. The settlers say he's one of the ringleaders of the rebellion."

"What rebellion? Nicaagat—Jack—is peaceable enough." Louder, so the Ute could hear, Thornburg said, "Come and join us for dinner, Chief Jack."

Jack reared back at hearing his *Maricat'z* name. "You know me?"

"All know of your mighty exploits, Chief," Thornburg lied.

"Why do you come?" Jack demanded.

Thornburg scowled at such bluntness. He had always dealt with Indians in a more roundabout fashion, in ways that pleased them. A pipe or two might be smoked before serious discussions began. But Jack had adopted a characteristic more likely to be used by a white man. Thornburg found it refreshing that he wanted nothing to do with beating around the bush and came right to the point.

"Your agent, Mr. Meeker, summoned us. He sent a letter to the Indian Commissioner, who sent one to the Secretary of the Interior, who had my commanding general order me to the White River Agency." Thornburg saw this confused Jack. "That's all right, Chief. It is confusing to me also. Why Mr. Meeker thinks there is any trouble when I can see there is none ought to be discussed fully with him."

"You go to reservation?" Jack placed his hand on the knife sheathed at his hip.

"Sir," whispered Rankin. "Look at their faces."

"They're clean enough," Thornburg said. "Is that what I'm supposed to see? No dirt?"

"They've wiped off yellow and black paint, sir. War paint."

"Are you telling me they are on the warpath and are trying to hide it from me?"

"We got four companies of soldiers to back up the agent, sir. That might not be what Jack wants, if'n he's the cause of the trouble."

"*If* there is trouble, Mr. Rankin," corrected the major.

"No need to go to reservation," Jack said loudly. He glanced behind him at the other nine Ute. They all shook their heads vigorously.

"I'm sure it is a needless burden on my men," Thornburg said, "but I have my orders."

"You camp here," Jack said, indicating the soldiers pitching camp near the Bear River. "Plenty to drink. Plenty to eat. Why not ride on to reservation, you and me and some horse soldiers? Maybe five."

"I beg your pardon?" Thornburg asked, startled. "You want me to continue to the reservation with only five troopers?"

"No need all go," Jack said. "Save you lots of saddle sores. You and the riding soldiers."

"I'm sure," Thornburg said dryly. Louder, to Jack, he said, "I have my orders. Riding on to the agency headquarters with only five soldiers would violate those orders."

The Ute spoke rapidly among themselves for a moment. Then Jack said, "Why you go? Why big chief tell you to do this?"

"Mr. Meeker has requested our presence, Chief Jack," Thornburg said. He saw a moment of agitation that the Ute leader hastily hid behind an immobile mask.

"Meeker speak to heap big chief in Washington?"

"Something like that," Thornburg said tiredly. He realized Jack could never understand the chain of command, or how Meeker had finally brought enough pressure to bear to summon four companies of troopers more than a hundred miles away to his aid. For all that, Thornburg wasn't sure he understood himself.

Jack chattered with his band, then asked, "You camp here long? Plenty water. You can hunt deer."

"Thank you for your kind permission, Chief Jack," Thornburg said. "We will be moving on at the dawn, however. All of us. On our way to the White River Agency."

"No," Jack said forcefully. "You no go to reservation."

"Tell you what, Chief Jack. I'll take my command to a spot five miles away from the agency headquarters, then accept your kind offer of escorting a small party to meet with Agent Meeker."

Jack and the others discussed this for another minute; then Jack turned back and nodded once.

"You stay, you rest and eat and drink. Then you go and stop before reservation. We show you way to Meeker in Middle Park."

"Your kindness will not be forgotten by the big chief in Washington, Chief Jack. Your name will be put up next to Chief Ouray's as a great leader of the Ute."

Jack snorted in disgust, nodded again, and wheeled his horse around. With a loud whoop, he and the other nine warriors rode back along the trail in the direction they had come.

"That was smart, sir," Rankin said. "Only five of us riding with ten of them would have been suicidal."

"I don't think so, Mr. Rankin, but keep a sharp eye out tonight. Have some of your scouts chase after Jack and find where he's camped, if they can without being seen. I want to know more about him and why he's so far from home."

"Yes, sir," Rankin said, calling to a couple of his better scouts.

Major Thornburg took off his hat and scratched his balding head. He didn't share his head scout's misgivings about Jack and his band, but something did not seem exactly right either.

"Might be Meeker's not so squirrely after all," Thornburg said to himself. He put his hat back on and went to be certain his sergeants had properly pitched camp and posted enough sentries to ensure the column's safety against any intruders.

Especially Ute warriors who had wiped war paint off their faces.

KIDNAPPED

September 27, 1879
White River Agency

"Go on, boy. Tell him," Nathan Meeker said brusquely.

Cray Eachin pulled away, not wanting to tell the Ute what Meeker had asked.

"He's been talking to Chief Johnson," Cray said. "He thinks you're going to ask him to give up his land, and he wants to keep it." Cray hesitated, because this was exactly what the Indian Agent wanted.

"I can take his land any time I want," Meeker said, anger mounting. "They are killers, murderers! They shoot at my employees and are hardly more than animals the way they live. What do they want grassland for but to raise their filthy horses!"

"I don't rightly understand why you don't like the Ute raising horses, Mr. Meeker," Cray said. "A good horse breeder, and the Ute are really good, can make a lot of money. Heaven knows, the settlers like Ute ponies, and prefer them to the broke-down nags that come over the Rockies from Denver."

"Don't blaspheme," Meeker said. His lips turned

to a thin line as his anger grew to even greater levels. "They are my wards and will do as I say. Tell him the cavalry is on its way, and if he doesn't do what I ask, the Army soldiers will make him a slave."

"What?" Cray stared at Meeker in utter surprise. "You don't want me to—"

"Tell him. Tell him the Army will put shackles on him and make him a slave if he doesn't let my crew plow his field. It's for his own good."

"Lying to him?" asked Cray. "You *are* just tryin' to scare him, aren't you?" Cray wasn't certain anymore what Meeker intended as a goad and what was true. Since Johnson had broken two of the man's ribs, Meeker had been erratic, but making a statement like this was sure to put a match to the fuse running all the way from New Mexico throughout the Ute reservation to North Park.

"It's not your place to question my decisions. Tell him."

Cray cleared his throat and chose his words carefully. He had learned to speak the *Nunt'z* language fairly well during his time with Towa. Some of the subtleties still escaped him, but more important than learning what to say, Cray had learned what not to say.

In Ute he told the brave, "The *Maricat'z* agent wants to give you a great gift." This caused the Ute to smile and nod eagerly since it had been so long since Meeker had distributed any of the supplies intended for the Tabeguache Ute. From the corner of his eye Cray saw how this appeased Meeker. For the moment.

"That is good," the Ute said in his own tongue. "I need fruit and coffee. I like coffee. And sugar."

"This is not the gift he gives you. He wants to

present you with a farm, all tilled and ready to plant when spring comes again." Cray had spent enough time in the Rockies to know how short the growing season could be. The first snows might come in weeks—or less. There was no time to do more than clear the boulders from the brave's field and plow it.

"I need grass for my horses," the brave said, turning more somber now that he realized the gift from the big chief in Washington was not what he wanted. "How am I to live if he takes my land and destroys the grass? Where will my horses graze?"

"Chief Johnson—Canavish—surrendered his land and allowed it to be turned into a farm. You should, too."

"Canavish got to fight the *Maricat'z* agent," the brave said, his eyes narrowing. "Can I break Meeker's arm or a leg? That might be worth having my pasture stolen."

Cray grinned and almost broke out laughing. It was an appealing notion. Trade a few acres of grassland for the chance to break some of Meeker's bones. Then he sobered. The thrashing Johnson had given Meeker had not changed the agent's mind about severalty. If anything, that beating had only made Meeker more determined to turn the entire Middle Park into a huge farm.

Cray got himself under control and said, "You have to let Mr. Meeker do as he likes. He is the agent."

"No." The brave crossed his arms across his chest and thrust out his chin belligerently.

"Please! He will call in the soldiers if you don't. That's what he told me," Cray said, trying to keep the pleading from his voice. He didn't do too good a job.

"Let the bluecoats come. It will not matter."

"Why not?" asked Cray.

"What's going on? He's not giving his permission, is he?" demanded Meeker. "That is of no concern if true. I'll have Mr. Price out there on his land within the hour. He will learn!" Nathan Meeker spun about and tried to stalk off. The pain in his ribs made the retreat less than intimidating, but Cray wasn't paying much attention to the agent. His eyes fixed on the brave.

"Why aren't you upset that he'll bring in the Army soldiers?" Cray asked again.

The brave sneered, spat in Meeker's direction, then walked off without answering. Cray felt a hollowness in his belly that wouldn't go away. Meeker was not bluffing. The agent had lost his mind with his insistence on plowing the entire Middle Park for farmland. If summoning the cavalry was what it took to force the Ute to his way of thinking, Meeker would do it.

What worried Cray more was the brave's response. He wasn't afraid of the military, and he ought to have been. More than once the Ute had seen the effectiveness of the soldiers against their traditional enemies. Ouray had made it abundantly clear to all the small bands in his loose confederation ranging from the south to North Park that they were to cooperate and not tempt fate by facing the bluecoated troopers. So why was this brave not cowed by the threat?

Cray Eachin started down the road from the agency cabin, heading toward the White River where Chief Douglass had his home. The cabin was almost as fine as the one Meeker used for his headquarters, and the land around it had been tilled, although the crops had not come in this year.

Douglass wasn't as eager to raise horses as Johnson and the others in his tribe, but Cray knew the chief had fought Meeker over plowing up all the land.

A few horses grazed near a dozen head of cattle behind Douglass's cabin.

"Chief!" Cray waited a proper amount of time before going to the front of the cabin. The door opened and the old chief came out.

"Maiquas," Cray greeted. "I seek your wisdom."

"Why bother?" Douglass asked rudely.

Such discourteous behavior was unusual from the chief, and took Cray aback.

"I need your help in convincing Agent Meeker he is wrong."

"Nothing will change his mind," Douglass said. "What do you want to say to him?"

"The way he is cultivating the entire park is wrong. There should be a balance between crops and pasture for grazing horses and cattle. For some reason, he is dead set against any of your people raising horses."

"They give us freedom," Douglass said, settling down on a plank bench. He took out a pipe and put tobacco into it. Cray noticed it was not the chief's old pipe, the one given him by Ouray. Douglass puffed a moment, then added, "He wants to enslave us by shackling our feet to the land. Ute ride. Ute hunt. We range from New Mexico to Wyoming."

"You think that's the reason?" Cray shifted uneasily from foot to foot as he watched Douglass puff away. The chief made no move to offer him the pipe. Cray took that as a bad sign.

When Douglass said nothing more, Cray went on. "I fear Meeker is going to bring in the cavalry. I do not want this and you shouldn't either."

"Let the horse soldiers come," Douglass said.

Cray stared at the old chief and realized why the Ute, chief and brave alike, were not concerned with Meeker's threats. They planned a rebellion against Meeker before any soldiers could arrive from their distant forts.

He stepped back, mumbled something about having to go, and then found himself staring down the barrel of a rifle held unwaveringly in Johnson's hand.

"Because I like you, you will enjoy our hospitality," said Douglass, "until there is no one left for you to warn."

Johnson poked Cray with his rifle and got him moving to a small outbuilding, where he was imprisoned. Cray put his hands against the wooden walls and wondered how long it would be until the Ute scalped Meeker.

AMBUSCADE

September 29, 1879
Milk Creek

"The day's hotter 'n a pistol," Major Thornburg complained, using his neckerchief to wipe away rivers of sweat wetter than the sluggishly flowing Milk Creek off to his left. He looked up at the tall bluffs on either side of the road leading south out of Williams Fork, where they had camped the day before. The rugged, rocky cliffs held the heat in the canyon and boiled away at the major and his men, tramping slowly behind.

"You want to take a break, Major?" asked Rankin.

"A break? It's only ten o'clock. We can cover another two miles before taking a rest." Thornburg looked closely at his head scout and saw something was eating at Rankin. The man was normally calm and collected, but now jerked about nervously, glancing over his shoulder every time they flushed a quail or a rabbit hopped across the pitiful excuse for a road, heading for the safety of its burrow.

"I want to send a couple scouts ahead, sir," Rankin said. "This kind of terrain gives me the collywobbles, all closed in the way it is. Since they didn't find the Ute camp after a couple days of hunting, them redskins might be hidin' out there right now."

"You reckon there might be Ute on the tops of those cliffs?" Thornburg squinted up at the rim, hunting for any sign of silhouetted Indians against the bright blue, clear Colorado sky. The only movement he saw was an eagle slowly wheeling upward on a rising column of air.

"They couldn't do much to us if they were up there, sir. It's down here I worry about. Ever since you met with Jack, I been keeping a special watch."

"And what have you seen, Mr. Rankin?"

"That's the worst of it, Major. I ain't seen nuthin'. At all. If Jack and the fellows with him were hunting, there would be traces of them all over the place. Blood attracting coyotes, a rifle shot now and then, something. It's like they just upped and vanished."

"That's not so bad, is it? They might have gone back to the reservation."

"We're only ten or fifteen miles from the edge of the White River Agency, Major," said Rankin. "If they wanted to do somethin' untoward, this is just the spot to do it."

"Why not wait for us to get onto the reservation?"

"We don't know what kind of mess we're ridin' into there," Rankin said grimly. "Meeker is crazy as a loon, from all accounts, writin' letters and makin' wild claims. He might still be in charge or them Ute might want us to think he is."

Thornburg had to laugh. "You believe Jack killed Meeker, has taken over, and doesn't want us riding down onto the White River Agency to find out his heinous crime?"

"Heard dumber things in my day, sir."

"I'm sure you have, Mr. Rankin, but we'll keep on. The heat is wearing us down, and I want to get through these canyons and out into Powell's Valley as soon as possible. There might not be much water in the White River this year, but it's got to be better than we're likely to find in this barren country." He listened to the fitful gurgling as the Milk Creek made its way down the floor of the canyon. Usually such a sound was cooling, refreshing, but today Thornburg did not find it so. If anything, the trickle promised to peter out soon.

"I been watchin' the arroyos, sir," Rankin said. "There's not been a drop of water in them all summer long."

"Then why are you watching them so closely? Are you afraid of a sudden mountain storm filling them with enough water to wash us away?" At this Thornburg did laugh. He could use the water, even that much, to take a bath. Every pore on his body was clogged with dust. When he spoke, he had to talk around a mouthful of grit, and eating was almost impossible. He might as well chew glass.

A flood would relieve the drought.

Thornburg looked back at the sky and knew it would never happen. Not today. Not from a cloudless blue sky.

"Some arroyos look like they've been cut up by a lot of riders," said Rankin.

"A lot?" asked Thornburg, perking up. "What do you call 'a lot'?"

"Can't rightly tell. That's why I told my scouts to be cautious. Might be hundreds."

"Hundreds? Or perhaps only a few who have come and gone repeatedly. Like Jack and his nine braves. If they raced up and down the arroyo bottoms, would that produce such a disturbance?"

"Might," Rankin admitted reluctantly.

"The Ute love racing their horses and betting heavily. From what you've told me of Chief Jack, he is a wild one and loves such pursuits."

"He's a wild one, all right," Rankin said. "That might be our salvation if the Ute decide to attack."

"Why's that?"

"Jack'd come right at us, no plannin', no subterfuge, just a lot of whoopin', hollerin', and shootin'."

"And we would cut him and his braves down quickly because we are a disciplined military force. This unit is one of the best I've ever commanded," Thornburg said. "Drunkenness is low and there have been virtually no desertions since I assumed command last year."

"Yes, sir," Rankin said, distracted. "We're getting into the pass. The cliffs are closin' in on both sides."

"So? What do you suggest?" asked Thornburg, miffed at his scout's insistence that Jack and the Ute were dangerous. The only tiny detail that troubled him was the way Jack and his friends had scrubbed war paint off their faces before meeting with him and issuing the peculiar offer for him and five soldiers to continue to the White River Agency. That request made no sense, unless some mischief was planned when he got away from his main force.

"The supply train's a mile behind the main column, sir," the scout pointed out. "If we got into a fight, we'd be cut off from our spare ammo."

"That would have to be a hell of a fight, Mr. Rankin. Every trooper has fifty rounds with him and there are a hundred and forty of us. We could fight a small war and not need the supply wagons."

"Sir, ahead. You see that arroyo? The one with the steep banks?"

"I do."

"If I wanted to ambush this column, that's where I'd have my men hiding. We'd be dead in minutes if we rode that way. A regular shootin' gallery since there's no way to go 'cept back or ahead."

"And you would have another detachment hidden along the road, such as it is?"

"We'd be shot at from three directions and unable to do anything but retreat back down a narrow path into our own men. The confusion would make it even easier for Jack to massacre us with no danger to himself or his braves."

"There would have to be a few more than the ten Ute we saw, Mr. Rankin," Thornburg said, critically eyeing the arroyo his scout worried so about.

"Yes, sir."

"This road is impossible," Thornburg said, coming to a quick decision. "Is it any better if we cut away from the arroyo, across country, and got through the pass on the far side?"

"It's better, sir, 'cause it makes me feel a whale of a lot better."

"Then lead the way, Mr. Rankin."

Major Thornburg passed the orders down the line for the soldiers to cut away from the stony road at a sharp angle and pioneer their own track through the mountain pass. The going wasn't any harder. And Thornburg had to admit that he felt better following his scout's advice. That arroyo did look risky.

AMBUSCADE— FAILED

September 29, 1879
Milk Creek

"We can attack now and bring great glory on ourselves," Nicaagat said. "If we charge straight ahead, the *Maricat'z* major will retreat through his own troops and cause great confusion. We can pick them off one by one then!"

"No," objected Chief Colorow. "You are too impetuous. This is not the way to kill *Maricat'z*. The white eyes always do the unpredictable."

"Listen to Colorow," said another sub-chief named Antelope. "He has killed many, many soldiers."

"I know he has," grumbled Nicaagat. "He has told me a thousand times of his great fights."

"All have given me great victories," Colorow said smugly. He folded his hands on his kettle belly and watched like the hawk circling above at the empty spot where the bluecoated soldiers would march along soon. "We must be careful with these walking and riding soldiers," Colorow said. "They fight harder than even the Cheyenne."

"That's not possible. They are *Maricat'z*," protested Nicaagat. "We should attack now."

"My plan is good," Colorow said.

Nicaagat glared at the older chief and finally gave in. Everyone spoke of Colorow's cunning in battle, how he always was victorious and danced the Scalp Dance with the most warriors, so few being killed in battle. Nicaagat thought this might be the secret of Colorow's reputation. More of his tribe lived to brag about their exploits, giving their chief the look of a great warrior.

"I am a great warrior, Jack," Colorow said, staring directly at Nicaagat, purposefully using his *Maricat'z* name as if he were reading his mind.

Nicaagat jerked as if he had been stuck by a pin.

"How do you know what I think?" he demanded.

"Colorow misses nothing," Antelope said proudly.

"He is an old man bilking the agents out of double rations," said Nicaagat.

"A wise warrior knows when to conserve his supplies and when to attack. And *how* to attack. See, Nicaagat, look, listen, and learn when I say this. The *Maricat'z* officer has over a hundred soldiers with him."

"We number three hundred!"

"We do," Colorow admitted. "That is a problem for us. How can every one of our valiant fighters take a scalp?"

"I want the scalp of his scout," said Antelope. "Twice he almost saw me. He is good. For a *Maricat'z*."

"Their greasy scalps will hang from many Ute belts before the day is over," Colorow promised.

"We fight from ambush and never let them return fire."

"That is the coward's way," cried Nicaagat, jumping to his feet. "We are Ute warriors. We should ride our ponies into battle, not hide behind weeds and shoot at them as if we were afraid of them."

"You should be afraid of them," said Colorow, getting to his feet also. He went to face Nicaagat and bumped his ample belly against a harder one. Nicaagat tried to stand his ground, but the impact staggered him. Colorow followed swiftly, bumping him with his belly again until Nicaagat reached for his knife to stop the abdominal attack.

"You see? I won repeatedly before you reacted. We will shoot from ambush. The *Maricat'z* will not know what to do. They will be confused. We will fire again. When they realize they have ridden into a trap, they will fight fiercely, as you were going to, Chief Nicaagat. By then, it will be too late for the bluecoats to save themselves. We will win, our warriors will have their scalps, and we can both boast of how we triumphed in battle!"

"What do you propose?" Nicaagat swung around and saw that Antelope had circled to a spot where he could fire at Nicaagat without hitting Colorow.

"The first attack is deadly, but it is only a diversion that allows us to ride our wonderful ponies around and attack from another, unexpected direction. We launch three attacks before they can respond with their first. *This* is how you win battles, Nicaagat." Colorow looked satisfied with himself.

"I will ride in this attack, the mounted one," Nicaagat declared.

"Of course," Colorow agreed. "There is none braver among us."

Antelope smiled, seeing how Colorow first insulted, then complimented the volatile Nicaagat. By the time the short lesson in tactics was completed, Nicaagat would have ridden into the Fifth World after the Hopis because Colorow said it was a good idea.

They returned to where the other braves waited in the arroyo for the soldiers to ride past. Colorow had explained it well. Let a quarter of the column pass—thirty or forty soldiers—then attack the center of their enemy's position.

Colorow craned his neck, and saw that the Ute were anxious but not agitated. They were trained warriors, knew fierce battle and how flowing blood changed a man. Outwardly calm now, they would become demons when the fight started. Colorow settled down onto his knees, then fell forward to sight along the barrel of his Winchester. He had taken it off a dead settler who, minutes before his death, had been contemptuous of the fat chief and his wild stories of war.

Colorow watched the empty space he had chosen patiently. Soon it would fill with a *Maricat'z* soldier, and he would have yet another kill to boast about. But as he mentally ticked off the seconds, he realized something was wrong.

"Antelope!" he shouted. "Go to the road and see what has happened to them!"

Antelope lived up to his namesake, jumping easily over a clump of weeds and sprinting out onto the rocky path where they had expected to see the soldiers appear. He disappeared down the road, returning a few minutes later.

"They cut off the road, Colorow. The major is taking the entire column away from the ambush!"

"What do we do now, Great Chief?" asked Nicaagat, sneering.

Colorow was silent for a moment. Then he smiled. "This is better. Take a hundred warriors with you, Nicaagat, and ride in that direction." Colorow quickly sketched out his new plan. Nicaagat laughed with joy when he saw how they would trap the *Maricat'z* column. He dashed off to get his fighters into position.

Colorow said, "Sometimes I think I am the greatest war chief ever. The *Maricat'z* officer robbed me of an ambush only to give me an even greater chance for victory!"

He pushed Antelope toward their horses. Nicaagat had to ride fast. Colorow and Antelope had to ride even faster if they wanted to be at the greatest massacre in Colorado history.

ESCAPE

September 29, 1879
White River Agency

Cray Eachin fumed and occasionally slammed his palms against the sturdy wall of Douglass's outbuilding. He tried to guess how long he had been imprisoned, but couldn't. Johnson had come to feed him twice, but those meals were sparse and left him hungrier than if he had not eaten at all.

Pressing his eye against a crack in the wall let him look south toward Douglass's cabin and get some sense of how the sun moved. After enduring several painful splinters in his forehead as he tried to follow the sun's movements, Cray gave up and tried to figure out some way of getting free.

It had taken him the better part of what he estimated to be a day to completely go over the small building. Whoever had built it had been an expert carpenter. Cray thought it must have been either Dresser or Price, since they were the only two men at the agency with the skill to construct so sturdy a structure. He had quickly found he could not even rock the building enough to put a wedge under the edge and possibly escape that way.

He spent hours damning them, then began the tedious job of trying to dig his way out. The ground proved too rocky and hard for that, so he switched to using a rock to scrap away part of a log in the wall, cutting at first a notch and then a deeper cut. When his hand began to cramp, Cray realized he might as well be pissing on the wall for all the progress he was making.

Disgusted, he settled down on a pile of rags and fell asleep. When he awakened he had the feeling it was night. A bit more effort trying to unhinge the door or otherwise get out produced only angry cries from a half-dozen Ute warriors on guard outside. When one opened the door and cuffed him back onto the pile of rags, Cray knew he wasn't going anywhere soon.

"I want to speak to Chief Douglass!" he shouted at his attacker.

The brave glared at him. "No."

"I want to know why he ordered me penned up like a pig."

"Johnson wanted to kill you. So did his two sons. Douglass said to hold you, that you were one of the good *Maricat'z*. Good, pah!" The warrior spat at Cray, then slammed the door. Cray heard the locking bar fall with grim finality.

He was still alive only because Douglass protected him. What was going on at the White River Agency?

Cray had plenty of time to sit and think and worry about it. The conclusion he came to was not a pretty one. Something was going on away from the reservation, probably having to do with Jack and his raiding. He was the most hotheaded of the Ute and the likeliest to get involved in unprovoked attacks on white settlements. That still didn't explain Douglass's attitude. If Meeker found out about Jack, he would certainly call in the Army.

Cray's mind took different roads, and always returned to one inescapable conclusion. Douglass and the other Ute were no longer cowed by the threat of soldiers coming onto the reservation because they were going to do something to Meeker to keep him from writing his letter.

"They're going to kill him," Cray muttered. "Have they already killed him? If they have, why am I still alive?" That didn't make any sense to him, but it got him to worrying even more. With Meeker dead, the other Ute Indian Agents would scream for troops to come swooping down on every reservation in western Colorado. Not even Ouray could restore order if Jack and Johnson—and Douglass—were intent on going to battle because of what Meeker had done to them.

A dead agent meant Washington would send more than enough troops to quell any rebellion, too. Having their bureaucrats killed was bad politics. It was even worse because the Ute were thought of as the peaceful tribe, the subdued Indians who always agreed to anything their great white fathers in Washington wanted. An uprising would be taken as a slap in the face.

Cray wondered briefly if Douglass intended to use him as a hostage or even a courier to take the word of Meeker's murder to the authorities. That didn't make much sense either, since the settlers would learn of it quickly enough. There were telegraph lines over the Rockies into Denver. A single telegram would alert the governor. It didn't take a courier for that kind of message.

Head hurting, Cray lay back and tried to piece it together logically. Everything he thought of became more and more fantastic, until he wasn't sure if anything he had considered was remotely right.

He sat up when the locking bar on the outside of the door began scraping open noisily. He jumped to his feet, waiting to bowl over the brave opening the door. If he could get away, he might find sanctuary somewhere nearby until he learned what was going on. Then he could warn Meeker and his family and the others at the agency.

The bright morning light momentarily blinded him, making him pause in his attack. Then Cray froze when he heard a voice he remembered all too well.

"Don't stand there. Hurry. They will be back in a few minutes. They are smoking a pipe, talking about what must be done."

"Towa!"

"Hurry!" the lovely woman cried. She grabbed his arm and pulled him from the small building. He stumbled out and looked at the clear sky. It was about ten o'clock. That meant he had been in the outbuilding a couple days.

She struggled to shove the bar back into place. Cray helped her. Unless the Ute checked on their prisoner, they wouldn't know he had escaped.

"Where can we go? To your father's tepee?" Cray didn't want to face Kanneatche, but he knew returning to the tent a hundred yards from the agency headquarters where he slept would be a mistake. The Ute would find him right away.

"No! My father and brothers are all getting ready for the warpath. They ride to join my uncle when they are . . . finished."

"Have they killed Mr. Meeker?"

"No," Towa said. The answer surprised him.

"What are they waiting for?"

"I do not know. Jack is north of here, doing something. Everyone along the Smoking Earth River waits for news from him and Colorow. When it comes, they will act."

"Colorow?" Cray laughed without any humor. "If he's involved, there's not much to worry about. He's a fat, stupid buffoon."

"He's a great warrior," Towa said, her lips thinning. Cray saw she was getting mad at him.

"I'm sorry. Let me thank you for rescuing me." He tried to grab her to give her a kiss, but she agilely eluded him. "What's wrong?"

"I am not your wife anymore," Towa said, her cheeks flushed. "I still love you, but you are not my husband. You must go, because I do not want to see you killed."

"If they haven't done anything to Meeker, they won't harm me. Douglass kept me here for a reason."

"They kill no one until Jack and Colorow tell them it is all right," Towa said. "Now go. Go back to the mountains. Your mine. Somewhere. Anywhere far away from the agency!"

"Towa, I—" Cray started for her, but the woman spun and ran off faster than a deer, leaving him standing alone beside the White River, the river the Ute called the Smoking Earth River. His heart almost skipped a beat when he imagined it flowing bank to bank with blood. White man's blood. Cray knelt, splashed water on his face, then looked around. He had to decide what to do.

Follow Towa's suggestion and hightail it, or warn Meeker? Cray thought a minute, and couldn't decide if there was anything worth warning the man about. He started walking with a long stride that devoured distance. It wouldn't hurt to look in on

Meeker and see if he was hale and hearty. If he was, then Cray would do as Towa said. He was fed up with Meeker's arrogant, crazy ways almost as much as he was with Towa and the Ute.

CHARGE!

September 29, 1879
Milk Creek

"Mr. Rankin," Thornburg called. "Have they gone away?" The major looked toward the arroyo that his scout had singled out as a possibly dangerous ambush point. The line of dutifully marching soldiers had made their way to higher ground well past the arroyo, but Thornburg had bad feelings that were growing, not going away, as they rode along, blazing a new trail.

"I reckon not, sir. Jack and the others mean to do us dirty," Rankin said.

"Then we must double-step it until we can get past any danger."

"Sir, listen!"

Thornburg cocked his head to one side and heard what his sharp-eared scout already had. Horses. Lots of them. All galloping. He had tried to convince himself that the chopped-up sandy bottom had been the result of Jack and his nine braves racing back and forth after laying heavy bets on their riding prowess. That fantasy evaporated like a drop of water on a hot rock in the sun. At least a hundred horses created the deep thunder, more felt in the gut than heard, rippling through the mountain pass.

"They're flanking us," Thornburg said, his mind considering all the possibilities. "We can't keep riding or they will cut us off from the supply wagons."

"What should we do?" asked Rankin, fearing that his commander would act on his dubious claim that they faced only Jack and a handful of other Ute. The entire Ute nation must be on the warpath to cause such echoes in the narrow canyon.

"Retreat," Thornburg said decisively. "Get the men back to the supply wagons where we can circle them and defend ourselves."

Orders rippled along the line and the soldiers smartly reversed their positions in the column and withdrew in an orderly fashion that might have saved more than a few of them.

"They're comin' at us from both flanks, sir," Rankin said, letting his binoculars drop on the rawhide cord around his neck. He no longer needed to look for the enemy. They were coming so fast they would ride over the Army position in a matter of minutes. "Open fire. We've got to hold 'em at bay till most of the boys get their asses back to the wagons and form a defensive perimeter."

"How far are the wagons?" asked Thornburg, pale now. He drew his pistol and cocked it.

"Three-quarters of a mile. I think some are havin' trouble fording the creek."

"That miserable little stream," grumbled Thornburg. "It held up the wagons with its deep mud but not the mounted troopers." This had separated his force, and might spell the doom for anyone caught on this side of Milk Creek.

"Sir, there, along the ridge. Indians. Give the order to fire on them."

"I'm sorry, Mr. Rankin, but I cannot. It runs counter to my orders. If they fire on us, we may defend ourselves. Otherwise, we can't shoot at all." Major Thornburg ran his thumb over the hammer of his drawn pistol, struggling with the conflict between his orders and keeping his men—and himself—alive long enough to see another sunset.

"That order's gonna be our death," Rankin said. He pulled his rifle from its scabbard.

"You are a civilian, Joe. If you open fire, there's nothing I can do but dismiss you."

"You want me to get this turkey shoot going, sir?"

"I have my orders, and I can't say anything like that to you," Thornburg said, still holding out some small hope that the charging Ute were not hunting for scalps.

Thornburg brought the column to a trot, but saw his scout was right. Rankin was an experienced Indian fighter, but General Sherman's orders had been explicit. Too many minor incidents had exploded into full-scale war because of the Army's tendency to shoot first and then parley. Thornburg swallowed hard when he saw how many Ute were closing in on his column. In spite of the smart about-face maneuver, his troopers were not going to reach the safety of the wagons. The Indians had outridden and cleverly outflanked his soldiers.

"Please, Major. Give the order," Rankin pleaded.

"Ride ahead and give my regards to Captain Payne. Tell him to circle the wagons and prepare all defense possible."

"What about you, sir?"

"Ride, Rankin. You have your orders."

Rankin stared at Thornburg for a moment, then

gave him a sloppy salute. He didn't hold much for being a soldier, but he had scouted as a civilian for more officers than he could remember. He knew what Thornburg faced.

Thornburg swallowed hard again and thumbed back the hammer of his pistol. His finger trembled as he curled it around the trigger, but still he did not give the order for his soldiers to open fire. He had his orders.

The Ute let out bloodcurdling cries and attacked. Whether one of his soldiers fired first or the Indians took a shot, Thornburg could not tell. All he saw was a wild-eyed warrior, war paint smeared in black and yellow stripes on his face, holding a smoking rifle.

"Return fire!" Thornburg shouted, lifting his own pistol and cutting loose with a flurry of shots. It became immediately obvious that the tepid response to the Ute's overwhelming attack was not going to save any of them. The Ute had attacked his column at a point where fifty of his men, both cavalry and infantry, were cut off from the remainder of his force. By dividing his force in this fashion, the Ute could circle him, slaughter almost half his command, then turn their attention to the rest at their leisure.

"Divide and conquer," Thornburg muttered.

"Sergeant!" he called to his top non-com. "Your squad, to me! Draw your carbines!"

The sergeant got his cavalry troopers together in a tight knot. As Thornburg watched, two were cut down by the increasingly deadly fire from the Indians. The major stood in his stirrups and saw that Rankin had penetrated the Ute force trying to cut the Army column in half. Joe Rankin was a good man. So was Captain Payne.

"Sergeant, prepare for a charge. If we don't

break the Indian line, the rest of the troops will surely be killed."

The sergeant blanched, but drew his carbine and passed the orders to the twenty chosen for this suicide mission. If they succeeded, most of the command would survive, and if they didn't the Ute would have an easy victory this day. Either way, no one in the squad was likely to be sitting around a campfire laughing about the mission.

Thornburg saw the infantrymen running in as good an order as possible straight for the wagons. Both flanks of the infantry unit were exposed and they took withering fire from the Indians, but Thornburg could slow down the Ute attack long enough to let close to thirty troopers find salvation. All he had to do was break through the Indians blocking the route back to where Captain Payne already prepared for a siege.

The major saw one side of the pincers closing faster than the other. That meant he had a brief moment, so very brief, when one side of the Ute trap could not adequately lay down supporting fire to the other. He had to attack quickly and force back the weaker side and allow his infantrymen and whatever cavalry troopers could make it through the gap their only chance for life.

"Charge!" cried Major Thornburg, leading his men directly into the knot of Ute threatening to cut off his men from the supply wagons and the remainder of his command.

Thornburg and thirteen of the twenty died, but the rest of the squad won through to the supply wagons and the dubious sanctuary inside their circle along with the thirty foot soldiers he had sought to protect.

ANOTHER LETTER

September 29, 1879—1:00 P.M.
White River Agency

"Are you writing yet another letter?" Arvella Meeker asked querulously. She peered down her pinched nose at the letter her husband penned in his cribbed, almost minute script. "Who is this one intended to arouse?"

"Now, dear," Nathan Meeker said, not looking up from his work. "You know how difficult it is keeping these savages in line. It is even worse trying to apprise my superiors of the serious nature of the threats we face every day so they understand what hardships we endure and what challenges we have already met."

"Who?" Arvella Meeker asked. "Who is supposed to be roused to action this time? You've written letters to everyone in Colorado and Wyoming."

"I have, and to no avail," Meeker said. "This letter will produce better results than the ones complaining about the whiskey sales by the settlers. I wrote previously to the Commissioner of Indian Affairs, but I am not sure he did anything, so I have chosen to write directly to the commander of Fort

Steele, asking again for him to dispatch troops immediately. The situation with Johnson and his boys is far out of hand and I require military might to back up my authority. Otherwise, the Ute will see me as a hollow man incapable of doing anything but issuing empty orders."

"You've written that major every few months for a year," Arvella pointed out. "What has it gotten you? Nothing. We have to deal with the Ute by ourselves. Admit it. The politicians in Washington care nothing about this reservation or the Indians on it. Only we do."

"We are doing a fine job of civilizing them," Meeker said, "but it is going slower than I had hoped, and so many of the people we are helping block us at every turn. You would think they would see how their lives could be improved by what we bring them."

"Ingrates," sniffed Arvella.

"What are you two arguing about now?" Josephine Meeker came into the room, buckets of milk sloshing gently as she walked. She put down the two pails on the kitchen floor, wiped her hands on her apron, and sat at the far end of the table. "Well?"

"That's no way to speak to your parents," Meeker said. "You must show more respect because you are an example for the heathens."

"They don't respect anyone, no matter how you act around them," Josephine said in a tone unconsciously mimicking her mother's.

"Your father is asking Major Thornburg to bring troops. Again."

"Haven't you written him before?" asked Josephine. "To no good end, I would say. The letters from the major I have seen were all quite condescending. He considers you little more than the boy who cried wolf."

"This one will light a fire under him. I have detailed every infraction committed on the reservation. If I cannot get soldiers out to stop the whiskey trade between the settlers and the Ute, then by God, I will get the entire Army here to keep the peace. I threatened Johnson and the others with military intervention if they did not behave. They have not."

"Has his son shot at someone else?" asked Josephine.

"Their arrogance requires that I do something more than make threats. As I told your mother, I must show them that I can back up my requests with force. I had thought it possible to deal with them as fellow human beings, but they are not sufficiently advanced yet for my appeal to their better natures."

"Better natures," sniffed Arvella. "They are godless heathens."

"Now, Mother, please," Josephine said. "If we work with their children, we might save them eventually." She rubbed her hands on her apron as she added, "There are so few who come by, though. Johnson's sons never show up for my classes."

"They're too busy shooting at Mr. Price and others trying to help them," said Meeker. "Why they aren't working in the fields is another matter. They cannot expect us to give them fields filled with robust crops. They have to work. That is the point of it all."

"Don't get started on depriving them of their horses, Father," Josephine said. "We've both heard your sermon. I see nothing wrong allowing them to keep a few horses."

"That will be a significant part of my letter to Major Thornburg. While you might disagree about how their horses lead them to a life of sloth, you must agree too many are a nuisance in a farming community." Meeker began writing again. Arvella and her daughter left him to his work and went outside.

"I should get back to the milking," Josephine said, squinting at the bright sun radiant in the cloudless sky. She frowned and pointed to a rider galloping down the road past the agency in the direction of Douglass's cabin. "What do you suppose has got into that one? He's going to kill that horse within a mile if he keeps galloping like that."

"They are always dashing about like chickens with their heads cut off," Arvella said, but she wondered also. This Ute rode a foam-flecked horse. The amount of lather told of a long, hard journey and unusual exertion on the rider's part. "He seems to be a messenger. Whatever could he be in such a hurry to tell Chief Douglass?"

"It can't be too important," Josephine said. "The Ute sense of time is as skewed as their estimation of distances. Their insufficiency makes me want to scream at times. I say for them to show up for class at seven A.M. and it means nothing to them."

"Do you need help with the milking?" Arvella asked.

"That would be nice, Mother. Thank you. Two of the Ute were supposed to be here to help this morning and never showed up. Now it is past noon and the cows' udders must be hurting them something fierce." Together, they walked toward the milking shed behind the cabin quartering the agency headquarters. They had barely filled two pails with milk when they heard thudding footsteps outside.

"Who might that be?" wondered Arvella. She went to the shed door and looked out. "Mr. Dresser! What's got you all hot and bothered?"

"Mrs. Meeker," gasped out the carpenter. "Th-they're killing everyone!"

"What are you saying, man?" asked Josephine. "Who's doing this?"

"The Ute. Douglass is leading them. They got a message from Jack. H-he's somewhere north of here and ambushed a cavalry detachment. Killed the lot of 'em."

"Come now, you are exaggerating," said Arvella. "Sit and drink some of this fresh milk. It'll settle your nerves, and you can tell us what has really happened."

"Mother, listen," said Josephine. "Gunshots."

The echoes of rapidly firing rifles rolled up the slope from the White River.

"I'm telling you, they've gone crazy," said Dresser. "Jack has killed all those soldiers, and now Douglass is going to kill us all!"

"What soldiers?" asked Arvella.

"Mr. Meeker sent for them. They were on their way here when Jack ambushed them. I don't know where. I couldn't hear that, but I know the Ute are on the warpath."

"Douglass would not harm us. Why, he is the most peaceable of the lot," Josephine said. "I would suspect the worst of Johnson, especially after what he did to my father."

"Do not forget," said Arvella, "that Johnson also shot at Mr. Dresser and that his brutish children fired on Mr. Price while they were attempting to plow the ingrate's field for him."

"I can detail even more outrages, Mama," Josephine said. "You might not have heard of—"

Arvella held up her hand to quiet her daughter. "Your father threatened many of the Indians with slavery if they didn't do as they were told. I don't know if he said this to Douglass personally, but he might have, to get him to obey."

"He'd never say anything like that to Douglass. Johnson, yes," Josephine said. "Father always thought Johnson needed extra inducement to do right, but not Douglass."

"Douglass is leadin' 'em," said Dresser. "I saw it with my own eyes. He killed two men out plowing the field just to the south of his. Summers and Glencannon. Gunned 'em down with so much as a by-your-leave." Dresser looked around like a trapped animal hunting for a way back to the safety of its burrow.

"Look," cried Arvella. "A few men from the fields. All of them are running."

"Over here, here," shouted Josephine, waving her arms.

Arvella cringed as the gunfire grew louder, warning her that the Ute were coming in this direction as they chased down the fleeing agency workers. Coming across the yard was a distraught woman. Arvella hurried out and put her arms around Mrs. Price as the woman staggered to her.

"Mrs. Meeker," the woman gasped out. "They killed my husband. And they scalped him! I saw it! They're killing us all."

"Into the milking shed," Arvella said, hustling the frightened woman ahead of her. "They won't see us here. We can figure out what to do once we are safely out of sight."

"They'll find us, no matter where we hide. We've

got to get off the reservation," Frank Dresser said, "before they slaughter us."

"Inside," Arvella said sternly. "I don't know if Nathan has heard the gunshots. I'll get him, and we can all hide together until he can decide how to handle this uncivilized behavior. I am sure he'll treat them most harshly."

"Mother, wait." Josephine grabbed her mother's arm and held her back. "Look. They're coming! So many of them!"

"Into the shed," Arvella said, her voice shriller than usual from the strain. "We'll trust to God that your father'll be safe. When they've gone, we will see what has to be done to put this right. I am sure he will be most angry." Arvella pushed her daughter ahead of her, then pulled the door shut. It didn't mute the sounds of gunfire.

The refugees huddled together near the milk cow standing in the center of the shed, contentedly chewing its cud. Arvella tried to take a lesson from the cow. It did not panic because there was nothing it could do to change the world around it. She had to remain calm, also.

But the gunfire! It swirled around the shed, seemingly coming from all directions.

Arvella stood and walked to stand by the cow, now growing restless. If gunfire had not disturbed the cow, something else was bothering it now. She sniffed and caught only the earthy scent of the cow, the shed, and the field beyond. Then Arvella realized what it was that spooked the cow. A touch of smoke in the air warned of fire.

She went to the back of the shed and pushed aside a loose board Mr. Dresser had been promising to fix for weeks and never had. Arvella saw the wall of flames marching toward the shed like eager soldiers attacking their enemy.

"They've set fire to our field. Quick, now. Everyone to the main house."

"No, you can't go," wailed Frank Dresser. "They'll see you and shoot you."

"Come now," Arvella said, her voice cracking like a whip with authority. "If we don't go, we'll be burned alive." She opened the shed door and herded those inside out, all except Dresser. He refused to budge.

"Don't go. It's a mistake," Dresser sobbed.

"Really, sir. I had no idea you could show such cowardice." Arvella sniffed in contempt at his weakness, then walked briskly away from the milking shed to the cabin for the shelter it would give. She had been wrong not rushing directly here to tell her husband what was happening. Now she had to get him out before the Ute burned down all their buildings.

Arvella rounded the corner of her cabin and stopped dead in her tracks. Three Ute, all decked out in war paint, held her daughter, Mrs. Price, and the others at gunpoint.

"What are you doing?" she snapped. "Let them go immediately."

"Mother, they—" Josephine was knocked to the ground when the brave holding her backhanded her on the side of her head.

"You savage!" Arvella Meeker stepped forward as Douglass and three other Ute emerged from the cabin. "You! Chief Douglass. What is the meaning of this inexcusable behavior? You should be ashamed of yourself!"

Douglass rattled out quick orders in his own tongue before turning to Arvella. When he faced her, the woman felt real fear for the first time in her life. His expression was not the one she remembered on his kindly, old face. Douglass glared at her with pure hatred blazing from his ebony eyes.

"Money. Get money. Now."

"I—very well," she said. "But you cannot harm my daughter or any of the others." Arvella looked to see that they were safe. Braves held Mrs. Price, Josephine, and two children firmly. They would be all right. For the moment. She was almost glad Frank Dresser had refused to join them. He might escape and fetch help.

"Money. Everything of value," Douglass said, shoving her rudely into the cabin.

"I keep it in a jar over by the pantry," she said. As she crossed the cabin, she saw a foot sticking out from behind the table where Nathan Meeker had worked on his letter. Arvella stopped and stared, eyes wide. That was her husband's boot. And it was not moving.

"Get money," shouted Douglass. He shoved her toward the pantry. Arvella saw the Ute inside taking everything they could carry off. She turned to beg Douglass to have them stop, then got a better look at the far end of the table.

Arvella held down her gorge, though it burned like fire in her throat. She had never seen a man mutilated so savagely before. And she would never be able to rid herself of the image of her husband, eyes gouged out, scalp taken, ears cut off. A wooden barrel stave had been savagely thrust into his chest.

Like an automaton, she opened the jar from the rear of the pantry and took out a thick sheaf of money intended to fund the operation of the White River Agency. It couldn't have been more than thirty dollars, but the Ute were taking more than the money. Any equipment of value was also being stolen.

In shock at seeing what remained of her husband, Arvella hardly knew what they did to her next. Afterward, all she understood was being taken a long way from the reservation and that Josephine kept begging her to tell what had gone on in the cabin.

Josephine begged until she found out firsthand what had happened to her mother. Then she, too, fell into frightened silence.

CHANGE OF COMMAND

September 29, 1879
Milk Creek

"Captain, Captain Payne!" Joseph Rankin clutched his arm where a Ute bullet had creased him. The blood oozed out and turned him into a gory mess, but the wound was not severe enough to slow Rankin down and get him scalped.

"Mr. Rankin," the captain of the Fifth Cavalry called. "Get into the circle of the wagons."

"No safer there," said Rankin, almost falling from the saddle just beyond the wagons. He grabbed his horse's reins and tugged at the balky, frightened animal to get it between two wagons to the promised safety inside the ring of wagons. "The major. He—"

"Catch your breath," Payne said. He looked out of the loose circle of supply wagons and saw nothing but a tide of Ute warriors coming toward them, screaming and waving their rifles in the air. "Catch your breath, while you can."

"Sir, please. The major was leadin' a charge to break through the Ute line tryin' to bottle us up."

Payne nodded but was not listening. He motioned to his officers to get their men into position. "Fire at will," Payne ordered. "Choose your targets well, men, and fire, fire, fire!"

Rankin's request for Captain Payne to go to Major Thornburg's aid was drowned out by the first volley from the soldiers. Then he stumbled forward as another slug passed within inches of his head, driving him to the ground.

Payne stepped over the fallen scout to protect him, his pistol coming up and firing in a smooth movement. The six-gun barked and a Ute warrior not five yards distant jerked around, the slug buried in his shoulder. A second shot to the chest took the brave from his horse. Then Payne was forced to take cover by the heavy fire. He flopped to the ground next to Rankin.

"Can you make it under the wagon?" Payne asked.

"I can do more'n that, Captain." Rankin grabbed a carbine dropped by a dead soldier.

Together they crawled to a place where they could see the tidal wave of approaching Ute warriors, all screaming and firing as they came. Bullets ripped chunks of wood from the underbelly of the wagon, but neither man took much notice. They were too busy picking targets and firing.

"I do declare, there must be a million of them," Payne said. "Where were they hiding?"

"They were waitin' in ambush for us ahead. The major avoided an arroyo where an attack would have wiped out all the cavalry troopers, but the Ute flanked us and tried to cut the column in two. The major's plannin' a charge to break through to save 'bout half his men."

"There they are!" Payne wiggled forward and stood exposed on the outside of the wagons. He fired methodically until his pistol came up empty, then scooped up a rifle dropped by a Ute warrior and began firing.

"This way, come on this way!" Rankin screamed to the struggling foot soldiers. "We'll lay down coverin' fire for you!"

He joined Payne outside the wagons so he could get a better field of fire. The Ute attack seemed to part, and Rankin knew the major was successfully holding open the two prongs of the trap. Then one side collapsed entirely, allowing the infantrymen the chance to scramble to safety.

"In, get in now," Payne ordered needlessly. "Grab some ammo and help us save the rest of your messmates!"

As one bloodied soldier stumbled past Rankin, the scout grabbed him and swung him around. The private's eyes were glazed over with all he had seen, but Rankin had to ask.

"The major. What happened to the major?"

The private shook his head, then began bawling. "He saved us. They shot him to hell and gone, but he saved us!"

"Get in there," Rankin said as kindly as he could. It made no sense, but he blamed the private for Major Thornburg's death and he blamed himself. He blamed everyone but the Ute.

"There are some cavalry troopers," Payne said, pointing.

"I recognize them. They were with Thornburg." Rankin helped the men to safety, but not a one of the cavalry troopers still rode. All had lost their horses to Ute rifle fire.

A sergeant stared at Rankin for a moment, then gave him the bad news he had known instinctively.

"The major's done gone and bought hisself a farm," the sergeant said.

"Get the doctor to patch your wounds," Rankin said.

"We goin' back to fetch his body? We cain't let him stay out there. Them savages will mutilate him. He's an officer."

"A fine officer," Rankin said, seeing the sergeant was suffering from shock. His words matched the blank face and the slumped shoulders.

"Get on in," Payne said. "There don't seem to be any more of them coming."

"Twenty-seven made it," called a lieutenant. "Not a one's arrived without at least one bullet hole in him, though."

"Come on," Rankin said, pulling at Captain Payne to get him back inside the protecting ring of wagons. "Unless there's someone outranking you, you're in command now."

Rankin saw the realization of what that meant hit Payne hard. Then the captain forgot about everything but staying alive as the Ute launched another attack.

"I've never seen such fierce fighting," Payne said as he emptied his pistol at the whooping, hollering Ute fighters. He reloaded, emptied his six-gun, and reloaded again. The barrel of pistol was hot to the touch, but Payne paid more attention to the next wave of attacking Indians.

The constant barrage took on an air of a rain-storm more than a gunfight, curiously lulling and almost soothing in spite of the deadly nature of the hail.

Payne shook himself like a wet dog. Rankin heard him mutter a quick prayer, and then Payne scooted back from the wagons to stand on an empty ammo box so every soldier in the circle could hear him.

"Hold your fire, pass it along, hold your fire!" Payne shouted. It took a few minutes before the ragged fire coming from his ranks died down.

"They're still sniping at us, Captain. Why are you ordering the men to stop shootin'?" Rankin took a few extra shots at distant Ute, but missed by a country mile.

"Let them use up their ammo," Payne said. "I need to see how bad they hurt us." Payne hobbled off to get reports from his officers. Rankin went with him as Payne made his way around the circled wagons. The farther they went, the more scared Rankin became.

No officers reported to Captain Payne. They were all dead or seriously wounded, and that included the doctor with the column.

"Sergeants!" he bellowed. "Assemble now!"

Four non-coms, two sergeants and two corporals, dragged themselves from their firing positions.

"Report!"

"Dead, sir. All dead or soon to be. Them Injuns done us dirty. They really shot us to hell and gone."

"Enough, Corporal," Payne snapped.

"Not all dead, Captain," reported a sergeant, "but mostly either dead or so shot up they ain't much good. And the Ute killed damned near two hundred of our mules. We ain't goin' anywhere with the handful of mules left us."

"Mr. Rankin?" asked Payne. "What is the situation as you see it?"

"Hopeless, Captain," Rankin said, not sugarcoating it. "This is the kind of place the Ute love for attacks. They're five hundred yards up into the pass and can shoot at us whenever the mood moves 'em. There's somethin' else, Captain."

"Something worse?" Payne almost laughed at the idea there could be anything worse than having all his officers killed or so wounded they were no good to him. The mules' slaughter meant they weren't going anywhere with the wagons.

"The wagons are almost a hundred yards from the creek."

"So?" Then it hit Payne what the scout was getting at. They needed water to maintain their defenses—and the water was a hundred yards away in Milk Creek, on the other side of a company of Ute intent on ventilating them if they stuck their heads up.

"That makes matters a damned sight worse'n I thought, Captain," the other sergeant said. "Most of our water barrels got leaks in 'em. If we could drink the water at all, with that much lead in it. We'd have to take a drink, then pick the bullets outta our teeth."

"Break out a few cases of ammunition, Sergeant, and make certain everyone has enough."

Payne cringed when a new volley ripped through the air above his head. The Ute were relentlessly firing at his increasingly small command.

"How long do you think we can hold on, Captain?" asked Rankin.

"I see no reason that we cannot last a good while, Joe," Payne said. "There are other units in the area. Major Thornburg confided to me how

Agent Meeker had been writing so many letters on so many topics that half the United States Army is in the field chasing down his phantoms."

"We could sure use a few of them ghost-chasers right now, Captain," Rankin said. "You know where they might be?"

Payne shook his head. Major Thornburg had not told him which units were in the area, only that many were.

"Might be over the mountains and patrolling along the White River. Could be some around Hot Sulphur Springs."

"They might as well be a thousand miles off," Rankin said, " 'less we get a message to 'em right away."

"We're better off than it appears on the surface, I think," Payne said. "We have order, we have adequate ammunition to fight any length of attack. Food? Cases of it. Water will be a problem in a day or two, but we might get a few soldiers to sneak down to the creek and fill canteens."

"The Ute seem mighty determined to kill us," Rankin said. "This is no quick raid."

"I tried to count the braves. We must be facing more than two hundred," Payne said.

"Could be a hundred or two more, sir," Rankin said. "Jack is a fighter, but he didn't think up this ambush. That means there are other chiefs with him, smarter ones."

"It doesn't matter who they might be," said Payne. "Not unless we care who's responsible for our deaths."

"Sir, the major's out there. Reckon he and his men are dead, but it'd be good if we could fetch him back for burial."

"I'll do what I can to retrieve his body and those

of the troopers with him. They are heroes and saved twenty-seven men who would otherwise have died. Right now what we do is dig in our heels and refuse to be budged. That might discourage the Ute enough to let us be." He looked up and saw the sun dropping past its zenith. It hardly seemed possible the attack had been going on for only a couple hours. The captain would have thought it had lingered the entire livelong day.

Rankin took a new rifle from a box, along with a double handful of cartridges, and went to take potshots at any Ute showing himself.

Payne made a slow circuit of the camp this time, talking to wounded men and directing that the dead be piled up off to one side. Burial details would be formed later.

He dropped beside Rankin under a wagon and stared across the stretch separating them from the Ute.

"You 'bout ready to send out a party to go after the major? I'll volunteer for it, sir."

"That won't be necessary, Mr. Rankin," Payne said in slow, measured tones. "I questioned three of the survivors of his charge. They all saw him go down with multiple wounds. One corporal said he thought he saw a brave scalping Thornburg. Another"—Payne swallowed hard—"another said he saw the Ute mutilating the body. There's nothing left to return home for burial, Joe.

"They are truly heroes."

"So are we all," Rankin muttered.

Payne laughed ruefully. "Only if we escape so we can report on our bravery."

"It's lookin' up, don't you think, Captain?"

"The Ute were driven off after their last assault. We have supplies, ammunition, and enough men to keep fighting for the foreseeable future. I doubt the Ute will show the endurance required for this fracas to turn into a siege. They are raiders, not true soldiers trained for this kind of fight."

"We did chase 'em off, didn't we?" Rankin said, looking for any bright spot to hang his hopes on.

"I—" Payne bit off his reply when he noticed the wind whipping down the slope from the Ute position. More than hot wind brushed his weathered face. He caught a hint of smoke on the breeze. "They're setting fire to the sagebrush. They're trying to burn us out!"

Rankin scuttled backward like a crab and got to his feet behind the safety of the wagon. Payne hurriedly joined him, already yelling orders to his troops.

"Get the wounded to the center of the compound!" Payne shouted. "Is there enough water to put out any fires?"

"No, sir, we ain't got 'nuf for drinkin', much less puttin' out a fire."

Payne hesitated, then said, "Get your saddle blankets. If the wagons catch fire, use the blankets to smother the flames. Do it in squads of three. One to beat out the fire, two to lay down covering fire."

The fire burned closer and Payne issued orders constantly, supporting, shooting at distant Indians, getting his men to the wagons catching fire.

"Sir, we can't hang on like you thought," Rankin told him.

"I'm afraid you are right," Payne admitted. "When it gets dark enough, you and three scouts sneak out and take a message to whatever settlement or fort that you can find. Get us reinforcements, Mr. Rankin."

"Hate leavin' you in such a pickle, Captain."

"We'll make it. The fires aren't taking hold yet and the wagons are only smoldering." He looked to the center of the circled wagons where dozens of wounded soldiers lay, somewhat protected by a breastworks built from the carcasses of mules. Corpsmen did what they could to patch up gunshots, and a doctor too injured to even sit up weakly called out advice on how they could best save their comrades.

"Still, sir. Feels like turnin' tail and runnin'," Rankin said. He did not add that it felt to him as if he was abandoning the men again, orders or no orders, as he had Major Thornburg.

"We'll be here to raise a cheer when you return, Mr. Rankin. Prepare your mounts, if you can find any horses still standing. I have a few pounds of lead to fire at the damned Ute!"

"Yes, *sir!*" Rankin replied, then ran to find his scouts and get them mounted on the best horses surviving. It still felt like he was turning tail and running, but he realized there was no way to save Payne and the rest of Major Thornburg's command without reinforcements.

Joseph Rankin led the other scouts out of the ring of wagons, past the Ute snipers, and back down the canyon. Then they split up, each heading in a different direction seeking what might not exist anywhere near: succor.

RELIEF

Pressley wobbled in the saddle, but kept riding. He kept telling himself it was better to be one of Rankin's scouts and entrusted with finding help for the embattled column than to remain behind and be massacred. Pressley felt a tad guilty about leaving Payne and the others to their almost certain fate, but he didn't want his scalp lifted by the Ute. There wasn't much hair on top of his head, but what was there he wanted to keep for a good, long time.

Joe had entrusted him and two others with finding someone—anyone—to relieve Payne, but the truth of the matter was that whoever went back to Milk Creek was likely to have a powerful big burial detail ahead of them. Pressley didn't see how Payne could hold out for even a day, much less the week or so it would take to march troopers back into the mountains to help.

He could have given up, but he was a dedicated scout and knew Rankin would never stop until he had found help for Payne. That knowledge kept

Pressley riding, as much to match Joe's expectation of him as to find reinforcements for Payne's troopers. He found himself heading toward Hot Sulphur Springs, not so much because he figured he could find any settlers willing to pull the Army's fat out of the fire as to get a telegram to Denver and let them know the trouble. There had to be support from some direction. Let Governor Pitkin figure out where it was supposed to come from.

As Pressley rode down the road toward the small town, his eyes widened in surprise. He rubbed them and thought he was seeing a mirage. Maybe too many hours in the saddle had taken their toll on his brain, forcing him to see what he wanted.

"Captain!" he shouted, waving his hat. "Hold on. I gotta talk. Help!" He waved his hat so hard the dust fell off in a gently descending cloud that choked Pressley for a moment. Then he dragged his spurs across his exhausted horse's flanks and got a halfhearted effort from the beast. But the scout kept shouting until he was hoarse.

The sergeant riding at the side of the Army column finally heard him and passed the word along to the company commander.

Pressley saw that the sergeant and all the other soldiers were black. Buffalo soldiers. Pressley didn't much care if they were green or had polka dots. They were U.S. Army cavalry and had to go to Captain Payne's rescue.

"Captain, Captain," Pressley croaked out, his voice almost gone now. "Big trouble. The Ute."

"Slow down, man," Captain Dodge, the white commander, ordered. He lifted his gloved hand and halted his column's advance toward Hot Sulphur Springs. "Catch your breath and tell me what's so danged important. By your look, you've come a ways."

"Sir, Major Thornburg. From Fort Steele. Dead. Most of his column's gone. All hunnerd forty men. Most were dead by the time I was ordered out to find help. Captain Payne, Fifth Cavalry, is hanging on by the skin of his teeth."

"What's this you say? What's happened?"

"The Ute, sir. Chief Jack. They ambushed us on our way to the White River Agency. We were ordered there to help out the agent."

"Nathan Meeker," Dodge said with no love in his voice. "He wrote so many letters, I was ordered out to stop the whiskey trade between the settlers and the Ute."

"This is more important, sir. They got plenty of ammo, but most are dead. All the officers save Payne are dead or too wounded to command. They shot us up good, sir. Ambushed us. The Ute intend to wipe out the entire column."

"I was on my way to the same place. Agent Meeker's White River Agency seems a breeding ground for rebellion, if he persuaded two different commands to send soldiers to aid him."

"I don't know what's goin' on at the reservation, but I do know Captain Payne's in powerful big trouble."

"I have no taste for stopping trade in whiskey," Captain Dodge said, "but I do for coming to the aid of a fellow officer."

"You got to hurry, Captain. Payne can't hold out long." Pressley took a swallow from a canteen handed him by the black sergeant, and nodded his thanks. "Truth to tell, he might be dead by now."

"Buck up," Dodge said. "You'll have to lead us back, if we want to get there in the shortest time possible. Sergeant! Send a courier into town and telegraph the colonel of a change in our destination and our mission. Pass along my regards, inform him of the situation with Major Thornburg's column, all the usual folderol. You know what he likes to hear as well as I. Make sure that the courier does not remain behind for a reply from the colonel."

"I understand, sir," the sergeant said, a grin pulling back his lips to show ivory-white teeth.

"Then you'll help, sir?" Pressley's heart hammered.

"Of course I will," Dodge said. Then he laughed. "Oh, you are wondering about my order for the courier not to accept any reply from our commander?"

"That's mighty strange, sir, 'specially since we can use danged near every trooper west of the Mississippi and maybe still not have enough to fight the Ute."

"My commander is not a man to confuse. I am reporting my new mission. I just don't want orders recalling me so he can discuss it with me."

"Oh," Pressley said, knowing what the captain meant. Some superior officers were better at warming desk chairs than they were straddling the damned uncomfortable McClellan saddles.

"Then it's just this, uh, company?" He didn't want to return to Milk Creek because of what he was likely to find, but he had to do his part. That was his job and he couldn't let Rankin down. But there seemed so few soldiers in Dodge's command to fight so many Ute.

"Suh," the sergeant said to him, "we're more than 'nuff trouble for the Ute."

"Column, wheel left!" barked Dodge, not waiting

for his sergeant or junior officer to give the command. To Pressley he said, "The sergeant is right. A company of buffalo soldiers is more than a match for ten times their number of Ute."

"If you say so, sir."

"Don't get the wrong idea about my company," Dodge said coldly. "They might be Negroes but you'll not find a harder-fighting, faster-riding cavalry unit in all the Army."

"Sir, they're gonna have to do that and more at Milk Creek."

"We shall," Captain Dodge said, bringing his troopers to a quick walk back along the trail Pressley had just ridden.

FUTILE WARNING

September 30, 1879
White River Agency

"What's going on, Towa?" asked Cray Eachin. "What're your people doing down on the reservation?"

"You do not thank me for saving you or bringing food," she said, throwing down a burlap sack at his feet. "You are an ingrate. I did right in untaking you for my husband."

"What's happened?" Cray said, his voice turning sharper. In spite of the problems at the agency, Towa was distracting him with personal matters. Cray wondered if she did it intentionally, or if it was simply her way of getting back at him for whatever he had done to slight her and make her leave him.

He took a deep breath and composed himself the best he could, then said, "I love you and think you love me, too, or you wouldn't have saved me or risked your life bringing me food. But I want to know what Douglass is doing."

"They are all gone," Towa said.

" 'They'? Who do you mean? The Ute?" He began rummaging through the food she had brought up to him at the mine shaft. It had been too long since he'd had a good meal, and nerves had kept him from going out hunting incautious rabbits or even finding roots or berries for a quick meal. Since hightailing it from the agency, he had hidden from the Ute and jumped at every noise, familiar or not. It was foolish, he knew, but he feared the worst.

"Meeker. The others at the agency. Douglass killed them all, except the women and two children."

"What happened to them? You mean Mrs. Meeker and her daughter?"

"Mrs. Price, too. Douglass gave them to his braves as prize for being good warriors."

"They're slaves now?" Cray closed his eyes for a moment, wondering if a woman slave of the Ute was the same as it was reported for other tribes, like the Apache and Sioux. He had never liked Mrs. Meeker, but would never wish such a terrible fate on her. Cray had taken a special dislike to Josephine Meeker, and she to him, but then she hadn't much liked anyone. Even such a disagreeable spinster woman shouldn't be humiliated and made a sex slave.

"Douglass has them in his village far away in the Shining Mountains where he is safe from the soldiers."

"I ought to do something to save them," Cray said halfheartedly. He was no fighter, and had no idea how he could sneak into a Ute camp that was alert for the first sign of a rescue and then get the prisoners out. It was made even more difficult a matter for him because he had never liked the acid-tongued, sarcastic women. Mrs. Price and a few of the other white women who had been with their husbands at the agency had been nicer to him, but only in comparison to the Meeker women.

Cray imagined what it would be like if he got to the camp and succeeded in releasing the Meeker women. The first thing they would do would be to take turns berating him for taking so long. Mrs. Meeker would lash out at him for his slovenly dress, and her daughter would pick up the chastisement by detailing his every social failing.

But how could he leave any white woman in the hands of the Ute who had killed their husband and father? He shook himself as his mind rolled over all the possible things he might do for them.

He hated himself for being a coward, yet he managed to believe it was more realistic thinking about getting someone else to save the women. He was one man against a huge Indian uprising such as had not been seen in Colorado during the past thirty years.

"What about the soldiers Jack ambushed?"

Towa shrugged. "The messenger brought word that Jack and Colorow had killed many bluecoats. I have heard nothing more. The killings along the Smoking Earth River are all that the warriors speak of now. That and how bold they are in battle."

"Bold," scoffed Cray. "Bold enough to kidnap and rape women."

"I will go," Towa said, stiffening at his comment. If she had been the least bit warm toward him before, she turned positively icy now. "I should not be here, helping you, feeding you. I thought it would be different. I was wrong."

"Wait!" He grabbed her by the arm. "Do you condone what Douglass has done? Douglass and Jack?" He found it hard to name Colorow with the

other chiefs, in spite of Towa saying how great a
warrior the corpulent brave was.

"You forget, Cray," she said, her gaze level and
as cold as any Colorado blizzard. "My father, uncle,
and brothers also took part. If you brand them
murderers, you brand me, too."

"No!" he exclaimed. "You didn't kill anyone.
You had no part in it. You saved me and would
have saved the others, if you had been able." He
read Towa's answer as plainly as if she had shouted
it, but she did not say it. She would not have saved
any of the others at the White River Agency.

She pulled free and turned.

"Towa, the Army will never allow this butchery
to go unpunished. Douglass and Jack aren't going
to remain free after killing Meeker and who knows
how many others. If it takes ten thousand soldiers,
Washington will send them."

"There are three thousand Ute warriors," she
said.

"Then Washington will send a hundred thousand. They will send as many as it takes to crush
your people as surely as Kit Carson smashed the
Navajo."

"They would move us from our land?" Towa
sniffed almost exactly as Arvella Meeker might.
"But then they do anyway. The treaty means nothing to you *Maricat'z.*"

"Your tribe will be moved far, far away," Cray
said, desperately seeking an argument to convince
her how hopeless it was for the Ute. He wanted
her back, but he needed her help finding
Douglass's camp and freeing the women prisoners
even more.

"Where would they move us?"

"I don't know," Cray said, his mind spinning like

a wheel in the mud. It was hard for him to come up with something that would scare Towa into helping him. "To Oklahoma, where they put most of the cantankerous Indians. Or maybe to Utah. Somewhere else, where all the men will be like Meeker and they'll force you to farm rather than hunt and raise horses and—"

"Stop," she said. "I do not like what has been done, but you offer no suggestions for stopping the killing."

"I don't know about things like this," Cray said, "but Chief Ouray does. Douglass and Jack respect him. If he told them to stop fighting, they would. That'll save hundreds of lives."

"He knows of treaties and many other things because he is wise," Towa said more thoughtfully. "The Ute listen to Ouray. So would the white soldiers."

"Yes," Cray said, a flood of relief washing through him. "Where is he? How do we tell him what's going on?"

"Do you think a chief as great as Ouray does not already know? His people are on the warpath. He has to know."

"He needs to know both sides, not just what Douglass might tell him."

"You do not lie," Towa said, warming to the idea. "You can tell him what you have seen."

"We can go south together. Wherever Chief Ouray is, we can find him and we can both tell him what's going on."

"We will have to find him to tell him this. I do not know where he is among the Southern Ute. Along the Uncompahgre River, perhaps. He has many houses given him by the great chief in Washington."

"We can do it," Cray Eachin said. "Together."

Towa nodded, but Cray failed to notice her lack of enthusiasm for traveling with him.

RESCUE?

September 30, 1879
Milk Creek

"Gunfire," Captain Dodge said to the scout. Pressley pricked up his ears and smiled for the first time since he had found the detachment of buffalo soldiers outside Hot Sulphur Springs.

"They're still alive!" he said. "There wouldn't be that kind of shooting if the Ute had overrun Payne's command—or what's left of it."

"Sergeant," barked Dodge. "Prepare the men for battle. We will have to make a concerted charge toward the circle of wagons. Mr. Pressley has described the arrangement to you."

"Suh, we kin get there easy 'nuff if'n we come from along the creek," the sergeant said.

"Mr. Pressley? Does that sound plausible?"

"Yes, sir. The sergeant's right. That's the best way to go, since the Ute pretty much surrounded the wagons. We can cross Milk Creek—it's shallow and muddy this year—and get to the wagons quick." Pressley frowned and then asked, "You want to bull on in like that? Wouldn't it be better to scout and find where the Ute's rear is and attack that way? You want to run 'em off, don't you?"

"I want to kill every last one of the red bastards," Dodge grated out. He snapped more orders, and the sergeant rode back along the column of soldiers, making certain every soldier was prepared for the fight to come.

"They're good men, the Negro soldiers," Dodge said. "I considered my assignment a punishment at first, but I've never ridden with a better company." The captain glanced over his shoulder at the sweating black faces, looking grim as they rode closer to the battle.

"Considering how many of them Ute are out there, they'll have to fight like demons," Pressley said. His hands began shaking as he remembered how completely Jack and his warriors had tricked Major Thornburg. The major had been an experienced field commander, and Rankin was about the best scout there was, and still Jack had boxed them all up in nothing flat.

"Are your nerves up to this, Mr. Pressley? You can hang back, if you wish. You've been through hell already."

"I've got to save them, if I can," the scout said. "I owe Rankin my life a dozen times over, and he gave me orders to bring back help. No matter what, I can't let him down. And I can't let down anybody who's lasted against the Ute this long."

"You have done well already, sir." Captain Dodge drew his pistol, then signaled for a slow advance until they reached Milk Creek. Sporadic shooting came from across the sluggishly flowing stream, but Pressley couldn't figure out where the Ute were. Then he looked up.

"On the bluffs! They're shooting down at us!"

His words were met with a hail of bullets from half a hundred Ute rifles. Pressley winced as a sharp pain twisted him around in the saddle. Grimly, he clung to the saddle horn, and his sanity, as a sluggish stream of blood flowed down from his left arm. He tried to raise it, but all the nerves were dead. It got harder by the minute to even stay on horseback, but the spinning, twisting landscape occasionally came into focus for him. Pressley fought.

Swinging his left arm like a lifeless club, Pressley let out a battle cry and got his horse galloping across the shallow creek with the rest of the buffalo soldiers.

"Onward, onward to victory!" cried Dodge, leading the charge. He fired repeatedly until his six-gun came up empty. Then he lowered his head, got his horse lined up right, and jumped the wagon nearest the creek to enter the ring of safety, such as it was.

"Push the wagon away," Pressley heard Payne order. "Let 'em in! They're here to save us!"

Pressley was dizzy as he rode forward, but saw three of the Fifth Cavalry unit troopers pushing a supply wagon back to make a gateway in the circle of wagons. Barely aware he was doing so, Pressley headed for the opening and burst through. But being inside the wagons did not lessen the number of Ute bullets singing past him. Pressley fell from the saddle and hit the ground hard enough to rattle his teeth when another slug struck him, again in the left arm. He had thought he was past all feeling there, but realized how wrong he was.

This wound hurt even worse than the first.

"What's your condition, Captain?" Dodge asked the beleaguered officer.

"Where's the rest of your men?" Payne asked,

looking around frantically. "There're more. There has to be! Don't tell me this is all you brought with you!"

"We have come to relieve you," Dodge said.

"But there's not enough of you," Payne muttered, dazed. He stumbled back and sat heavily, ignoring the occasional Ute bullet sailing past his head and smashing solidly into the mountain of rotting mules they used to protect the wounded in the center of the camp.

"We will fight our way to freedom, sir," Dodge said stiffly. "Mr. Pressley informs me you have plenty of ammunition and supplies. With my company of rested soldiers, we can—"

"You're it? There aren't any more to relieve us? We're going to die!" moaned Captain Payne.

"Calm yourself, man. Come on." Dodge grabbed the agitated Payne and pushed him away from the main body of men. Pressley lay on the ground nearby, able to hear everything that was said, although standing took more energy than he could muster.

"Report, Captain Payne."

For a moment, the wounded captain fought the rising panic. Then he settled down.

"Captain J.S. Payne reporting. We're down to fewer than forty men after being besieged by the Ute. I don't think there's a man among us who hasn't at least one bullet hole in his hide. We're keeping the most seriously wounded in the center of the compound."

Dodge wrinkled his nose at the stench rising from the barricade formed by the dead mules.

"We have three horses left alive. The Ute have the high ground around us since they took positions there around sunrise this morning. I have no idea why they let you ride in, unless they want to kill more bluecoats."

"Your confidence is shaken, Captain," Dodge said stiffly. "We'll win free and get your command away from the skirmish."

"Skirmish? This is no skirmish. It's a goddamn massacre!"

"Captain, please. You don't want to demoralize the troops." Dodge looked at Payne with some distaste. Conditions were terrible, but they were not yet hopeless.

"There's nothing more I can do to their morale that the Ute haven't already, if that's your concern," Payne said. "We might have plenty of ammunition—it's enough for three times our number now—but we haven't had any water for almost twelve hours. We're getting mighty thirsty. I wish you'd brought more than your canteens with you."

Dodge looked over his shoulder in the direction of Milk Creek.

"When it gets darker, I'll send some of my men out to fetch water."

"No!"

"Sir, please," Dodge said. "My men might be of color, but they do not lack for courage under fire."

"You don't understand," Payne said. "It's not cowardice that'll do them in if they go. It's the Ute. We've tried repeatedly, and cannot get past their snipers. I've lost a dozen good men trying."

"We'll wait for sundown for my soldiers to try," Dodge said, as if speaking to a young child. "Now come and tell me what supplies I can count on. What are in the wagons?" Dodge's nose wrinkled again. "And how did the wagons get burned?"

"The Ute started a fire in the sagebrush, but it burned out before it destroyed any of our wagons.

Then we set fire to other wagons, thinking to rob new attacks in such a fashion of their fuel."

"Let me get this right," Dodge said. "You set fire to your own wagons so the Ute couldn't?" He looked at Payne as if the man had gone mad.

"It's like setting a counterfire," Payne said, his voice taking on a dull monotone as he explained. "Rob the big fire of fuel and it dies down fast. We thought it would work if we burned the wagons and charred the side facing outward."

"Did this unusual tactic work?" Dodge ducked as a bullet ricocheted past his ear.

"Must have," Payne said. "We're still here and the Indians stopped trying to burn us out."

"Who is the most senior among your command?" asked Dodge. The two captains walked past where the scout lay beside a decaying horse carcass, trying to keep from taking a third bullet.

Pressley heard Payne's mumbled response, but was too tired to keep his eyes open. He slumped down, occasionally awakening as someone fussed over him. Time drifted by in spurts and surges, but Pressley was never quite aware of anything but the dull, throbbing pain that suffused his entire body. When he came fully awake, his left arm was bandaged and tightly wrapped against his body to keep it from flopping about. Pressley sat up and looked around.

Since his arm was bandaged, he expected to see everything put right in the camp. If anything, it was worse than when Dodge had led his buffalo soldiers into the ring of supply wagons. The two captains stood a ways off, arguing. Occasional slugs ripped through the dusk, but no one took notice of them, as if this were the most natural—and unavoidable—circumstance in the world.

Pressley forced himself to his feet, and took a few shaky steps before catching himself against a wagon.

"Sir, what can I do?" he asked, not sure if he directed his question to Dodge or Payne.

"Pressley, isn't it?" asked Payne. "You've done well."

"Joe Rankin taught me good, sir. How long 'fore we get the hell out of here?" A deathly silence feel between the officers, causing the scout's heart to hammer in his chest. "We *are* bustin' outta here, aren't we?"

"The Ute have us pinned down for the moment," Captain Dodge said. "We decided to wait them out. It would be highly unlikely that they would press the attack another day or two. Like all Indians, they are raiders, and not trained to fight a battle over any length of time."

"Seems they've done a right fine job so far," Pressley said. He clamped his mouth shut when he saw the look on the officers' faces. They were lying for the sake of morale among their troops. They had no more chance of breaking out with their combined command than Payne had before Captain Dodge and his buffalo soldiers showed up.

All he had done was thrust more troopers into the jaws of the deadly Ute trap. Pressley sank down, back against a wagon wheel, stunned with the knowledge that he was responsible for the fate of not only Payne's men, but Dodge's now as well.

"I'm sending a few of my men out to fetch water for the garrison," Dodge said.

"Don't," said Payne. "They'll be killed. The Ute sneak up like shadows in the dark, Dodge. You can't see them. One minute no one's there, the next they're shooting up anyone fool enough to poke his head outside the ring of wagons." Payne spoke with a frantic note fed by his failed attempts to get water from Milk Creek.

"We need water. The wounded need it," Dodge said.

"It's suicide," Payne insisted.

"Let me try, sir," Pressley said. "I'm as sneaky as any Ute. I got out once. I can do it again."

"Not with your game arm," Captain Dodge said. "I asked for volunteers from among my men. Five are ready to go."

The rattle of empty canteens banging together could be heard over the intermittent gunfire. Pressley turned slowly to keep the pain in his arm to a minimum. Five buffalo soldiers were festooned with canteens dangling by cords from around their necks, making them look as if they wore them as some futile shiny silver armor.

"Sergeant Murdoch has told you what needs to be done. Good luck, men," Dodge said. He glared at Payne to keep the other captain silent. The five men saluted and hurried off to ready themselves for the stealthy trip out to Milk Creek.

Pressley started to say something about how much noise the banging canteens made, and how hard it would be carrying that many back after they had been filled with water, but he saw that Dodge brooked no argument. Pressley wasn't clear on the chain of command, but it seemed to him that Dodge ought to be under Payne's command. But Payne wasn't in full control of his emotions after enduring so many hours of combat. Pressley had seen how battle shook up some men—and officers. A few shots meant nothing, but the constant barrage wore on a man's sanity after a day or two.

Pressley knew. He had seen it during the Civil War.

"Go on, get us enough of that muddy water to wet our whistles," Captain Dodge said, trying to be lighthearted about his orders. The five buffalo soldiers dropped to their bellies and began wiggling out from beneath the wagons.

They had not gone twenty yards when a shot rang out, followed quickly by a shriek of pain. Then all hell cut loose. Pressley shielded his eyes from the glare from dozens of rifles firing—all in the direction of the men trying to reach Milk Creek.

Captain Payne said, "May God have mercy on their souls. If they are taken alive, the Ute certainly will show them no pity." He turned and hobbled off to alert the soldiers along the side of the compound facing the creek of the failed foray.

Dodge stared into the now-silent dusk after his soldiers, grinding his teeth in frustration, saying nothing.

THE LONG, HARD RIDE

October 1, 1879
Rawlins, Wyoming

Joe Rankin fought to keep from falling from the saddle. He had ridden for twenty-eight hours straight, taking a rest only when his horse flagged. If the horse died, he would never deliver the message of the Ute attack and get help for Captain Payne.

The world swung in wild, weird patterns whenever Rankin tried to focus his bloodshot eyes. He eventually gave up, closed his eyes, and fought to keep from falling asleep in the saddle. If he did that, the horse would slow and eventually stop. Worse, he might be tossed off. As tired as the horse was, Rankin was in worse shape, and could never hope to run down a mount intent on escaping from the punishment he gave.

A big, fat raindrop spattered coldly against his face, to run down his cheek. Rankin reached up with a shaky hand, and felt the mud forming behind the drop as it made its way across his leathery face. He tipped his head back and let the icy rain hammer into his face, reinvigorating him.

Over a day in the saddle. Solid. Little rest. No food. Only whatever water he could find along the way, and too often damned little because it was so dry. Rankin tried to remember why he did this to himself because it was so easy to believe Payne and the rest of the troopers were dead by now. There had been so many Ute. Hundreds. And Major Thornburg had been killed saving a handful of soldiers, along with most of the other officers in subsequent attacks. The troopers of the Fifth Cavalry were good, but without officers to bolster their spirits, Rankin was not sure they would survive.

"Why'd the Ute attack like that? It wasn't a quick raid, in and away, grabbin' what loot they could and then going to get drunk an' bragging about it. They kept up the fight. Why?" Rankin asked the questions into the teeth of a rising wind, to keep himself alert and awake. The land needed rain, but he did not need the wind slowing him down as he rode.

Rankin was in such bad shape he thought he heard mumbled answers to his questions coming from a distance. He pulled down his hat and leaned into the wind as the rain grew heavier. If Rankin had been less determined to reach Fort Russell, he would have found shelter.

"Keep walkin'," he said, patting his tired horse on the neck. "Keep headin' toward Rawlins."

"Hey, mister, you want to stable your horse till the rain's done?"

It took Rankin a second to realize the voice was not a hallucination. He wiped the water from his eyes and peered into the increasingly thick rain for the source.

"Who's there?"

"It's me, O'Connor. I work at the stable down the street."

"Street?"

"Mister, you all right? You're in town."

"Rawlins?"

"Well, yeah. Where'd you think you were?"

"Mr. O'Connor, can you direct me to Fort Russell?"

"Piece of cake. Just keep ridin' the way you're goin' and you'll be there in fifteen minutes. Course, you'll be drenched. I got a slicker at the livery, if you want that."

"Thank you, Mr. O'Connor. Thank you!" Rankin snapped the reins and got the horse into a faltering trot. He could rest, but not now. When he reached the fort. When he told them of the horrors happening down in Colorado. He donned the yellow slicker, promising the young man he would return it when he could. Rankin put his heels into his balky horse's flanks and got it moving through the driving rain, traveling slowly down the road toward the fort.

Before he knew it, the sentry at the main gate called out a challenge to him. Rankin responded, and was soon dripping on the floor in front of the commanding officer, General Wesley Merritt. The one-star general stared at Rankin as he weaved about, unable to stand upright.

"Why don't you sit?" General Merritt suggested, pointing to the lone chair beside the desk.

"Sir, I can rest later. There's been an ambush. Major Thornburg's command from Fort Steele's been wiped out, purty near. The major's dead and

Captain Payne was holdin' off the Ute the best he could."

"Sit down before you fall down," Merritt said sharply. "I don't want you passing out until you report in full."

Rankin collapsed to the chair, but sat on the edge, fearing he might relax so much he would fall asleep.

"A hundred forty men, sir. Most of the major's command were dead when I lit out. The survivors were most all wounded by the time Captain Payne ordered me and three others scouts to get help. We scattered, the others huntin' for help nearby, but I figured Fort Russell was the only hope for Captain Payne."

General Merritt listened in silence until Rankin began repeating himself as he struggled to make the officer understand the real dangers faced by Payne and the rest. The general held up a hand to quiet the scout.

"Mr. Rankin, you have performed service above and beyond what anyone could have expected from you."

"You'll go to the captain's rescue?"

Wesley Merritt stared at Rankin for a moment, then said, "I choose to believe that question comes from your extreme exhaustion. Of course I will go to his aid. I will have two hundred cavalry and a hundred fifty infantry on the trail at dawn tomorrow."

"Infantry will slow you down, sir."

"I am aware of that. They will ride in wagons. Speed is obviously of primary interest if we are to save any of those poor wights. Don't teach this dog to suck eggs, Mr. Rankin."

"Sorry," the scout said, his eyelids sagging. He

heard the general rattling on about provisions and the fastest route to the ambush site along Milk Creek, but Rankin faded fast. Leaning forward, he rested his head on the desk, and was asleep in seconds, content that he had done what he could.

It was up to God and General Merritt now.

IN THE MIDDLE OF WAR

October 3, 1879
White River Agency

"We would never have been allowed to talk to Ouray, even if we had found him," Cray Eachin said. Towa hunkered down by the cooking fire, eyes averted and the set of her body telling him she did not want to talk. No matter what the woman—his wife—wanted, he had to talk to fill the ominous silence settling all around. Since Towa had released him as her husband, Cray had felt the need to do *something*. Talking to Ouray and stopping the killings by Douglass and Johnson and the rest might not be enough, but it was all he could do.

"He was somewhere else, and we'd have had a merry old time chasing him down. Do you think Ouray had any part in the rebellion?" Cray's question fell on deaf ears. Towa methodically went about preparing their dinner. "I don't think so. He has too much to lose. All the Ute have too much to lose."

"Jack doesn't. Colorow doesn't," Towa said.

"But what about Douglass?" Cray was glad he had drawn her out, even this little. "He stands to lose all his land when the Army gets around to coming down on him."

"The bluecoats will never find him, if he does not wish to be found," Towa said. "He will fade into the mountains and be seen only when he wants."

"But he is giving up so much! The land at the reservation, all his belongings, the gifts from the government. All are forfeit because he killed Meeker and the others. And . . ." Cray's voice trailed off when he came to talking about Mrs. Meeker, her daughter, and the other woman. He had heard the stories about the treatment they were likely to receive, and Towa had done nothing to sugarcoat it.

Slaves. Sex slaves.

Cray stared at Towa, and wondered how she could be part of a culture that saw nothing wrong with taking women captives and raping them. Towa had shrugged it off as if it were inconsequential, even when he had asked how she would like it if another tribe kidnapped her. Her only comment had been that Ouray was half Jicarilla Apache. Such intermixing of the tribes always came about during wars.

"I've got to do something," Cray said. "If I can't find Ouray and beg him to intervene, there has to be something else."

"Talk to Douglass," she said. For a moment, he wasn't sure if Towa had let her sarcastic tongue answer before her brain had come to a real answer. Then he started thinking about what she said.

Douglass had not killed him outright. That

meant the old chief had some feeling for Cray. He could go to Douglass and ask for the white women's release in exchange for his testimony. Cray bore no ill will against Douglass, and even liked the old Ute. That he could speak to Douglass in his own tongue would count for something also. Cray might not be the most eloquent spokesman for the Indian Bureau, but he could get the women free before the Army came down on the renegade Ute. In any fight, there was always a chance the women and two children would be hurt or killed.

Cray wondered if death might not be better than enduring the shame of their capture and mistreatment. None of the women would ever be readily accepted into polite society if it were known how they had been used by their captors. And he had seen some men who had been taken into other tribes as young children. They belonged to neither world, no matter how much the Indians claimed they might be part of their tribes.

"I've got to try," Cray said. Towa looked up, startled. She opened her mouth and then clamped it shut, turning away from him. Cray couldn't read what that meant and Towa wasn't talking much to him.

"Where is Douglass's camp? You don't have to take me there since it would be dangerous for you."

"Why? I am Ute. My uncle is a big chief riding with Jack and Colorow. My father and brothers will protect me."

"Kanneatche? He's probably too drunk by now to stand upright. He was one reason Meeker was always writing the Army to complain about the whiskey trade."

"He is my blood."

"Sorry, I didn't mean to insult you. He's your father, no matter how much of a drunk he is." Cray didn't keep the bitterness from his voice now. Towa wasn't acting like a wife at all. He was glad she had rescued him, but he had no idea why she had stayed with him afterward. Towa had not allowed him to so much as touch her without flinching away, as if he carried the plague.

Towa began eating without offering Cray any. He started to ask, then grabbed his gear and stormed off.

"Where are you going?" Towa called after him.

"To talk to Douglass." Cray was perversely pleased to hear her protests, but they died down when his long stride carried him down the side of the mountain and across the plowed land that had once been Johnson's pasture.

The utter desolation of the reservation land worked on Cray's imagination until he was sure a Ute warrior would leap up from behind every bush and rock. All he heard was the soft whistle of the wind through the valley and the distant gurgle of water in the White River tumbling along to quench the parched ground. The autumn rains had yet to come here, but from the thick gray clouds roiling along the far northern horizon, he guessed rain did fall somewhere. It would eventually roll downhill and fill the river.

Just as the Army troopers would roll down and inundate the White River Agency.

Cray considered all the places nearby where Douglass might have pitched a temporary camp, and decided he would go farther afield for his war camp. With only a slight twinge of conscience, Cray snared one of Johnson's incautious ponies and jumped onto its back. He had ridden enough without a saddle to be in control from the moment he mounted, no matter how the pony tried to buck him off.

Without knowing exactly where he headed, Cray rode northward. Now and then he looked down and tried to find tracks in the dirt, but he wasn't much of a frontiersman. However, he would have had to be blind to miss the dozens of fresh hoofprints in the road curving off to the east, across the oxbow in the White River. He sucked in a deep breath and got the horse into a trot. He didn't know what he was riding to, but he thought it had to be Douglass's secret camp.

The pounding drum alerted Cray Eachin that he neared the Ute encampment long before he smelled the smoke from the fire or saw the sparks tumbling upward into the cold night air. He had spent the day following the Ute tracks, and now that the time had come to find Douglass and ask for the release of his hostages, Cray found himself getting cold feet.

Towa had spoken out of anger at him. The more he thought about it now, the more he had to believe she wanted him to ride into Douglass's camp and be turned into a pincushion by a hundred arrows and ventilated by twice that number of rifle slugs.

"I'll show her I can do this." His hands trembled, but his resolve firmed. Towa didn't believe he could do anything useful. He had failed to find gold or silver, and he had never gotten on well with her father. He wasn't much of a hunter, and had killed the bear more by accident than design. He had not even had the gumption to spirit Towa away and find a preacher to perform a real marriage.

Cray jumped to the ground and tethered the nervous pony to a sturdy sagebrush. He had no idea if he would be better served riding in boldly or sneaking around to find Douglass and speaking with him in private. Whatever he eventually decided, it wouldn't hurt to scout a little to find out what he was getting into.

Cray was under no illusion that he was better at sneaking around than the Ute and wouldn't be seen by a sentry, if any were posted. But he saw no guards as he slipped toward the bonfire in the dying light of the day. The closer he got, the louder the drumming. Cray flattened himself against a rock when pounding hooves came in his direction.

A double line of Ute warriors thrust lances in the air. Some had scalps dangling from them. The double line wheeled about and went back through camp, splitting to gallop on either side of the fire. The riders came around and rode back through, whooping and shouting like madmen.

Cray watched as Douglass's wife Jane came out, holding a pole with three scalps as high as she could over her head. The riders rushed past, and then came back while she stood proudly. Cray swallowed hard, realizing he was watching a Ute Scalp Dance. The chief's wife held the scalps her husband had taken in battle, and the other riders, some with their wives riding behind them, rode past to show their kills.

Without realizing it, Cray reached up and touched his own head. The greasy hair would look as bad as any of the scalps carried by the Ute braves if it were removed. But Cray still felt he had to do something to rescue the white women taken prisoner by Douglass's braves.

The chief sat in front of his tepee, smoking his pipe as he watched the Scalp Dance move into its next stage. The warriors dismounted and began dancing around Jane and the fire. The squaws separated and went to the far side, all carrying their husbands' booty.

Cray swallowed and knew the dance would be over soon. This one went from noon till sundown, and then the warriors would sit around, smoke, drink, brag about how courageous they were, and whip themselves into a frenzy for the next day's fight.

Looking around, Cray tried to find where Mrs. Meeker and the others were being held, but couldn't figure out which tepee was used as a prison. He had not been seen yet, and considered sneaking around until he found the white women. Visions of heroically rescuing them by slashing through the hide side of a tepee and leading them back to the agency flashed through his mind. Then Cray realized it could never happen that way.

He sucked in a deep breath, then moved around in the gathering shadows until he crept up near Chief Douglass.

"Great chief," Cray called out, hoping only Douglass heard him. "I want to beg your mercy."

Douglass turned slowly, still puffing on his pipe. His eyes widened slightly when he saw Cray. He made no move to offer Cray a puff on the pipe, which would have been proof positive there was a chance of negotiating the women's release. Douglass puffed a couple more times, then shook his head. He turned back to watch the festivities as they wound down and his wife began a slow walk back, the pole with the three scalps still held above her head.

Cray realized the old chief had not killed him before the attack on the agency and its employees because of friendship. And friendship had again saved him, possibly for the final time. If Cray tried to press the issue of freeing the white women, the other Ute in the camp would lift his scalp as surely as they had with Nathan Meeker, Frank Dresser, Price, Glencannon, and the others.

He wanted to sit beside Douglass and argue, to reason with the old chief. Then common sense hit Cray. He backed away, looked around, and faded into the shadows as the Scalp Dance ended and the warriors began milling around the bonfire. Cray hurried off to find his horse, damning himself for a coward.

He had ridden all this way only to turn tail and slink away into the dark, hoping no one would spot him. But there had been nothing he could do. Just as with Towa, there was nothing he could do.

The ride back to the White River Agency seemed ten times as long as when he had ridden into the mountains searching for the women.

BURNED WAGONS

October 5, 1879
At the Mouth of Coal Creek

General Wesley Merritt passed the order down the line to halt when his scout came riding up, elbows flapping around wildly. Merritt had ridden with this scout before, and knew he was not likely to be spooked easily. He looked scared out of his wits now.

"General," the grizzled scout said, eyes wide. He licked dried lips and obviously struggled to get the words out. "Up in the mouth of the canyon. It's purty bad."

"How bad, Jed?"

"Real bad, General," the scout said. "No survivors. Counted a dozen dead bodies and the wagons was all burned up."

"Mr. Rankin said Captain Payne had circled the wagons. There were thirty or so in the supply train. How many did you see?"

"Not that many. Ten wagons maybe, not in any kind of defensive circle that I could see. Fact was, they was strung out for danged near a quarter mile, with the mules all cut free from their harnesses.

No sign of the animals anywhere. And there wasn't no more than twenty folks all scattered round. But they was scalped. Ev'ry last man."

"Were they in uniform?" asked General Merritt. He saw surprise light the scout's face.

"Now that you mention it, nope. They was stripped. Most of 'em was, that is. But the few what was still dressed wore reg'lar clothes, jist like me."

Wesley Merritt tried to keep from smiling. Jed wore a tattered black-and-green flannel shirt and buckskin trousers. A floppy-brimmed, tired black hat turned brown with trail dust dipped down on either side of his head mimicking earmuffs. He was hardly a fashion plate, even for a mountain man. Then the general sobered.

"This must be another wagon train that was ambushed," he said. "Did you search for any identification? No, of course you didn't," Merritt said quickly, realizing the sight of so many dead freighters had brought Jed hurrying back with the news. He would not have wasted one precious second searching the bodies. "You did as I ordered and reported back straightaway."

"You said it, General," Jed told him. "You want to lead the troops to the ambush site?"

"Did you spot any Ute lurking about?"

"No, sir, nary a redskin to be seen. The place was as quiet as, well, as quiet as a grave." Jed paled a little under his leathery skin. General Merritt tried to remember if Jed was likely to have seen so many dead men before, and decided he wasn't. Things had been peaceful way too long, except for the occasional cowboy hurrahing Rawlins and drunken Indians shooting at settlers. This was Jed's first massacre.

Merritt hoped it was his only one.

"I need a moment to consider what you've told me," General Merritt said, humming tunelessly to himself as he mulled over his scout's report. He did not want to ride into an ambush, but he trusted Jed's abilities, although the scout obviously had been scared spitless by what he had found ahead along the road. Joseph Rankin had been explicit in his description of the attack on Major Thornburg's troopers, and this train had to be a victim of yet another Ute attack.

He lifted his canvas-gloved hand until he got the attention of the sergeants back along the line, then lowered it and pointed directly ahead.

"Lead on, Jed," the general said. "Keep a sharp eye out for any sign of the Indians."

"You don't have to tell me that twice, General. My whole body's one raw nerve right now, just tinglin' and twitchin'."

They rode in silence until the burned-wood odors caused General Merritt's nose to wrinkle. He slowed the advance, split his troops to either side of the road, and only then did he ride forward with the scout beside him.

"See what I mean, General? All dead."

General Merritt rode to the front of the small supply train and found the driver of the first wagon, who had probably died before the others. The Ute had fired on him, hitting him a dozen times, to force his wagon to block the rest. The ambush had proceeded quickly then, the other drivers unable to escape past the front wagon blocking the rocky road. On the narrow roadway, there was no hope that they could have turned the bulky wagons around to retreat, even if a fully laden wagon pulled by a mule team could have outrun a Ute warrior on horseback.

Wesley Merritt reached over, pried loose the blood-soaked shirt, and fished around in the shirt pocket, hunting for some identification. He found a thick sheaf of papers, all glued together with the man's blood. Carefully prying the bullet-riddled pages apart, he made out the shipping orders the best he could.

"I don't know if this poor wight is George Gordon or if Gordon was simply shipping the material to the White River Agency. However it is, everything being freighted to the Ute reservation has been stolen or burned."

"So this ain't the bunch we're supposed to rescue," Jed said, stating the obvious. "Then where are they? The soldiers, I mean."

General Merritt shook his head, then looked farther up Coal Creek Canyon in the direction of the branching Milk Creek.

"Bugler!" he called. "Front and center."

The bugler trotted up, looking pale. He couldn't keep his eyes from sneaking away to stare at the driver's corpse and how it had been almost cut in half by the savage Ute gunfire.

"Sound Officer's Call," the general ordered. "And everyone else, listen up for any reply. Go on, son. Sound the call."

The bugler licked parched lips, put the bugle to his lips, and let loose with a few shaky notes that firmed and then echoed full-blown along the canyon walls.

For a few minutes, the call rolled on, dying away as fast as the men in the wagon train had. At the general's nod, the bugler repeated the blast. Before he could sound the call a third time, an answering bugle call came from deeper in the canyon.

"It sounds as if there *is* a command left to save,"

General Merritt said. He took a deep breath, then called in a forceful voice, "Column, forward! Full trot!"

CEASE-FIRE

October 5, 1879
Milk Creek

"They are harder to kill now," complained Nicaagat, sitting on his heels and glaring at his fellow chief. Colorow leaned indolently against a large rock, licked his fingers after devouring his second entire rabbit, then belched in appreciation. He rubbed his belly, belched again, and lay back with his fingers laced behind his head to stare up at the bright azure sky dotted here and there with billowing lead-bottomed clouds that promised rain soon.

"They are going nowhere," Colorow said confidently. "My plan worked perfectly. The black-white soldiers came to save them, we let them in, and trapped all of them. You kill them one by one if they try to fetch water from the stream, or whenever you want, with no danger to yourself. What more could a warrior ask?" Colorow laughed as he rolled onto his side and propped up his head to look down at the supply wagons. "They even set fire to their own wagons! We didn't have to waste the effort of making a fire with flint and steel. They burned themselves out for us! What fools they are!"

In spite of himself, Nicaagat had to laugh. This produced an answering deep laugh from Colorow, who took limitless glee in the plight of the bluecoats below on the canyon floor. There was much to enjoy, killing those *Maricat'z* soldiers! And the vaunted black-white soldiers had not been of any help to those bluecoats already penned up. They did not shoot straighter or fight any harder than any other trapped rat because they had no water.

"That was clever on your part to have braves sneak close, then yell as if they were attacking. It scared them into torching their own wagons to keep us out." Nicaagat joined Colorow in another gale of laughter as they remembered how inept the soldiers had been, how frightened they were of the mere sight of a Ute warrior.

"We could never have taken them then because they were determined to live forever," admitted Colorow. "Now, they are too frightened to sleep. Before long, they will fall over dead from their own mistakes. A terrified guard will shoot at another, and they will kill themselves out of exhaustion."

"How many have you killed?" asked Nicaagat. "I have killed nine!"

Colorow belched again and sat up, his big belly rolling as he moved. He looked around the small camp to see if he had a large enough audience, but the other Ute were intent on watching for the *Maricat'z* to poke their heads up to be shot. It did not happen as often now because there were fewer of them.

"Who knows how many I have killed?" Colorow finally answered Nicaagat, seeing that he had no one to boast in front of other than his friend. "I cannot keep track."

"I have the scalps as proof of my courage in battle," Nicaagat said. He lifted the string of scalps dangling at his waist, then let them fall back against his sinewy thigh.

"Scalps, pah. Who needs scalps to prove your skill? Didn't I tell you where to send our warriors so the *Maricat'z* could not escape? Wasn't I right allowing the black-white soldiers to join the others, so we could trap them all? Outsmarting your enemy so others may take their scalps is the true measure of a heap big warrior. That skill is worth more than any scalp hanging at my belt."

"Colorow, look." Nicaagat stood and waved to a rider galloping along the road below, bent low for speed. "That is one of the lookouts you positioned a mile down the road. Why do you think he is racing along like that?"

"Perhaps the *Maricat'z* have reinforcements on the way and that one is reporting their arrival. It is good that I insisted we have sentries along the road after I ambushed the other wagon train from Hot Sulphur Springs." Colorow rubbed his greasy hands over the flannel shirt taken from one of the bodies in that supply train. He smiled crookedly, remembering how poorly those *Maricat'z* had fought. The attack—the one he had planned—had gone perfectly, most of the freighters dead before they realized they were in trouble. Even the ones who had fumbled out rifles and shotguns had been unable to fire them accurately. They had all died without a single Ute brave being injured or killed.

"Yes, it is good to be warned," Nicaagat said, looking glum. He had wanted all rifles pointed at the bluecoats cowering inside their ring of burnt wagons. Sentries scattered all over the canyon took away the hope of a quick victory over the trapped soldiers. Unlike Colorow, he preferred the quick, overpowering raid to the drawn-out fight. He wanted to see fear on the face of his enemy when he killed him, not exhaustion. If the rider working his way up the steep slope to where they camped reported reinforcements, that meant the fight would drag on for days more. Perhaps weeks, weeks that could have been spent raiding white settlements and stealing back the horses they had traded to Peck.

"What do you have to tell us?" called Colorow to the rider, a young buck from the Uncompahgre.

The brave reined back hard, his pony's hooves kicking up a dust cloud.

"Many, many *Maricat'z* are coming. Bluecoats, both on foot and horseback."

"Ah, cavalry and infantry," mused Colorow. "They fight well, but they bleed red like all the other white men."

"There are hundreds of them. Can we fight so many?" the young sentry asked apprehensively.

"We killed that many down there," Colorow said, pointing at the circle of wagons. "I have another brilliant plan that will bring us all much glory. As we did before with the black-white soldiers, we let them 'rescue' the other *Maricat'z,* prance about while they pat each other on the back and think they have been successful, then we tighten the garrote around their necks again. We can keep them all bottled up for days, until we kill them."

"But these new soldiers are rested, and we are tired from waiting and watching," protested the sentry. "They will fight like devils."

"*Nunt'z* fight like a hundred devils, tired or rested," snapped Nicaagat. "If Chief Colorow says we can kill them, we can! *I* can kill them by myself!"

"We have more than enough ammunition from raiding the other wagon train," Colorow said, ignoring Nicaagat's outburst as mere bravado. "Keep me fed, and I will show you the way to great victory. We will scalp and strip every last one of the bluecoats." He laughed.

"There, there they come. Hear the bugle call?" The rider spun around as the Officer's Call echoed up from General Merritt's position farther down the canyon.

"From below, in the circle of wagons, they answer quickly. Good. If we had scalped their bugler, they wouldn't be able to lure the new *Maricat'z* into our trap," said Colorow. "The more soldiers, the more scalps we can take."

"We let them come in without shooting at them?" asked Nicaagat, his finger rubbing along the stock of his rifle. "That seems wrong. We can kill many of them."

"Let them enter, thinking we have left," Colorow said. "When they settle down and ready themselves to leave, we kill them."

"No one is to fire," Nicaagat said, spreading the word. "No killing until I give the word. We trick them as we did before." He glanced at Chief Colorow to see if this suited the corpulent tactician. It did.

"Wait," Colorow said. "Another sentry comes. From the other direction along Milk Creek." He frowned as he peered at the rider—at the riders. He spotted no fewer than five Ute galloping along. These were not the braves he had positioned to warn of any escape attempt on the part of the trapped soldiers.

"Those are not our sentries. They are warriors coming to join us," chortled Nicaagat. He did a small victory dance. "All the other tribes join us in our fight. They want to share our glory and gain much honor for themselves and their tribes."

"I don't think so," Colorow said slowly, squinting as he identified the riders. "Chief Ouray sends messengers."

"Ouray? He would never fight. He has no belly for it anymore. These warriors will—" Nicaagat clamped his mouth shut when he realized what Colorow was saying.

"They come with orders from Ouray," Colorow said. "He would not send his most trusted courier unless he and the other principal chiefs had heard of our fight and had come to a conclusion about the tribe's future."

"What of the *Maricat'z* riding to rescue the others, the ones we have been fighting?" asked the sentry.

Colorow said nothing as Ouray's most trusted lieutenant, Saponowera, drew rein and stopped a few yards away from them. The young warrior glared at Saponowera as the possibility he would no longer be permitted to fight grew with every heartbeat.

"Maiquas," said Colorow, smiling cheerfully. "We welcome our brothers from the Southern Ute."

"Chief Ouray does not want a fight. You will stop," Saponowera said, his voice ringing out across the camp so all the warriors could hear him. "The full might of the Ute tribe will fall on your heads unless you stop this fight. Now!"

"We are *Nunt'z!"* shouted Nicaagat. "Do we fight among ourselves? No! What right does Ouray have to tell us to quit after all the atrocities done to us on the reservation?"

"You will stop fighting because your chief commands it," Saponowera said coldly. "Not one bullet more will be fired. Leave. Return to your homes."

"Our homes?" Nicaagat sneered. "The White River Agency is not our home, it is our prison."

"Quinkent has killed Meeker. There are no more *Maricat'z* alive there. Go home. Go back to your *carniv* along Smoking Earth River in peace."

"So, Father Meeker is dead," murmured Colorow. "Much good comes from our raiding." He glanced over at Nicaagat, who wanted to continue killing, no matter that the reason for their rebellion was now worm food because of Quinkent's swift knife. For a moment, Colorow considered defying Saponowera—and Ouray. He enjoyed being hailed as a great chief, and Ouray had always slighted him, making fun of him and telling the other Ute that he was only a blowhard. It would be good to show old, tired, fearful Ouray that there was great glory to be gained in fighting once more.

With Nicaagat doing the actual killing, Colorow thought their fight could last for years.

Saponowera glared at Colorow until the corpulent chief bowed slightly and turned to gather his gear. Then again, there was the problem of Ouray and the many warriors he commanded. Colorow was too wise to want Ute to fight Ute.

To Nicaagat, Colorow said, "It is time to leave."

"But the new soldiers! We can kill them with the other *Maricat'z* below. Our complete victory will be stolen from us if we quit now."

"It is time to leave," Colorow repeated, knowing that the telling and retelling of this fight would cement their reputation as warriors more than actually killing the trapped *Maricat'z*, their black-white allies, and the new bluecoats racing to their rescue.

"We have done well. Let's talk to Ouray and see if we cannot do even more with his blessing."

Nicaagat grumbled, and went to spread the word not to shoot any more of their enemy. As the young firebrand left, Colorow went to Saponowera and looked up at the mounted messenger. It was time to soothe ruffled feathers and forge new alliances.

"I tried to stop him," Colorow lied. "He threatened me and all the others. Nicaagat has tasted blood—and likes it. You might suggest that Ouray watch Nicaagat carefully."

Saponowera snorted in disgust, tugged at the reins, and turned his horse back south.

Colorow heard the triumphant cheers from General Merritt's soldiers riding to the rescue of the Fifth Cavalry survivors, and wondered if the commanding officer knew how lucky he was. The Ute would have killed him eventually because Colorow's plan to trap yet another detachment of soldiers was perfect. In a few minutes Colorow struggled to mount his horse and rode hard to catch up with Saponowera, to make certain Ouray's messenger understood that Colorow had nothing to do with the killing of the *Maricat'z* soldiers.

Unless Ouray wanted to declare war on all the *Maricat'z*.

PANIC

October 7, 1879
Howardsville, Colorado

"Get out of town! You all got to get out of town!" the man shouted, holding open the doors to Jimmie Soward's saloon. Wild-eyed, the husky man looked around the room. He was disheveled from having ridden in the snow and rain and had mud spattered high on his scuffed boots. Two six-shooters were jammed into a broad leather belt cross-draw fashion so he could draw them while on horseback. But the expression on his face was what alarmed the men in the saloon.

Seldom had they seen anyone more panicky.

"What's the matter?" Jimmie called from across the room. "We're finishin' the counting on ballots."

"Ballots?" the man asked. He stepped into the narrow saloon and slammed the doors with a loud crash behind him. He fell back, leaning against them so no one could follow him in without creating a ruckus. The man put his hands on the butts of his pistols, making Jimmie a mite uneasy. He had seen drunks wound up tighter than a two-dollar watch without getting the feeling he got staring at this gent. Here was a man about ready to blow his cork.

"We're the San Juan County seat and we held an election today," Jimmie said, edging along behind the bar so he was nearer the bung-starter he kept handy in case of fights. He wished he had his trusty Smith & Wesson now, because he couldn't hope to stop the crazy-looking gent with a mallet from across the room. Only a hunk of lead could hope to put an end to a man who might want to end his career by shooting up a saloon full of election judges. "You can't go tellin' us what to do."

"But they kilt everybody in Animas City. The Ute! They slaughtered every last soul."

"What's that?" This got the full attention of the men at the table with the ballots spread in front of them.

"They're on the warpath. You got to leave. Hightail it now, or your scalp'll be danglin' from one of them lances they carry. I tell you, they're killin' ever'body they come upon."

The man staggered to the bar and leaned heavily. "I been ridin' all day and I'm parched. I got to get my message to Governor Pitkin up in Denver."

"That's a powerful long ride from here," Jimmie said, taking out a bottle of his best whiskey. He poured a shot for the messenger. "Who're you carryin' the message for?"

"For everyone who hankers to keep on breathin'," the man answered, knocking back the drink. "Every white man in the state, that's who. For every white woman who don't want to be kidnapped and raped by those savages, and the white men who want to stop that from happenin' to their wives and mothers. The Ute are movin' fast toward Silverton, and I got to get the message to Antelope Springs."

"Why the Springs?" asked Jimmie, confused. He poured the man a second drink. It vanished down the man's gullet as fast as the first drink had.

"There's troops there, and ammo. Supplies! All will be needed to put down the uprising." With that, the man spun and rushed from the saloon.

"Wait!" Jimmie called. "You didn't pay for the drinks." He talked to empty air. He started to go after the man, but stopped when one of his friends at the table called to him.

"Let him go, Jimmie. You heard him. Animas City's gone, massacred. We're next."

"Who was he? I never seen him before," protested Jimmie. "Why should we believe him?" The bartender talked to an empty room. The men counting the ballots had left them on the table in their haste to get out of town. Jimmie walked over, pawed through the ballots, tallied them in his head, and said in amazement, "I'll be danged. Who'd've thought *he* would have won?"

"Hey, you, up there on the pole," shouted a rider with a rifle in the crook of his arm. "You hear anything about the Ute?"

The telegraph lineman twisted around and peered down at the small knot of men riding along the road to Silverton. He frowned at the way they were armed and looking so bristly. His boss had warned him about highwaymen coming up from New Mexico, but these gents didn't look like robbers. They had the air of a lynch mob.

"I've been up on poles the livelong day. What are you talking about?"

"The Ute killed every solitary soul in Animas City and are moving by the thousands to Silverton. This is the worst Injun massacre in Colorado history, and it's happening all around us. We're goin' to help defend the city. You want to come with us?"

"I don't have a rifle," the lineman said, slipping his leather belt down from where he had looped it around the pole to support him. He dropped rapidly to the ground and brushed off his hands.

"We'll give you one, 'less you want to just hightail it."

"How many Ute?" the lineman asked.

"We heard more'n ten thousand. Could be more, and they're all out for blood. We don't have time to lollygag. Either follow us or get out of the area to somewhere safe." The riders galloped off.

"Where's it safe?" the lineman shouted after them. He got no answer. He looked up at the telegraph wire he had been repairing, then went to his buckboard and got the team moving. He wasn't going to stand around waiting for the redskins to kill him.

"Looks like we're in time," a man with a Greener goose gun said. "Silverton ain't burned to the ground yet."

"Yet," said another. "Let's see what they're doin' to barricade the city."

The men from Howardsville rode down the slopes into town, getting nothing but curious looks from the local citizens.

"Why ain't you all gettin' ready to fight for your lives?" shouted one of the posse.

"You been out in the sun too long, mister?" asked the town marshal, coming up with his hand resting on his six-gun. "You might want to put down that shotgun. Wavin' it round like you're doin' makes me mighty uneasy."

"The Ute! They butchered everyone in Animas City. The messenger going to Antelope Springs warned us, said the Indians were marching on you and—"

"Whoa, hold your horses, mister," the marshal said. "There hasn't been no massacre. I heard tell of a messenger being sent to warn about possible Ute trouble by the folks over at Animas City. They want the governor to send them some arms and supplies, but there's no killin' goin' on. The Ute are still peaceable enough, in spite of what's bein' said."

"But he said there was a massacre. Everyone in Animas City was kilt in their sleep and scalped and—" The angry man bit off his recitation to ask, "Why'd he lie?"

The marshal scratched his head, then said, "The gent they sent has a powerful thirst. Don't reckon you were in the Howardsville saloon when he busted in with this startling news, were you?"

"Well, sure, we was countin' ballots."

"Did you buy the gent a drink?"

"Two. He got two free ones from Jimmie!" shouted another member of the rescue posse.

"Reckon he riled you just to cadge a couple free drinks." The marshal laughed at their confusion. Then he said, "Since you boys rode all the way to help us, I suppose you ought to get a drink apiece to thank you. But that's all!" The marshal laughed as he crossed the street to enter the nearest Silverton saloon.

* * *

"So, we're settled on the terms of the bet?" asked the cowboy astride his nervous horse. The Southern Ute racers crowded close, trying to spook him. He had raced them before and knew their tricks. Before the race started, they couldn't do too much, but when he got out of sight of the bettors as he rounded the far turn was the time he had to be alert to a whip coming for his face or one Ute sacrificing himself by bumping horses to let another win.

"We go around track twice," the lead Ute said. "Winner takes all."

The piles of blankets, almost fifty dollars in gold coins, and a few other items were stacked on the ground at the finish line. It was a decent bet and he had a better than even chance of winning. He had seen the Ute racing among themselves and knew his horse was stronger over a two-mile distance than any of theirs.

"Let's race!" cried the cowboy, putting his heels to his horse's flanks as he spoke. Jumping the gun was cheating, but he did it before they could. Let them protest. He was already halfway to the first turn. He kept his head down as the cold autumn wind whistled past his face and left the skin all tingly and red. The horse he rode was strong and wanted to run today.

He felt completely alive.

He easily circled a stand of aspen trees at the far end of the track, well ahead of the Ute, and headed down the backstretch. He glanced back, seeing the Ute gaining on him, but his horse had stamina as well as speed. There was no doubt who would win.

The final turn came and went behind him as he flashed across the finish line. He saw a half-dozen cowboys riding up, looking agitated.

"Ben, hey, Ben. Haven't you heard?" shouted one he had met a few times in the only saloon in McPhee.

"Heard what? That I just beat these three fair and square?" Ben laughed. It was good to be alive. Alive and a winner.

"Up north, at the White River Agency. The Ute massacred the agent and every other white man there. Then they kidnapped two kids and took all the women as slaves!"

The three Ute drew rein behind him, exchanged looks, and then shied from him.

"Wait," Ben called. "You can't take that. I won those blankets. And that's my money!"

The other cowboys were already going for their guns. The Ute dropped the money, but kept the blankets as they galloped off. He stared after them, wondering what was going on. He knew these Ute, and they'd never kill anybody. Try to steal his winnings, yes, and cheat during the race, but never kill anyone. Ute were the peaceful Indians. Everybody knew that.

Then he read the truth on the faces of the men who had come to warn him. He joined them as they rode in the opposite direction from the retreating Ute, hunting for a place to hole up until the soldiers at Fort Lewis could be contacted and General Hatch could get his troopers into the field after the killers.

ARRIVAL

October 11, 1879
White River Agency

"Look sharp," General Merritt ordered. "We will be riding into the heart of the Ute power."

Wesley Merritt felt good about the quick rescue of Captain Payne and the other survivors. Simply blowing a charge on the bugle and riding up had lifted the Ute siege of the embattled men. Merritt had ordered squads out to find the Ute and engage them until a larger cavalry force could be projected against them, but the Indians had left. The simple appearance of Merritt and his companies of fresh, determined troopers had been enough to frighten off the cowards.

That did nothing to lessen the damage done to the Fifth. Payne had done an admirable job holding on to his command after Major Thornburg had been killed in battle. The stench of the decaying mules and horses, not to mention the soldiers who had died early in the siege, had been enough to sicken Merritt after a few minutes. How Payne and the others had endured it only added to the valor of their behavior.

They had survived because they were U.S. Army, and General Merritt was proud of them and their determination not to surrender or die. The Ute had cut them off effectively from Milk Creek, making thirst as deadly an enemy as any Indian sniper, but the cans of fruit had provided some liquid for the soldiers, and more than one of Captain Dodge's buffalo soldiers had sneaked to the creek and back with a few canteens to give just enough water to keep the men's spirits buoyed and their tongues from curling up with dehydration.

Since leaving a few men with Payne to act as guides until the captain returned to Fort Steele, Merritt had actively hunted for the Ute, finding their tracks as they had raced south toward the White River Agency. But their spoor was easier to find than the Ute themselves. They were like smoke on the wind, swirling about half seen, only to vanish entirely if anyone reached out to touch them.

General Merritt had found enough white settlers along the retreat that had seen the fleeing Indians, but no one had concrete information to give him. All he got were rumors and more rumors. The settlers were willing to spin wild tales of Ute depredation, but none of their stories had panned out. Still, one thing was mighty clear.

The Indians were on the run—and he was the one herding them.

"Can't see any sign of them, General," said his scout, Jed, squinting as he shielded his eyes from the bright wintery sun. "Mighty unusual to be so quiet down in the park, if you know what I mean."

Merritt knew, and it chilled him. The massacre had spread quickly, from all accounts. The large raiding party that had pinned down Payne's unit was only part of the uprising. Every last informant he had found on the way to Middle Park had told of vast killings and slaughters of hundreds of innocents.

As quiet as Middle Park was near the tumbling water in White River, Merritt knew the stories might have more than a grain of truth in them. If anything, it was too quiet. More than once he and his troopers had ridden through ghost towns. He was not a superstitious man, but always looked over his shoulder as he left such abandoned towns. The feeling of someone watching him, maybe alive or possibly dead, always gnawed at the edges of reason.

General Merritt got the same feeling now about the White River Agency. He rode ramrod straight as the column wended its way down the road toward the river.

"The Ute call it Smoking Earth River," Jed almost whispered.

Merritt was relieved that the scout felt something of what *he* did about the terrain and its lack of living creatures. Even the rabbits refused to budge from their burrows.

"I see more'n that smokin' now. Lookee there, General." The scout pointed along the river to a dozen cabins that had been burned to the ground.

Wesley Merritt turned and stared across neatly plowed fields bare of crops, along surveyed roads, and at the split rail fences showing the beginnings of civilization that Nathan Meeker had brought to the park. But the children running along, throwing stones at squirrels or laughing on their way to school, the men toiling in those fields, the women hanging up laundry—it was all missing. The White River Agency was more like a cemetery than a living, breathing community.

The wind whipping down the valley carried more than a hint of winter with it. There was the clammy feel of death on the wind.

"The headquarters is up that way," Merritt said. "That's where I'd put it."

"Reckon so, General," Jed said. "Looks to be the most traveled road goin' up to it."

Merritt dispatched men in squad strength to explore the entire area, with orders not to engage any Ute they found but to report back immediately. Having his men ambushed and killed the way Major Thornburg had been was not part of his way of doing things. In spite of his caution, the scouts saw nothing. Nothing at all. He and Jed, with a few junior officers trailing them, rode to Meeker's headquarters.

"It was a nice place once," Merritt said, staring at the burned-out shell of a cabin.

"Heard tell they moved it from Powell's Valley when the agent decided not to stay there."

"More water here," Merritt said distantly. His nose wrinkled at the unpleasant stench hanging in the air. He dismounted and went to the cabin. The smell grew stronger until the general found the source.

"Is a burial detail called for, General?" asked Jed.

Merritt nodded. "It looks as if they mutilated the bodies after they killed them—or perhaps it was before they killed their victims." A dull anger built inside at any fighter who could drive a barrel stave into his victim's chest and then decapitate the dead. "Identify the bodies, if you can."

"Sir, we found another body out back. Shot in the back. I think I recognize him," said the lieutenant. "It's Shadrick Price. My brother worked for him when he was up north, in Steamboat Springs, at Mr. Crawford's spread."

"Meeker hired locals whenever he could," said General Merritt. "Find a list of the agency personnel, Lieutenant. Match the bodies with the names, if you can, then report to me."

"Some might have escaped, sir," the lieutenant said. "There's a trail of blood running off into the foothills."

"Track it," Wesley Merritt said grimly. "No one rides alone. At least five troopers in every group. I will not have any in my command ambushed."

"Good idea, General," Jed said. "Major Thornburg was too trustin' of them red devils."

"Captain Payne said the major followed his orders and refused to fire until the Ute fired on him. That spelled his downfall. My orders come directly from General Sheridan and give me far greater latitude. We will engage only in strength and will fire first, if the opportunity presents itself for a successful skirmish." General Merritt looked around and saw his officers understood the orders. He shooed them away to poke through the embers.

Two hours later the lieutenant returned with another body.

"Sir, this one's Frank Dresser. He had papers on him identifying him. We found him in a cave in the mountains."

"Dead?" asked the general, seeing the man's body draped over the back of a horse.

"Damnedest thing, sir. And excuse my French. We tracked him by the trail of blood to the cave. He was curled up there, his head on his folded shirt like he had gone to sleep, and looked as peaceful as could be."

"But he was dead?"

"As dead as a mackerel, sir," the lieutenant said.

General Merritt sighed. Price, Dresser, Arthur Thompson, Glencannon, Summers, a man found two miles north of the agency carrying a letter from Meeker—and Nathan Meeker himself. All dead.

"Any buildings left standing?"

"One to the west of here, sir," reported Jed. "Looks to be one of the Injuns' houses. Prob'ly Chief Johnson's, from a signpost out front. Ever'thing else has been set on fire."

"An oversight on the Ute's part, I am sure," Merritt said dryly. He heaved a sigh and came to a conclusion. "Bury the men and be sure to put appropriate markers on the graves. Use one of the plowed fields. That'll save on the digging."

"Yes, sir," snapped the lieutenant, looking at Dresser's body and resigning himself to a tedious and repugnant duty.

"Has anyone found the women?" Merritt asked.

"Reckon not, General," said Jed. "I been keepin' a sharp eye out, too. I know how them red devils are 'bout women and children. All the bodies we've found were white men. Don't look much like they even fought back."

"They were taken by surprise," General Merritt said, his ire rising. "And I believe the women were simply . . . taken."

"What do you want to do now, General?"

"We'll go back to Powell's Valley," Merritt declared. "We'll establish a cantonment there, and then go hunting for the women once we have a secure base. I trust our luck retrieving them will be as successful as relieving Captain Payne's command."

The scout and officers exchanged looks. They

weren't convinced there would be any such outcome, not after seeing what the Ute had done to the employees of the White River Agency.

CHIEF OURAY

October 12, 1879
San Juan, Colorado

"I've got to see the chief right away," Cray
Eachin pleaded. "I've been on the trail for almost
a week, and it feels like I've ridden a million
miles." He felt a rising tide of frustration, especially
after his earlier failure to find Ouray. Cray had
heard the old chief had been in Denver when he
and Towa had come hunting for him to tell him
of Douglass's attack at the White River Agency. But
now he knew Ouray was back from his travels.

Saponowera stared at him and said nothing.

"Look, I know where Chief Douglass—Quinkent—is holding the hostages. Ouray doesn't want
trouble with the white soldiers. If we work together,
I can get Mrs. Meeker and the others free. That'll
remove a lot of trouble between the Ute and the,
uh, *Maricat'z.*"

"Do you speak *Nunt'z?*" asked Saponowera.

Cray did his best to convince Ouray's minion
that he knew enough about the Ute to be of use.
He had kicked himself constantly since leaving
Douglass's camp without even attempting to res-

cue the captive white women. Cray had gone over
a dozen different excuses, some of them terrible,
to alleviate the guilt he felt. Telling himself they
wouldn't endure any worse than they already had
shamed him the most. He should have done
something, even to the point of trying to take
Douglass captive and swapping him for the
women. A dozen other crazy ideas had occurred
to him as he rode south, seeking out Ouray by
following the vague rumors of his location passed
along by riders he met on the road. He had finally found a man who had seemed honest and
claimed that Ouray was heading back to Los Pinos
Agency as they spoke.

Saponowera grunted but did not reply.

"I tried to find Chief Ouray before, but he was
somewhere else," Cray said. "My wife Towa and I
were here but the chief was gone." He bit his lip
when he realized he was babbling. It meant too
much not to try to enlist the great chief's help.

"Towa is your *piwán*?"

Cray didn't trust himself to answer other than
quickly nodding.

"This is why you speak the Old Language so
well?" asked Saponowera.

"She is everything in my life," Cray said, pushing
away the emptiness left by Towa's departure. He
had failed at everything he had ever tried. He had
left New Orleans because his family was dead and
nothing held him there but bad memories. He had
never found gold or silver, no matter how hard he
dug. Working at the agency for Nathan Meeker had
not been his forte, and keeping Towa happy had
not either. He missed her, and wondered where she
had gone after he had set out to rescue the white

women and the two children taken prisoner by Douglass.

"Come," Saponowera said, spinning and walking off quickly. The invitation took Cray by surprise, but he hurriedly followed. They stopped when they reached the edge of town. Saponowera stared down the road leading to Fort Lewis. Cray started to ask what they waited for, but he held his tongue.

In a few minutes, a buggy kicked up a cloud of dust at the bend in the road leading into town. Cray saw Chief Ouray riding beside the driver, shivering as he huddled under a Navajo brown, gray, and white patterned Two Gray Hills blanket against the chilly autumn weather as if it were midwinter.

"You wait here," Saponowera said. The Indian stepped forward and spoke rapidly with Ouray. Only when Saponowera motioned for Cray did the young man go to speak with the great chief of the Ute.

"You worry about Quinkent," Chief Ouray said.

"I worry about what the *Maricat'z* will do if Chief Quinkent does not return the women and children he kidnapped."

"He thinks they are spoils of war," Ouray said.

"The cavalry will kill Douglass—Quinkent—unless the women are returned safe and sound."

"What can you do to bring this about?" asked Ouray.

"I know where Douglass's camp is," Cray said. "I saw him, but could do nothing to release the women. With your help, perhaps Saponowera carrying a message from you, I am sure Douglass will release them."

"I know all this," Ouray said. "I stopped Nicaagat and Colorow from attacking the cavalry to the north of the reservation."

"You did?"

"Saponowera carried my request to stop. General Merritt found no one to fight, saving *Nunt'z* lives. And *Maricat'z* lives," Ouray said, almost as an afterthought.

"I didn't realize you had—"

"I have done much to calm the winds of war blowing through the Shining Mountains," Ouray said. He heaved a deep sigh of resignation. "It is taking much time, but the storms are dying down. When the new *Maricat'z* agent comes, things will happen more quickly."

"New agent? To replace Nathan Meeker?"

"Charles Adams will parley soon," Ouray said. "I am pleased that you speak the Old Language well and that you think to save lives, both *Nunt'z* and *Maricat'z*. It is to your credit you have risked your own life for others."

"Thank you," Cray said, head spinning.

"Know this. I am not an old, infirm chief. Your women will be freed. If they are not, Quinkent, Nicaagat, Colorow, Curicata, and all the others will feel my might." Ouray reached out and slowly tensed his hand into a fist. Cray heard the crackling as Ouray squeezed down on the invisible defiance to his will.

"Thank you," Cray said again.

"Will you be my representative? Will you join Saponowera in dealing with Chief Quinkent?"

"You want me to speak for you?" Cray was startled. This was not a role he had ever considered filling—or being offered him.

"We want the same thing, for lives to be preserved and the fighting to cease. You have determination and speak the Old Language passably well."

"I—yes," Cray said.

Ouray smiled, touched his driver's arm, and the buggy rattled off into town, leaving Cray and Saponowera standing in the road. Somehow, Cray had never felt more important.

DEALS & PROMISES

October 21, 1879
Plateau Creek

"He's moved his camp from when I scouted it," Cray Eachin said to the new Indian Agent, Charles Adams. Adams, in spite of being a portly man who looked as if he spent all his time in a library with his nose stuck into a book, rode well. The only one in the party who bothered Cray was the German, Count von Doehoff, a member of the German legation in Washington who had been visiting Adams when he had been ordered by Secretary Schurz to negotiate the release of the captives. Cray found Adams a bit academic and standoffish, but surprisingly knowledgeable about the Ute and their ways. That was a good thing since Saponowera and two other chiefs had come along with the group.

But the German? Cray saw him as nothing but trouble, the way he asked his impertinent questions and bedeviled Saponowera with stories of German military superiority in Europe. For some reason, the German ignored Captain Cline and his aide from Fort Lewis and gravitated toward Adams and Cray.

"We know where the new camp is," Adams said.

"Is there someone in the camp telling you what's going on? How are the captives?" asked Cray, realizing that Adams knew far more than he had revealed so far. Cray glanced at Saponowera, who rode with his eyes straight ahead. Ouray's right-hand man also knew everything about Douglass's new camp. Cray could tell by the way the corners of his mouth twitched upward in a sly smile when Cray was asking Adams for more information.

"Let's just say that Chief Douglass—Quinkent—does not move his tepee without others knowing it. The three women and two children are safe in his camp," Adams said. "Put your mind to rest on that score. Concentrate instead on arguments to convince Douglass that he should release them."

"I thought Ouray had sent instructions for Douglass to release them all," Cray said, looking at Saponowera. "Douglass won't go against Ouray's direct order, would he?"

"Ouray has sent such orders," Adams said, choosing his words carefully because the German rode closer, listening attentively, "but Chief Douglass seems a bit hesitant to believe Ouray is serious. It is our duty to convince him to put an end to this awful kidnapping right away."

"What are you going to say about all the men killed at the agency?" Cray saw Adams and Saponowera stiffen slightly at this question, and knew he trod on dangerous ground. There must be some difference of opinion between the two—between Ouray and Washington—about punishment for the massacre. Even more disturbing, von Doehoff smiled wolfishly and reached up to touch a bright pink scar on his cheek, as if remembering some European war and the toothsome bloodshed. Cray began to worry that the count would be intent on doing more than observing, simply to get a chance to see the Ute and the cavalry in some horrendous battle. The description of the carnage Jack had wrought on Major Thornburg's column had turned the German positively rhapsodic.

"We will deal with such matters as they arise. There is Plateau Creek, isn't it?" called Adams to their guide.

"Do you plan attacks?" asked the German. "If the red men do not give you the women and children, will you bring in artillery? I would see the mountain howitzer in use against the savages. It has been well employed against your Apache in Arizona where the terrain is similar."

"That will not be necessary," Adams said lightly. "General Merritt has only cavalry and infantry at his command, and moving in mountain howitzers is not something to undertake without great need."

"But the cannon will remove the enemy efficiently," von Doehoff said, obviously enthusiastic for the display of such power. "It is their tactic to mount a frontal charge. Into a well-maintained artillery battery, such an attack would prove fruitless, even suicidal. Therefore, the obvious weapon of choice is the howitzer."

"You don't know the Ute," Cray explained. "They are great fighters, but if they faced such a cannon, they would simply vanish into thin air, like dust in the wind. It would be futile dragging around such a heavy weapon and pointless to fire it. They ride their horses as if they were part of them."

"You are an expert on warfare with the red man?" asked von Doehoff, riding closer to Cray.

"Well, no."

"He is quite the expert, and so modest," Adams chimed in. "Do tell him all you can, Mr. Eachin. Take your time doing so." Adams's smile flickered so fast the German failed to see it. Cray realized he was being given the job of keeping their aggressive observer occupied until they reached Douglass's village so Adams and Saponowera could talk in private. If he did not prevent von Doehoff from butting into their conversation, they might fail to come to an agreement over what course of action to follow.

Cray rambled on, telling tall tales and relating what stories he could remember other miners spinning. The German ate it all up as if it were the Gospel truth, and stayed clear of Adams and Saponowera until they reached the creek.

"Quinkent's camp is there," said Saponowera, pointing upstream toward a stand of lodgepole pines.

"Sentries?" asked Cray nervously.

"There are none," Adams assured him. "Come along. Look sharp now."

Cray listened with half an ear to von Doehoff telling about European battles he had witnessed during the Crimean War. Somehow, the man never quite detailed any fight he'd personally engaged in, making Cray think the man was always the observer and never the participant. Cray hoped it would be that way with them all today. If Douglass got angry, they could find themselves in plenty of trouble fast.

As they rode past a large tepee, an Indian woman pushed someone back inside and hissed like a mad cat. Cray heard a woman calling out in English, but could not make out the words. It sounded as if he had found where Josephine Meeker was being held, possibly along with her mother and Mrs. Price. Of the children he saw no trace.

"There," Saponowera said, pointing to an even larger tepee in the center of the village. He easily dismounted and walked to the flap, throwing it open. The Indian did not wait to be invited in, ducking low and swinging inside. Adams and Cray were slower to follow. Sitting in a large circle near a fire pit filled with warming embers were dozens of warriors, all passing around a pipe.

"We seek Chief Douglass, known to you as Quinkent," Adams said. Saponowera walked quickly around the circle, eyeing each of the braves. Only a few returned his hard stare. The rest averted their eyes, as if they were guilty of terrible crimes and knew it. The boldest of the Indians were the ones Cray knew would give them the most argument, and in the case of real conflict, be the most dangerous.

"He is not here. You wait," said one brave near the door. "I will get him."

Cray grabbed the German's arm and kept him from drawing his side arm.

"Don't do that," he cautioned.

"He'll fetch more red men and kill you all," protested the German count. Cray noted that the man did not include himself in the supposed massacre. It must have violated European ethics to kill anyone who was a mere onlooker. This made Cray laugh harshly. Von Doehoff had much to learn. If Douglass wanted to attack, he would kill them all, no matter their status. Cray had heard of a war chief in northern California killing a general under a truce flag while they were supposedly talking about the terms of a peace treaty.

But Cray couldn't believe that would ever happen

here, not with Ouray's personal emissary among the peace delegates. The other two Ute chiefs stood impassively, staring ahead and saying nothing. Their presence, along with Saponowera's, cowed the Ute more than anything the German might say or do.

"Sit. We smoke," Saponowera said, taking a pipe from one warrior's hands without it being offered. He puffed, then passed the pipe around. Adams sat cross-legged and took the pipe, expertly smoking it before giving it to Cray. For an hour they sat quietly, smoking and watching the restless braves with them. Rather than settling nerves, the longer they smoked, the more fidgety the other Ute became.

Then Douglass swept into the tepee like some primal force of nature.

Again Cray had to stop Count von Doehoff from drawing his pistol. To keep the German occupied and less likely to cause trouble, he whispered, "That's Chief Douglass, the Ute we're here to negotiate with."

"We will talk," Douglass announced without fanfare. More than half the warriors rose and left silently. Cray had already decided who were the lesser braves and who were likely to take part in peace talks. He had not been far wrong in his choices. The most nervous of the braves were those leaving now.

He guessed Charles Adams hadn't missed a one.

"Chief Douglass, I bring you greetings from Chief Ouray and orders to immediately release the captives you have taken," said Adams.

Such bluntness caused Douglass to rock back.

"I will not release them! They are slaves taken in battle."

"Ouray is not happy with this. You will cease all fighting, as Jack and Colorow already have."

Douglass looked past Adams to one of the chiefs sitting beside Saponowera. "I see one of Colorow's sons has come to bring me this message."

This took Cray aback. He had not realized one of the chiefs riding with Saponowera was Colorow's own son. Closely studying the man showed few of his father's features, making Cray wonder if the mother had been from some tribe other than the Ute.

"The rest of the mighty Ute nation urges you to stop your fighting and to give back the three white women and the two children," Adams said matter-of-factly, but Cray heard the edge of steel rattling along the sides of the words. Adams glanced in the direction of the cavalry officer, who sat behind the circle to one side of the entrance flap, not partaking of the pipe and not saying a word. Cray wished he knew more about the officer now, because he might be called upon to back up Adams's veiled threats with real force.

Cray knew Captain Cline was attached to the Uncompahgre Agency as a military advisor, but had no idea if he could order troops into battle on his own against the Ute or had to go through his commanding officer, General Hatch.

"We will no longer fight," Douglass said. "Those we hated and who hated us are dead. Those who are our friends remain." Douglass looked directly at Cray, who smiled. The chief did not show any friendliness, but Cray took his words to mean that, with Meeker dead, they had no problem with returning to the reservation. Cray found he bore no malice toward Douglass either, in spite of what the chief had done. Douglass had gone out of his way to be certain Cray was not injured. An added point in the chief's favor was the way he had reacted to Cray's abortive attempt to parley and free the women by sneaking into the Ute camp during the Scalp Dance. It would have been easy for the chief to call attention to the interloper.

Cray involuntarily reached up and touched his scalp. It might have been hanging from the chief's lance.

"That is good that you lay down your rifles and stop your war. Ouray approves of your wise decision. He will be even happier when you release your prisoners."

To Adams's words this time, Douglass spat and shoved the pipe away when it came to him. "You take the children. We keep the women."

"No, you will not. Do you want many soldiers to attack?" asked Adams. He glanced in Captain Cline's direction. The officer glared at Douglass, but said nothing and made no overt move toward the pistol holstered at his side. Somehow, this struck Cray as more menacing than if Cline had jumped to his feet and waved a cavalry saber around. There was a stony determination, a surety of outcome, a solid assurance that the women would not remain with the Ute in Cline's unemotional demeanor.

"We want them away from Middle Park," Douglass said. "We want General Merritt and his soldiers to leave Powell's Valley. That is our land by treaty."

"That is possible," Adams said, nodding thoughtfully. "It will be done—after you release your prisoners."

Cray listened with half an ear, knowing that Douglass would give in eventually. He saw a squaw poke her head in and look around, then back out hastily. It was the same woman who had kept Josephine Meeker in the tent as the peace negotiators had ridden into Douglass's camp.

Saponowera bent close and whispered in his ear, "That is Susan, Ouray's youngest sister."

Cray realized then who Ouray's informant must be. The squaw looking after Mrs. Meeker, her daughter, and Mrs. Price was slipping messages out to her brother. He felt a relief wash over him. The women were in safe hands.

"Then it is decided," Adams concluded. "You will release your prisoners and we will escort them to Montrose, where they will be welcomed as Chief Ouray's guests. He and his wife Chipeta will not release them until you are satisfied that General Merritt's troopers have withdrawn from their camp."

Douglass nodded once, signifying the conference was at an end.

Outside in the late afternoon chill, Adams said to Cray, "I will go to the cantonment and speak with the general. I have the authority to remove him, and I shall. You will accompany the women. Mrs. Meeker's son Ralph will stay with his mother and sister at Ouray's house."

"I didn't know the Meekers had a son," Cray said, past surprise now. He knew so little about the people at the agency because Meeker had irritated him so. Now he wished he had known more so he could have been more effective helping Adams free the captives.

"He is on his way from Greeley as we speak and will do much to ease his sister and mother's grieving, I am sure," Charles Adams said, sucking in a deep breath and puffing up his broad chest. He looked out over the rocky hills to the grassy meadows beyond and smiled. "This has been a good day's work, sir."

"But?" asked Cray, hearing something unfinished in Adams's words.

"Who will pay for the deaths of so many fine men?" Adams asked, turning glum once more. "Because the hostages are free does not mean justice will not be served. But at what cost to peace in Colorado?"

That was something that had never been mentioned to Douglass, and Cray realized it would be the next sticking point in the talks, a point that might cause the entire rebellion to flare up again.

SAFE . . . AND LOST

October 25, 1879
Uncompahgre Agency

"Do you think Mrs. Price will ever stop crying?" Cray Eachin asked Josephine Meeker, who rode beside him in stony silence as they made their way back to San Juan.

"Why should she?" the young woman snapped. She peered at him as if he were one of her abductors and responsible for all the ills that had befallen her. Her squinty eyes looked piglike and her lips thinned to a razor slash that made her even less becoming. Josephine's hair was matted and dirty and she was covered with small cuts, either from abusive treatment or the dog-work chores she had been forced to do while in Ute captivity. "You have no idea of the atrocities perpetrated on our bodies. For her, it was doubly difficult since she'd just found her husband so brutally murdered."

"Why isn't it just as bad for you?" Cray asked. "Your father was murdered. Mutilated."

Josephine Meeker sniffed and looked away from him.

"I want to know. Are you stronger than Mrs.

Price? What makes you that way?" He wondered if
there was something in Josephine Meeker's moti-
vations that he could use to soothe some of the
pain he was feeling over Towa. Cray had not lost
her as these women had lost husband and father,
yet he felt more like Mrs. Price than Josephine
Meeker over Towa leaving him. He wanted to cry
for the loved one he had lost.

"I have my faith," the woman said curtly. "And
my mother needs me. And my brother is waiting
for us at Chief Ouray's house."

"It's good to have family," Cray said, his mind
turning to his own parents and siblings, now long
dead back in New Orleans, and as always, to Towa.
He hoped she would be at the Uncompahgre
Agency so he could speak with her again. They had
not parted on the best of terms.

Cray mentally changed that. They had parted on
terrible terms. Towa had not even spoken to him
as she left, and all because he couldn't find the
right words to say or the right thing to do. He
wasn't Ute and lacked the knowledge of how one
brave could keep several wives happy. Cray had
tried to keep just one and had found it impossible.

Or had he really tried? The winter at the mine
had been difficult, but he had rather enjoyed it,
the parts where they weren't close to starvation or
freezing to death. Towa had not seemed to mind
then either. If she had not been with him, she
would have been at the White River Agency in her
father's tepee. Cray had to believe she would rather
be with him than Kanneatche.

If she had been white, Cray would have said the
lack of gold or silver had caused her to leave, but
such things meant nothing to the Ute. They simply
did not understand what the precious metals meant

to a white man, a *Maricat'z*. If he had hunted better, was a better shot, had given her the things a Ute warrior would have, perhaps this would have insured her staying with him.

He didn't know.

"There," called Captain Cline, riding at the front of the small party. "I see the chief's house."

"You'll be with your brother soon," Cray said to Josephine.

"I haven't seen Ralph in a spell," the woman admitted. "He and Father did not see eye to eye on very many things. That's why he did not come with us from Greeley to help the savages at the White River Agency." She swallowed hard, then sniffed derisively again. "It saved him."

"Your father died doing what he believed in." Cray said the words, but found himself identifying more with the Ute. Nathan Meeker had been a zealot intent on "civilizing" an already civilized tribe. He should never have gotten on his hobby-horse about forcing them to go against their nature by turning into farmers. There was nothing wrong with hunting and raising horses. Then Cray realized how astute Meeker had been, how sharp and clear his vision of the future.

With so many white settlers pouring into the parks west of the Rockies, the Ute were being pressed into ever smaller areas. They could continue to hunt for a few more years, perhaps even ten or twenty, but then the settlers' towns would be spreading like wildfire and driving the game the Ute depended on into the higher mountains.

As the buffalo had been killed on the plains, the elk and deer would vanish under civilization's onslaught. All that would abide was the land. Meeker had wanted to teach the Ute how to farm that enduring land so they could feed their families, if not immediately, then in a few years. His methods were suspect, but his foresight had been impeccable.

Cray had a sinking feeling that the Ute had lost their best chance of remaining on their tribal lands by killing Meeker and the others at the White River Agency.

"Ralph!" called Josephine. She kicked at her horse's flanks and trotted forward to greet a tall, gangly man who looked like a younger version of Nathan Meeker. The young woman slipped from the saddle and fell into his arms.

Cray watched, a lump in his throat. It was good to have family. Mrs. Meeker was slower to follow, but soon the three were huddled together, arms around one another. Cray rode over to Mrs. Price, who had dried her tears for the moment, but looked as if she would burst out crying again at the slightest provocation.

"Is there anything I can do for you, ma'am?" he asked.

"No, I am fine," she said, obviously distraught at seeing the Meeker reunion. It reminded her how her husband was dead and buried, just as it reminded Cray of how alone and without family he was.

"Captain Cline will look after you. Chief Ouray's known for his hospitality." Cray realized he should not have mentioned any Ute name. Mrs. Price began crying again, leaving him to wonder if he could do any worse in tending to business. Charles Adams had entrusted the party to him, and he had seen the survivors safely to the Uncompahgre Agency and Ouray's large, rambling house, but Cray had no idea what he was supposed to do now.

He dismounted and tethered his horse behind the house, considering that the hospitality might extend to him so he could curry the horse and feed it some of the grain he saw in a pan near the barn. He looked up when he sensed someone moving quietly up behind him.

"Towa!"

"Hello, Cray," she said. "I am here to talk with Ouray on the behalf of my father."

"Is Kanneatche trying to get out of responsibility for the Meeker massacre?" Cray's words carried a sting to them he had not intended. "I'm sorry. I didn't mean it that way."

"That is all right. Yes, my father has asked me to speak with Ouray to tell him he is innocent of the killings."

They stood and stared awkwardly at each other for a moment. Then Cray asked, "How long are you going to be here?"

"I am leaving now. Chief Ouray was most kind and offered to help however he could. He knows the new Indian Agent will require someone to punish but is not sure who it will be."

"Adams isn't looking for a scapegoat," Cray said, defending the man for no reason other than to keep Towa here, talking to him, near enough to reach out and touch if he had the nerve. His hand twitched, but he could not find the gumption to so much as take his wife's hand.

"Adams speaks for others in Washington. You have not heard General Hatch. *He* wants someone to pay for the deaths."

"I don't have anywhere to go right now—officially, I mean. I told Mr. Adams I'd see the Meekers and Mrs. Price here. I saw them here and now I'm at loose ends." Cray danced around asking outright to accompany Towa back to her father's tepee, but he felt in his gut that it was wrong to simply invite himself. She had to say it was all right for them to be together.

And she didn't.

"They leave for Greeley in a day or two," Towa said. "I overheard Arvella say this to her son."

"They can reach Greeley without me." Cray waited for Towa to say something more, but it did not come.

"I must leave now, Cray."

"Come with me," he urged. "I'm selling the coal from the mine and not bothering to look for gold anymore. I've been hearing rumors of the narrow-gauge railroad coming over the Rockies from Colorado Springs and into the western part of the state. Even narrow-gauge roads need coal to run their locomotives. It's not the same as finding silver and getting filthy rich, but it could mean a decent living."

"I am happy for you," she said. Towa's face was impassive. She held her hands clasped together in front of her and did not move a muscle.

"But you won't come with me," Cray said, crestfallen.

"No."

Towa stepped back as if she were afraid he might try to grab her. She gave him a look that was indecipherable, then hurried away. Cray started to call after her, but his throat seemed paralyzed. He just didn't understand. He stared at her until Towa rode from Ouray's house, heading toward the White River Agency.

She never looked back, but Cray watched her until the road curled around and she vanished from sight. Even then he stood and stared. The hardest thing he had ever done was not jumping on his tired horse and galloping after her to beg her to take him back.

THE OTHER SIDE

October 27, 1879
Jack's Camp

"It's good of you to come along on such short notice, Mr. Eachin," Charles Adams said. Cray tried to interpret the man's mood, and found himself getting a little apprehensive about it. Adams looked like he was ready to jump but was trying to keep from showing his uneasiness. "This is important work we're doing, and I need a first-rate interpreter to avoid all confusion."

"I understand how a mistake can turn the western part of Colorado into a bloodbath," Cray Eachin said. "Another bloodbath," he hastily amended.

"You are a smart fellow and know these people well."

Cray almost turned and rode off when Adams said that. He knew nothing about the Ute. Nothing. His failure to figure out what Towa wanted from him proved that beyond a shadow of a doubt. His sympathies might lie with them over the way Meeker had tried to completely change their way of life, but know about them? Really *know*? Cray couldn't honestly make that claim.

"I knew some folks at the agency, too," Cray said, remembering how snippy Josephine Meeker had been and how distraught Mrs. Price was after being released. But it was Nathan Meeker who kept coming to mind, and how little Cray had liked the man. For all that, he was sorry to see him dead in such a grisly fashion.

"Keep your feelings to yourself on that score," Adams said sharply. "We need only learn from Jack what the Ute side of the matter is. How do you rate his veracity?"

"His—oh, you mean how likely is it that he'll tell the truth?" Cray thought for a moment. He had almost fired from the hip, but Adams needed more than that. "Jack'll tell what he thinks is the truth, if only from his own skewed, boastful perspective. If you ask Colorow what went on, nothing of what he says will be right. That chief and the truth are total strangers."

"I am not sure Colorow is in the camp where we go. General Merritt learned that Jack's camp is above Powell's Valley, not far from the road leading down to Middle Park where Meeker and the others were murdered. Is there any reason Jack would choose this spot for his bivouac?"

"He hunts in those hills and knows every rock and tree," Cray said. "He might not want to be far from the reservation either, since he still has horses running free there."

"Johnson's horses have been rounded up by the soldiers," Adams said. "This has caused some friction, to say the least. But they are not likely to be returned until this entire matter is settled."

"There," Cray said, pointing. "I see the tops of a half dozen tepees. That must be Jack's camp."

"So it is." Adams looked behind them to the squad of soldiers accompanying them. He waved and the last two troopers halted, to wait there in case they had to ride to General Merritt with word that the fact-finding mission had been massacred. Somehow, Cray was glad to see Adams was taking the matter of dealing with Jack so seriously. It never paid to underestimate the firebrand Ute.

"Maiquas," Cray called in greeting when Jack came out from the largest tepee. The Ute chief hesitated, as if he considered running for the woods. Then he puffed out his chest and strutted forward arrogantly. Jack put his hand on the knife sheathed at his hip, but made no move to draw it. The threat was obvious to Cray, though. Jack might talk, but he wasn't going to put up with any nonsense from Adams, cavalry detachment or not.

"I know you," Jack said to Cray in Ute. "You took Kanneatche's daughter for your squaw. Then she left you because you could not hunt and provide for her."

"Agent Adams wishes to speak to you about all that has happened and what you know of Father Meeker's death." Cray spoke stiffly, formally, trying to avoid what might be Jack's way of needling him so he would make a mistake. Still, the words stung Cray. All the Ute seemed to know of his problems with Towa—better than he did himself.

"I promised Ouray that I will speak with Adams and tell him all I know of this," said Jack. "Let us smoke a pipe as we talk."

To Charles Adams, Cray said quietly, "He wants to smoke while you talk. That's a good sign. Jack wants to be friends, or at least he wants to give that impression."

"Of course he wants to be friendly," Adams said dryly. "Someone has to pay for killing all those soldiers, and he doesn't want to be the one. If I consider him my friend, I won't get him into trouble. At least, that's what he apparently thinks." Adams shook his head slightly, then dismounted and went to greet Jack with a hearty handshake.

They went into Jack's tent, skirting a small fire, and eventually sitting around the fire pit as they waited for the Ute chief. Jack fumbled in a pouch, filled a pipe, used a twig from the fire to light the tobacco, puffed it to life, and then passed it before speaking. His every movement seemed deliberate, as if he wanted to impress on them how reasonable he could be and that he wasn't the wild man the newspapers had made him out to be.

Cray wasn't sure where the truth lay. Probably between those two extremes, since he had never seen Jack any way other than wild-eyed and whooping and hollering to impress his followers.

"You will tell Washington what is said here?"

"Yes, I will, Chief Jack," said Adams, passing the pipe after a puff or two.

"Then I will tell my story," Jack said pompously. "I tried everything to avoid a fight, but Meeker said he had told soldiers to come and they would bring with them ropes and shackles to imprison us all. We would be slaves for all the *Maricat'z* to abuse."

Adams started to speak and then stopped himself. Questions would come later. He took out a notebook and began scribbling in it as Cray translated.

Jack smiled when he saw the agent begin taking down all he said.

"I could not stop Meeker, and he said many of us would be hurt or killed, the others made prisoners. This frightened me and gave me great fear for my people."

"What did you do then?" asked Cray.

"I rode north to the mouth of Coal Creek Canyon to speak with Major Thornburg. I asked him to keep his troops away from the reservation, because so many soldiers would frighten the women and children. I asked him to come to the agency with only a few of his men. He refused my offer. He wanted to make war on us, because of what Meeker had told him. I know Meeker lied to him, saying that the Ute had killed many who worked for the agency."

Jack puffed solemnly on the long-stemmed, big-bowled pipe, staring at the inside of the cured-hide-wall tepee as if he were looking across the Shining Mountains.

"I dickered with him. So many soldiers coming to camp would be wrong at the agency, I told him. Major Thornburg agreed to come only halfway to the reservation, then wait there while I gathered other chiefs for a big powwow."

"Others like Colorow?" Cray forced himself to keep from smiling. The corpulent chief must have thrown in with Jack because there was food to be had.

"Yes, Chief Colorow wanted to attend, as did Quinkent, but the major lied as much as Meeker. Barely was I out of his sight when he broke his word. He did not camp, but rode on, heading for the agency along the Milk Creek road with many of his men. His whole command would frighten women and children all along the way, so Colorow had the idea we should talk again. We rode along the road and waited for them, but they avoided us and took another route."

"They avoided you?" asked Adams. "Why would they do that?"

"They thought to kill us because they formed a skirmish line. Colorow and I were shocked when the soldiers shot at us. Some of our young men were killed because they did not expect this shooting. All we wanted to do was talk to Thornburg, to find why he lied and rode on to the reservation with all his soldiers."

"You returned fire?" asked Cray. "When the major's men shot at you, you simply defended yourself?"

"Not at first. I sent couriers to Quinkent, who was still at the agency, telling him what had happened. Colorow suggested that we attack, but I tried to speak again to the major. I did not want to fight. He would not listen, so the young warriors listened to Colorow because he is a great war chief."

"I'd like to speak to Chief Colorow later," said Adams. "Is he in camp?"

"I do not know where he is," Jack said, obviously lying.

"That's all right," Cray interrupted. "We're interested in *your* side of the story, not his. Not right now."

Jack nodded sagely and continued. "I speak only the truth to you. The couriers told Quinkent some of the young warriors were killed and this frightened him. If the soldiers killed braves intent only on peace and hunting, what would they do when they reached the agency and listened to Meeker? He would convince Thornburg he had to kill us all, women and children and braves alike."

"So Douglass—Quinkent—then killed Meeker

and all the agency employees?" Adams frowned at this.

"I have heard this is so. Quinkent should speak for himself."

"What of the freighters from Hot Sulphur Springs you massacred? George Gordon and twenty others bound for the White River Agency with food and blankets?" asked Adams.

"I know nothing of this," Jack said firmly. "Maybe Thornburg killed them to steal their clothes. Maybe General Merritt did. I do not know because I was not there."

"General Merritt found a burned-out wagon train when he came to Captain Payne's rescue," Adams said.

"Then it was Thornburg who killed these men with their wagons and mules," Jack said, looking smug that he had solved the enigma.

"Sir," Cray said softly to Adams, "it might be for the best to simply let Jack tell his story about Thornburg's death. If you get him off on another track, we might be here forever and never find out anything. He's an expert at spinning tales and turning the facts around to put himself in the best light."

"I agree. Please tell him." Adams continued scribbling notes to himself on all that Jack had said.

Cray translated and Jack nodded, happy to get back to the story of his bravery.

"I wanted nothing but to return to my home along the Smoking Earth River—the *Maricat'z* call it White River—but the major chased me and my men. They shot at me and those with me. I defended myself until many warriors from other tribes who had joined me in my hunt for deer and antelope fought alongside against the renegade bluecoats. The major and his company of soldiers thought to kill us with their ambush, but we fought back and killed him!"

"Was he advancing or going back toward his supply wagons when he died?" asked Adams.

"He ran from us, as Colorow said he would if we fought hard enough. We followed, to make certain the other soldiers did not attack us. We forced them to circle their wagons and fight from hiding. Every time they tried to attack, we killed more of them, their mules, their horses."

"So you had them boxed in?" Cray asked.

"We dared not let them out or they would have attacked us. They were a hundred yards from Milk Creek. Every time one tried to go to the creek for water, we shot him. Colorow said we could keep them from hurting us if they were not allowed to drink from the creek."

"So it worked out," Adams said. "What of the burned wagons?"

Jack smiled at this question, barely restraining an outright burst of laughter. "They set fire to their own wagons! We laughed, Colorow and I, until our sides hurt. They thought we were going to attack them, so they burned the wagons to keep us away."

"How long did you keep them at bay?"

"They kept trying to charge, to attack us," Jack said. "Colorow had many schemes, being a great and wise war chief, but I wanted only to prevent them from reaching the agency where they might harm Quinkent and the others of our tribe."

"Mighty kind of you," Cray said. Jack nodded in agreement, not hearing the sarcasm.

"I saved my people by fighting the soldiers there along Milk Creek. The bluecoats tried over and over to break through to kill us, but I kept them pinned down. They would shoot one of my warriors, I would kill two of them!"

"For how many days did you lay siege to the soldiers?" asked Adams.

Jack ignored the question and rattled on about how his green warriors had been blooded in battle, found booty, and even gained great stature for their bravery.

"What about Captain Dodge?" asked Adams.

"The *Maricat'z* with the black-white soldiers? Colorow was clever. We did not fight them, but let them ride to the circle of wagons, thinking they were saving what remained of Thornburg's soldiers. We let them enter, then closed in around them, keeping them from killing us!"

"And General Merritt?"

"My scouts reported that General Merritt was coming with many soldiers. I was ready to fight them, too, to keep them from harming my braves, but Saponowera came then, bringing orders from Chief Ouray that there was to be no more fighting. I did not want to obey, because these new soldiers, the black-white men, and those who had followed Thornburg would pour into the park and harm our women and children, but who am I to ignore a command from our greatest chief?"

"Who indeed," murmured Adams.

"I could have fought General Merritt and all his men, but Chief Ouray said to leave, to return to my home. So I did."

"That explains why General Merritt reached Captain Payne so quickly," Adams said softly to Cray. "Jack and the others pulled back and didn't try to stop his advance."

"To hear the general's story, he fought every step

of the way," Cray said. The general and Chief Jack had a lot in common.

"There is much chaff to be blown away before we find the kernel of this tale," Adams said. He made a few more notes to himself, but Cray could not read what the agent was writing to put into his report.

"What do you know of Meeker's death at the agency? What of Shadrick Price, Frank Dresser, and all the other men there?" asked Cray.

Jack shook his head vigorously. "I know nothing. Quinkent fought Meeker at the White River Agency. I fought Major Thornburg along Milk Creek."

"So you were a brave and cunning warrior, and Colorow mapped out the tactics you used against Major Thornburg?" asked Adams.

"No one is as great a chief as Colorow when it comes to planning," Jack said, puffing out his chest. "And no Ute is as fierce in battle as I am!"

Long into the night Cray Eachin and Charles Adams listened to the stories of daring individual combat, of the menace presented by the renegade soldiers, both white and black, and of Jack's greatness and how he knew nothing of Meeker's death, other than what he had heard secondhand. Adams came away believing Jack innocent—of the Meeker massacre.

PROMISES OF PEACE

October 28, 1879
Powell's Valley

"My head hurts from listening to so many conflicting stories," Charles Adams said. Cray Eachin wasn't sure if the agent was joking or if he meant it. They had stayed in Jack's camp the prior night after hearing the tall tales he spun about his heroism and how great Colorow was at planning the attacks on Major Thornburg's troops. Cray had come away thinking he might have misjudged Colorow's abilities, though a niggling doubt remained about how clever Colorow really was. Jack was proud of the number of soldiers he had killed, but still feared what might happen to him because of it. Praising Colorow might be a way of shifting the blame, should that become necessary in a criminal trial.

"It might be worse now, sir," Cray answered. "Mixing all the Ute chiefs together is a certain way to get the lies flying fast and furious, especially since no one is likely to accept blame for massacring Agent Meeker and the others."

"That particular crime seems well solved," said

Adams. "Chief Douglass held the captives, and they will testify next month when General Hatch begins formal hearings. How Douglass might wiggle out of any guilt for the killings and mutilations is something between him and his god, but it will not be much of a question for the court to answer."

"Jack was straightforward about killing Major Thornburg, too," Cray said. "He should swing for that."

"I'm not so sure that's in the cards," Adams said thoughtfully. "Politics will rear its ugly head before the dust settles, I fear. We will bring many of the guilty to justice, but not all."

"But he admitted that he killed Thornburg! You heard his story, and it is entirely twisted around! Captain Payne reported that—"

"Ah, yes, Captain Payne. He won a medal for his bravery under fire. He might inherit Major Thornburg's command also, but his sworn statements concerning the assault and subsequent siege are not likely to be well received by the Ute."

"Of course not, since it damns them," Cray said, getting confused. Adams spoke in riddles. Jack had confessed to killing the major and leading the Ute who had killed so many others of his command. Jack had held down what remained of Thornburg's command, and Captain Dodge's, and had probably attacked Gordon's wagon train and killed the freighter and all his drivers. General Merritt would testify that George Gordon's wagon train had been ambushed by the time he found it. Who else but Jack—or Colorow—could have done that? It was absurd to believe Jack when he suggested that Merritt might have done it to steal the civilians' clothing.

"You translate, son, and let me worry about how

this will look before a military tribunal. Ah, there's General Merritt."

Adams waved to the general, coming from his tent. Cray looked around the valley and saw the places where Meeker had begun the tilling, only to abandon the area in favor of better irrigated land to the south in Middle Park. Some of the plowed fields were already overgrown with weeds as they struggled to return to their natural state. For Cray's money, the valley looked better without the farms.

Meeker had done so much to provoke the Ute, yet he'd had their best interests, as he saw them, at heart. Cray felt a pang of pity for the dead agent, but no sympathy.

"General Merritt, how good to see you again," said Adams. "I hope you don't mind that this is turning into a small powwow. Jack will be here soon, and he said he would send a messenger to fetch Chief Douglass."

"Hello, Charles," Wesley Merritt said in greeting. He shook hands warmly with the agent and looked over his shoulder in the direction of a recently erected tepee. "I got wind of the meeting when Saponowera showed up this morning. He seems to have his ear to the ground when it comes to anything having to do with Jack or Douglass."

"He's Ouray's best negotiator," said Adams. "I'm surprised Ouray himself did not come since we will decide on charges soon. He would want to head off any big confrontation in court since he is such a news-savvy Indian."

"He has his supporters in Denver as well as in Washington," General Merritt said obliquely. "I'm sure Saponowera will do well to present Ouray's case."

"Should we gather in your tent or outside? It is

a chilly day and looks like rain." Adams peered at the heavy clouds slipping down the western slope of the Rockies and into the valley.

"It won't rain or snow for a spell," Cray said. "You're going to have a powerful lot more Ute here than just Jack, Douglass, and Saponowera."

"How's that?" asked Adams. Then his eyebrows rose when Cray pointed to columns of riders making their way up the floor of the valley toward the cantonment.

"How many chiefs are there?" asked General Merritt, astonished at the number of Indians coming to his bivouac. "If each group has only one, that'd be a dozen or more. I have plenty of soldiers to stand guard, but if we have to fight them all, it'll get mighty bloody mighty fast."

"That won't be necessary," Cray said hurriedly. "Ouray is guiding them all."

"But why so many?" asked Adams.

"Being a chief doesn't mean too much," said Cray. "Every family group has one. The only one they all listen to, both Northern and Southern Ute along with the Tabeguache, is Chief Ouray. He doesn't want to slight any of them by denying their chiefs the right to sit in on this conference."

"Do we have to treat them all like kings?" General Merritt snorted in disgust at the idea. "I have better things to do than listen to hundreds of so-called chiefs all deny they knew anything about the Meeker Massacre or what happened to Major Thornburg."

"You will listen, if it means you don't have to fight them all," Adams said sharply. "The idea is to have them let off steam as well as find a way of fixing blame for what has happened." Adams rubbed his well-fleshed buttocks and grunted. "I don't look forward to sitting on the ground for however long this will take."

He glared at the general, defying him to argue with the path he had chosen to deal with the Ute and their legion of chiefs.

"We can spread out a horse blanket for you," Cray suggested. "That'll be softer."

"I'd prefer a chair inside a tent to sitting on the cold ground when it might rain or snow at any time," Adams said. "My old bones are still creaking from sitting all night in Jack's tepee, but if the number of chiefs requires it, we will gather outside." He paused long enough to be sure Wesley Merritt had nothing to add, then pulled up his collar against an increasingly brisk wind blowing off the mountain slopes.

"Could your men start a fire, sir?" asked Cray. "That would go a ways toward giving Mr. Adams a spot of relief."

"Lieutenant!" barked the general. "See to it right away. Bonfire, and a chair for Mr. Adams."

"Wait," Adams said. "As much as it will pain me, I can sit with the Ute on the ground. I don't want to seem above them, not yet. I don't want to get off on a bad footing with them."

"Let them get used to it," General Merritt said sharply. "They slaughtered good, decent soldiers. I intend to see that they pay for their crimes."

"There, there, General," Adams said. "You'll have your day in court, I am sure. Right now, all I need from you is your presence to give backing to my words."

"Whatever you want, Charles," said General Merritt. "If you need me to take some of them out and execute them, I'll gladly do that also. By God, I'll do it myself with my own pistol!"

Adams laughed, but Cray did not hear the usual humor in the man's laughter. Everyone knew how strongly Wesley Merritt had been affected by the sight of the Fifth Cavalry survivors when he had rescued Payne's command.

"*Maiquas,*" Adams said, greeting Ouray's representative, having learned a few Ute words. "I am pleased to see that so many powerful chiefs have come to talk."

Saponowera said nothing, but Jack spoke up right away.

"I have spoken to you all night."

"You have, and a fascinating account it was, too," Adams said, placating the volatile chief. "Is that Chief Douglass I see coming up the trail? Yes, it is. Please, Mr. Eachin, invite him to join us. Is there anyone with a pipe? I am sure General Merritt has tobacco to share with our friends."

Merritt grumbled as he went to find tobacco for the pipes appearing as if by magic from a half dozen Ute pouches. It took the better part of an hour before the bonfire blazed, crackling and snapping and sending sparks skyward, and the Ute had settled down around it enough to smoke and listen and talk.

True to his word, General Merritt brought a chair for Adams after a few hours, and the Ute were more inclined to talk rather than bristle. The Indian Agent gratefully sat in it, elevating him above the others. Cray sat close-by to translate for him—and to get a kink in his neck from looking up. He wondered what the Ute thought about this since they, too, had to look up to Adams.

"Great Chiefs, no one wants a war," Adams said slowly as he carefully chose his words. A murmur of agreement went around the circle. "There have been mistakes made and some valiant warriors have died. But there have also been those who died who did not deserve it. Father Meeker harmed no one. Shadrick Price and Frank Dresser and the others all worked for the agency, tilling the fields and doing as they were told. They harmed no one."

"They stole my pastures!" cried Chief Johnson. "Meeker promised me land, then took it to cut the earth to grow his weeds!"

"I am aware of the circumstances surrounding your loss of land, Chief Johnson," Adams said. "Mr. Meeker was not as diplomatic as he should have been in regard to your land. However, nothing he did merited death and mutilation."

The arguments why the Ute had done what they'd done to Meeker and the others at the White River Agency went around the bonfire, but Adams kept them returning to how brutally Meeker had been killed.

"Does any here want to fight the *Maricat'z* soldiers?" asked Saponowera when it came his turn to speak. "Ouray does not. I do not. They are like drops of water flowing down from the tall mountains. One dries up under the sun and two more follow. We can never stem the trickle. When it becomes a flood, it will drown us all in war we can never win. Ouray wants peace."

"There will be peace, Chief Saponowera," Adams assured him. "Washington knows the Ute are a peaceful, peaceable tribe and that this is an unfortunate accident caused by a handful of your people."

Cray sputtered as he translated. What had happened was no accident!

Adams glared at him and continued buttering up the assembled chiefs.

"There will be more soldiers than those bivouacked here now," Adams said.

"No!" cried Douglass. "No more soldiers."

"They must keep the peace, unless all gathered here will agree to a new treaty. The hostages have been freed. What Washington must guarantee now is that there will be no more rebellion, no reprisals, no more killing of innocents."

Cray listened to the chiefs argue in their roundabout fashion, but all agreed that they did not want General Merritt and his bluecoats camping on their land permanently. It only remained for the Ute to agree to whatever terms were necessary for the Army to withdraw and let them live in peace on their own land again.

Charles Adams eventually persuaded the chiefs to agree to a special commission that would settle all matters.

TESTIMONY

November 12, 1879
Los Pinos Agency

"General Hatch looks upset," Cray Eachin observed.

"He has sent so many telegrams to Washington that the wires have melted," Charles Adams said with no enthusiasm. "It's an old chestnut to be tossed around with him. He thinks the Department of the Interior comes up with pointless projects that blow up in their faces; then the Army has to come in and clean up afterward. He doesn't want any such occurrence again."

"That happened this time," Cray said. "It got bloody fast after Meeker took away Ute pasturelands. Chief Johnson is a hothead and Meeker ought to have known he would never suffer the loss quietly."

"That's why the general wants the Indians put under the Department of War where he can deal with them directly. There are many in Washington who favor this."

"The Army wouldn't be needed if Meeker hadn't

tried to force the Ute into being farmers," Cray said.

"He was overly enthusiastic, true," Adams said, "but Mr. Meeker did what was asked of him. His methods might be in question, but his orders are not."

"Washington wants the Ute turned into farmers and their horses taken away?" Cray's eyebrows arched at this. He had considered all the arguments, and somewhat reluctantly had decided Johnson and the others were right. To strip the Indians of their horses was a death sentence. A slow one perhaps, but certainly a death coup for their way of life. They had once roamed out onto the Great Plains and hunted buffalo, fought the Sioux, and roved throughout Colorado. Without horses, this far-ranging would have been impossible.

"There's Chief Ouray," Adams said, changing the subject. "I must talk with him before the hearings."

"Are these just hearings to gather facts or is it a trial?" Cray asked. "If you want me to translate, I need to know."

"Just translate the best you can, son," Adams said, again not answering. He bustled over to speak briefly with Ouray after the chief had climbed down from his buggy with its beautifully matched team.

Cray saw the other Ute chiefs riding up. Johnson was the first to arrive, but Douglass came soon after, decked out in fine white man's clothing. In a way, Cray was surprised to see Douglass appear. He thought the chief would have hightailed it for the high mountains where he could hide out. Instead, Douglass seemed in his element, talking with the others and seeking out what attention he could from the handful of reporters present.

"Are you Eachin?" asked a stiff-backed, smallish lieutenant with a big, bushy mustache and dark skin that tended toward an unhealthy grayish tone. "My name's Valois, and I will be recorder and legal advisor for the hearing."

"I suppose I'll be translating as much as I can," Cray said, thrusting out his hand. The lieutenant stared at it and shook it tentatively, as if Cray had been gutting a deer and had not cleaned off his fingers. "Yep, I'm Cray Eachin. I was married to one of *them.*"

"We must begin right away," Valois said, his distaste for working with a Ute sympathizer obvious. "The general is anxious to be done with this sordid affair."

"He must not have much experience dealing with the Ute if he thinks it'll be over quick," Cray said, trying to lighten the tone a mite. When he saw that Valois did not smile, he hastily added, "The Indians move in their own time, in their own way."

"Truth will be told and it will proceed according to the general's timepiece," Valois said brusquely, pushing past Cray to get into the agency headquarters.

Cray followed and looked around. Los Pinos was older and better established than the White River Agency ever had been—or likely would be. A dozen rooms opened off halls in either direction from the main room, where General Hatch already sat behind at a short table, fingers drumming restlessly on the wood top. A few chairs along either wall to the sides provided space for observers, but a large open area remained in front of the table.

"Lieutenant Valois, bring this session to order," barked General Hatch. "I want the proceedings to be as succinct as possible. No drawn-out statements will be permitted as this is only a fact-finding session. Do I make myself clear?"

"Yes, sir," the lieutenant said. Valois took a deep breath and called the hearing to order in a stentorian voice that rattled the windows and carried outside to where the Ute chiefs still palavered. The Ute took no heed of the small lieutenant's summons.

Cray settled in alongside Charles Adams, who seemed irked that his own talk with Ouray had been interrupted.

"Gentlemen," General Hatch said loudly. "We are here to establish the facts in certain matters, not the least of which are the death of Major Thornburg and Agent Meeker, and the abduction of three women and two children following those deaths."

Ouray stepped forward from his post beside Adams and stood before the general like a silent force of nature. Ouray had dressed in a black broadcloth coat with a black string tie. A silver ornament had been woven into a long dark braid of hair and dropped across his chest, where it bobbed as he moved. For several seconds, Ouray said nothing as he waited for the general to give him the go-ahead. General Hatch seemed taken aback at Ouray's opening move, without being summoned by name to testify.

"Yes?" General Hatch blinked, unsure what to do. He certainly recognized Ouray, but had no idea what to do with the chief since his move violated the rules of order.

"I am Ouray, chief of the Ute. Long ago I went

to Washington and there I spoke with your great chief because I learned the *Maricat'z* tongue as a young boy. I told him I was not chief of all Ute but only a chief, that no one could be chief of all Ute. He took me to a window in his wonderful big white house and told me to look out.

"I saw tents so close together that there was no room to walk between them. In each tent lived five men. This was the finest Army ever assembled, your great chief told me, the biggest and strongest ever to march across the country, and if he said I was to be chief of all my people, then I would be. The power of all those soldiers would be as my power, if I urged my people to live in peace."

Ouray paused and let the implication soak in. He was chief of all the Ute because the Army of the United States backed him.

"Get on with it, Chief Ouray," grumbled Hatch. "Your authority is not and never has been questioned by anyone present at this hearing. We have witnesses to call. Unless you get to the point, I must rule you out of order."

Ouray went on, as if he had not heard the general.

"I returned from Washington with that promise and many more. I brought money with me to help my people. Indian Agents came to dispense gifts of blankets and food. Houses were built for many of us. We owe much to the generosity of the great chief in Washington, but I no longer owe my position as chief among Ute chiefs to him.

"I have the backing of many powerful *Nunt'z* to enforce my will. And it is my will that we shall decide what is to be done about the attacks on Major Thornburg and Nathan Meeker."

"Well, I am glad that's out of the way," General

Hatch said, his fingers impatiently playing an unseen piano along the edge of the table. "Who are you calling first to testify?"

"Two are here," Ouray said.

"What's that? Only two? I thought you called all the responsible chiefs here."

"Perhaps they are on their way, General," suggested Adams, getting to his feet. "At any rate, Douglass and Johnson are outside."

"That's Chief Douglass?" asked Hatch, indicating the chief just outside the window.

"Yes, I pointed him out to you this morning," Adams said testily. "We might have time for him to finish his testimony today if we begin now."

"I should hope to hear from more Ute than Chief Douglass today," General Hatch said, glaring at Adams, as if the agent tried to undermine his authority. Hatch seemed not to notice that Ouray had already stolen away much of his thunder and established a chain of command through the Ute chiefs.

Cray sidled closer to Adams and whispered, "How much do you want me to translate? Chief Ouray will likely give a good translation for Lieutenant Valois. His English is a lot better than my Ute."

"Alert me if anything Ouray says varies widely from the testimony itself," Adams said. Cray nodded and stepped back to stand beside the chair Adams had staked out as his exclusive property before the hearing began.

"Quinkent!" called Ouray.

Chief Douglass came in, looking as if he led a fine parade. He looked around as he strutted forward, then stopped in front of General Hatch and struck a pose like the orator who was his namesake.

"Tell us—" began Ouray.

"A moment," interrupted General Hatch. "This man is not sworn to tell the truth."

"Sworn?" Ouray looked perplexed.

"An oath is required," Lieutenant Valois said. "He must swear that he will not lie."

Ouray thought for a moment, then said, "There is an oath Quinkent has taken that will do for this hearing."

Quinkent reached up and took a feather from his braided hair. Cray whispered to Adams, "That's a feather dedicated to his god, Sunawiv. It's got his name on it so he can be identified when he goes to the Happy Hunting Ground. If he swears on that feather, it's the same as using a Bible."

Adams caught General Hatch's eye and nodded, to indicate this was acceptable.

Quinkent rattled off a long speech in his own tongue, which Ouray started to translate, then paused.

"There is no direct translation for some, but Quinkent—Chief Douglass—has affirmed there is only one spirit governing heaven and earth, that Sunawiv watches both earth and heaven and guides Quinkent to tell only the truth."

"That's not it," Cray said, "but I can't get any closer. There're words being used I don't know or can't translate."

"Thank you, son," Adams said, motioning Cray to silence.

Quinkent struck his pose again, one hand gripping his left lapel and his right waving about in the air, and launched into a long recitation, most of which Cray had already translated for Adams during earlier meetings. Ouray reported easily and accurately on everything Douglass said.

"He's getting to the part about the threats Meeker made," Cray whispered. Adams perked up. He had been drifting off, lost in his own thoughts while Douglass repeated what they already knew.

"Chief Quinkent says that Agent Meeker promised blankets and food, but delivered only intimidation. Meeker said he would bring in soldiers to tie up anyone who did not work and others would be put in shackles and used as slaves."

"Poppycock," muttered General Hatch.

"That's a good translation, sir," Cray said suddenly. He subsided under the general's cold glare.

"Meeker wrote letters filled with lies about Quinkent," Ouray continued, "and told newspapers how bad Quinkent was. Meeker was going to use the soldiers to put Quinkent in chains and then kill him."

"Mr. Meeker might have been a bit zealous for his position as agent, but I cannot imagine he would ever say such a thing, even as a goad to get someone working," said the general.

"He's only telling you what Douglass said, sir," Cray declared. He refused to be cowed by General Hatch. From the corner of his eye, Cray saw that Valois took down everything being said, including the challenges to General Hatch's authority in running the meeting. The general realized his superiors would scrutinize the minutes and that he had to appear as if he was in control of the hearing.

"I see. Continue." Hatch nodded brusquely, as if he had requested Cray's comment and was pleased to receive it.

Quinkent dropped his pose, turned his back to the general, and sat on the floor in front of the table.

"What's wrong with him?" demanded Hatch. "I have a few questions to ask."

"He's only responding the way he would in council, sir," explained Cray, refusing to be cowed by the general's choler. "He said his piece. Now he expects the council members to have their say and discuss what he's testified."

"That is so, General," said Ouray. "If you wish to ask questions, I will ask that Quinkent answer." The chief spoke at length with Douglass, getting him back to stand in front of General Hatch at the table. The general took out a cigar, chopped the tip with a small knife, and rolled it about between his palms, then lit a match and began puffing on the cigar until it billowed choking blue fumes into the closed room.

"Ask him if he participated in the massacre," Hatch finally said.

Chief Ouray frowned, not quite understanding what was meant.

"General Hatch wants to know if Douglass had any part in killing those at the White River Agency," Adams supplied.

Ouray translated, and Douglass quickly replied in English, "I know nothing about this."

"Does Chief Douglass know who did massacre Meeker and the others?" asked General Hatch.

"I saw the white women go to the milking shed after many shots. I went to my tepee. A young brave had a wounded foot. I tended it, although Canavish is our medicine man and should have been called."

"Did you have any part in planning the attack?" asked Hatch.

"No." Douglass's response in English was short and abrupt. Douglass fell silent, pursed his lips, then spoke several minutes more in his own tongue.

"He has nothing more to say," Ouray translated.

"Then we shall adjourn for the day," Hatch said,

pulling out a watch and studying its open face carefully. He snapped shut the case and tucked it back into a pocket, rapped sharply on the table, and said, "Dismissed until nine A.M. tomorrow morning."

"This might be for the best," Adams said to Cray. "I need to talk to Ouray."

Before Adams could approach the Ute chief, General Hatch marched out from behind the table and put his arm around Adams's shoulders, as if he intended to give him a bear hug.

"Time for a talk, sir. We can have dinner while we discuss this matter at greater length. There's much I need to say." Cigar clamped between his teeth and puffing like a steam engine, Hatch directed Adams away from the chief and out the door, crossing the spacious yard to the agency housing.

"Chief Ouray, is there anything I can do for you?" asked Cray, using the best *Nunt'z* he could muster. Ouray had impressed him with his solemn, businesslike conduct as much as General Hatch had made him a little embarrassed to be a *Maricat'z*.

"I must find the quarters assigned to me during my stay," Ouray said. "After I tend my team."

"I'd be happy to do that for you, Chief."

Ouray nodded once, then walked off with a slow, stately gait, passing Douglass and Johnson, who chattered like magpies just outside the agency headquarters building. Cray led Ouray's team to the corral and let them loose, then went to the barn to get curry brushes.

He stopped in his tracks when he saw Towa inside the barn. His heart skipped a beat and he started to call out to her, but a short, stocky Ute brave rose from one of the stalls, naked except for the straw sticking to his body.

Cray fought for words, but he felt as if his tongue had been stung by a scorpion. His throat was paralyzed. It was obvious what Towa and the brave had been doing. He backed off and went to water Ouray's horses and see that they had enough grain to keep them happy, knowing this would give Towa and her brave time to leave.

It got mighty cold long before the bright autumn sun sank behind the western mountains.

DECISIONS

November 13, 1879
Los Pinos Agency

"I call this hearing to order." General Hatch rapped smartly on the table with his knuckles. The booming sound filled the room and echoed outside to where the Ute stood around talking as they had the day before.

As before, Cray Eachin sat beside Adams, but today his mind was a thousand miles away from the proceedings. He hardly heard Lieutenant Valois call Johnson to testify, but he did perk up when he noticed how the Indian had chopped off his hair. When he had seen Johnson earlier, the chief had worn a big floppy hat that hid his head.

"Sir, do you see that?" Cray whispered to Charles Adams. "Johnson's hair being lopped off like that means he lost a son in battle."

"So it seems," Adams said. "This might be more interesting testimony than I had anticipated."

Ouray again translated as Johnson—Canavish—told how Meeker had taken his land and plowed it, then moved the entire agency south to Middle Park, where Johnson had built a new house, only to have it taken from him again so the agent could plow the ground to put in a field for crops.

"This is extraordinary," General Hatch said. "Do you believe Agent Meeker had any personal hatred for you, Chief Johnson?"

The translation went on for some time. Cray tried to follow what Ouray was saying, but could not. He got the feeling that Ouray was asking far more than Hatch had wanted to hear answered. Finally, Ouray launched into the translation of Johnson's reply.

"Chief Canavish told the plowman to stop, but he said he could not. Canavish went to his house where Agent Meeker stood. Again Canavish protested, but Meeker told him he would go to the calaboose if he protested, that he had always found him to be troublesome and a bother."

"What did Johnson say then?" asked Hatch, interested more than he had been the prior day.

"Canavish said he would ask for a new agent. He took Meeker by the arm and pulled him away. Canavish wanted only to go back to his house after settling this matter."

"Where was Chief Johnson during the massacre?" asked Hatch.

Ouray spoke with Johnson a full minute, then said, "He was in his camp."

"How far was that from the agency?"

"He would have to travel two full days, if he took his lodges. One day if he did not."

"In what direction from the agency?"

"South."

"Ask him if knows anyone who took part in the massacre."

Ouray asked Johnson what General Hatch wanted to know, then answered succinctly, "He does not."

"Did he have any sons who took part?" asked Hatch. The general had been at Fort Lewis long enough to know Ute tradition, and could not help but notice how Johnson's hair had been hacked off.

"No."

"Does he know the names of any Indians who fought with the soldiers?" asked the general.

"No."

General Hatch's lips thinned to a line.

"Enough of this." Hatch dismissed Johnson with a wave of his hand. Johnson sat on the floor in front of the table. "Who is next?"

"Does it matter, General?" asked Adams, standing. "I know these men have not told the truth. I have smoked pipes with them and heard other stories. In spite of the oath they have sworn to their god, they are not being truthful."

"No Ute will speak against another of his tribe," Ouray said. "The laws of your country say you cannot be forced to testify against yourself."

"I want the truth!" barked Hatch. "Isn't there anyone who will tell me the truth behind these murders?"

"Sir," said Lieutenant Valois in his shrill voice. "Chief Ouray is right. No Indian can be compelled to testify against himself. They have the same rights as a white man."

"Am I wrong, or did they take an oath to their god Sunawiv to tell the truth?" asked Hatch. He glared at Ouray, demanding an answer from the chief.

"He's caught between our justice and that of his own people," Adams said to Cray. "No Ute could testify truthfully and live long."

"General Hatch," Ouray said slowly, "Quinkent

and Canavish made that oath because you ordered them to."

"Very well," Hatch said. He shuffled through a stack of papers, then pulled out a thick wad. "Since we are not going to find the truth among these . . . chiefs, I have here a deposition recently taken in Greeley, Colorado, from the three women who were abducted."

"I protest!" cried Ouray.

"Sir?" Hatch's eyes went wide. "On what ground? These statements were given and sworn to before a notary public."

"The oath of a woman is worthless among Ute." Ouray backed down slightly when he added, "I will reserve judgment on the testimony until it is read to me."

"Very well, Chief," said Hatch. He shoved the papers across the table to Lieutenant Valois. "Read these depositions to the members of this hearing, Lieutenant."

"First is the testimony of Mrs. Price, the wife of a carpenter on the reservation. A complete attestation is part of the record, but certain parts are pertinent," Valois said. "Mrs. Price swears she was outraged by an unnamed Uncompahgre Ute as well as Johnson. No one struck her or otherwise injured her, but Johnson and an old Ute told her they might let Mrs. Meeker go because she was so old, but that they would keep Miss Meeker and the children as slaves."

Cray watched the Ute seated on the floor in front of the table as Valois read the testimony. He knew many of them understood English well enough to know what was being entered as evidence against them, but their expressions remained impassive throughout.

Further damning depositions from Arvella Meeker and her daughter Josephine were read. Cray closed his eyes and shuddered as Valois read how Mrs. Meeker had been violated by Douglass, his wives and children taunting her and threatening her with violence afterward. The outrage perpetrated on Josephine Meeker was similar in scope to that endured by her mother and Mrs. Price.

"What is Hatch going to do?" asked Cray. "He knows Johnson and Douglass lied, and now he has the women's statements entered into the official record. It's come down to a matter of who's telling the truth, and I don't think anyone can believe Johnson or Douglass is the least bit truthful."

"I don't know what he will do," said Adams. "He is not going to please anyone however he rules, I fear. I hope it does not ignite new fighting if it goes dramatically against Douglass and Johnson. The Ute are fierce warriors when aroused. The deaths of Major Thornburg and so many of his men show that."

"They can be underhanded, too," said Cray. "They didn't give Meeker or anyone at the agency a chance to fight back. They ambushed the lot of them."

"Shhh," said Adams. "I think the general is going to issue a verdict."

"I have heard the evidence and weighed it carefully," General Hatch said. "I must declare truth to be the first victim at this hearing. Chief Ouray, will you consent to accompany the members of this commission to Rawlins and hear the testimony of Captain Payne, Joseph Rankin, and other soldiers present at Milk Creek?"

"No."

General Hatch reared back as if Ouray had struck him.

"I will not travel anywhere but Washington."

"So you will allow Washington to settle this matter?" General Hatch looked relieved. Ouray was making it easy for the general, taking it from his hands and dropping the hot potato into the laps of the politicians. "How many chiefs do you want to go with you?"

"Eight," Ouray said.

"Excellent, sir. I will draft a message to Secretary Schurz for your approval stating that you and a number of principal chiefs, not to exceed ten, will give testimony there. I shall continue gathering evidence here to expedite matters. Is that satisfactory?"

"It is," Ouray said.

"Then I call Chief Colorow of the Nupartka Ute as the next witness."

Colorow entered the room, looking solemn and in complete possession of his emotions. He stood stolidly before the general, but did not take the oath, this having been established as meaningless to the Indians.

"Chief Colorow, what can you tell me of Jack?"

"Nicaagat," Ouray translated as Colorow spoke, "did not live at the White River Agency. Agent Meeker refused him food and blankets and did all he could to chase him away."

"Did you ever witness any of this dissension?" asked the general.

"Nicaagat spoke often of the trouble there, but Colorow lives to the north of the agency and knows nothing of it himself," translated Ouray. "The women in Nicaagat's band were ashamed to ask Meeker for rations because he would deny them and humiliate them, calling them lazy and no-accounts."

"Tell us about the fight with Major Thornburg," General Merritt requested. He sat back and watched as Colorow began a long, impassioned description of the fight.

"Colorow says he and Nicaagat talked to the major, only to have him attack them when they were not expecting it. They were taken by surprise by his treachery, but fought bravely. With many warriors following him, Colorow positioned them in such a way to prevent the major from effectively attacking again."

"He admits planning the attack on Major Thornburg's troopers?"

"Yes," said Ouray. "He is proud of the fight and his part in it. Nicaagat fought well against the soldiers also. After the first fight, they were afraid to leave because the soldiers might follow and kill them. However, they did immediately obey a message I sent with Saponowera ordering them to stop fighting when I learned what had happened at the White River Agency." Ouray looked pleased that Colorow and Jack had obeyed so swiftly. Cray knew it was the best thing the chiefs could have done for their own survival since Merritt's column had moved in quickly and would have made short work of even three hundred warriors.

"I wish Major Thornburg were here to give his side of the skirmish," mused the general. "At least we would hear some truth. Thank you, Chief Colorow."

Colorow pulled his blanket around his broad shoulders and walked slowly from the room. Cray watched him go, marveling at the way he had carried himself and testified like some elder statesman. Cray was certain the battle at Milk Creek had not happened the way Colorow described, but from a slightly different perspective, he could see Colorow's point.

For the rest of the day testimony was given until, when the sunlight slanted bloodred through the far window in the agency headquarters, Hatch glanced at his watch and said, "We have heard enough to come to some preliminary conclusions. The hour is late, but we shall wrap this up quickly."

Hatch shuffled the stack of papers in front of him, then took one from Lieutenant Valois. He glanced at it, smiled slightly, and handed the paper to Charles Adams.

"These twelve men are to be charged in the matter of the massacre and subsequent ravishment of Mrs. Nathan Meeker, her daughter Josephine, and Mrs. Shadrick Price. Please read the list, Mr. Adams."

"First: Chief Douglass. Next: Johnson. Next: Pasone, who took Miss Meeker for his *piwán*."

Cray watched the chiefs sitting on the floor as their names were read. Douglass looked startled, but Johnson acted as if he had heard nothing but gentle rain beating softly against the sides of his tepee. The remainder of those cited were old men who had remained at the agency, choosing neither to ride with Douglass nor go north to fight with Jack's band. Cray thought they were more victims of circumstance than anything else, but knew proving they had taken part in killing Meeker and the rest of the agency employees was going to be almost impossible. No Ute would testify against another, and only the Ute had survived, other than the women and children, who were not eyewitnesses to the worst of the killing.

"We now go on to—"

"A moment, General Hatch," said Chief Ouray. "I held my tongue before. Now I must speak. You say the Ute Tribe is a nation. That is always said when you want land from us. The law of our nation does not accept the testimony of women."

"Lieutenant?" The general looked to his legal advisor for assistance.

"The Ute are wards of the United States," Valois said in his high-pitched voice. "If they are, as Chief Ouray says, a separate nation, they must be considered as a conquered nation."

This made Cray sit straighter.

"If we are a conquered nation," asked Ouray, "who conquered us?" When no one answered Ouray, he went on. "You know the law of your nation, Lieutenant, and I know the law of mine."

"Well, yes," said General Hatch, uncomfortable at the legal problems he was creating. "I think it is safe to say that the military action taken by Jack and Colorow might have been justified. We are in no position to verify their stories, Major Thornburg having been killed. Therefore, the only matter remaining to be resolved by this commission is the matter of the deaths of Nathan Meeker and his employees. Do you agree, Chief Ouray?"

Ouray nodded agreement.

"This session is adjourned for the day," barked Hatch.

"He's swapping one crime for the other," Cray said to Adams, outraged the officer would do such a thing. "General Hatch is saying he will forget the charges that Jack attacked and killed those soldiers from ambush if Ouray allows the trial to go forward against Douglass, Johnson, and the other ten."

"He's a better diplomat than I thought," Adams said tiredly.

"Jack and Colorow will get off scot-free this way!"

"Yes, they will," said Charles Adams, standing.

"But—" Cray sputtered.

"Keeping the peace is our highest calling. If some must die so that the majority can live without protracted conflict, so be it." Adams walked out, but Cray couldn't help noticing how he looked as if he had lost rather than won.

GUILTY

January 15, 1880
Los Pinos Agency

Cray Eachin sat cross-legged on the floor, smoking a pipe and talking with a young brave from Colorow's band. For months, Cray had wanted to know if his first impression of Colorow was accurate, and he still was not sure. Colorow made himself out as a mighty warrior, a clever general moving troops in the field against overwhelming odds—and triumphing—but Cray saw him only as a blowhard whose only purpose in life was to cadge food from as many people as possible. For the months since the Hatch Commission had adjourned, Cray had worked informally at the Los Pinos Agency, taking on chores that Charles Adams delegated and acting as translator when bilingual Ute were not free for the job. The biggest complaint reaching him concerned Colorow and the way he extorted food from the white settlers.

"He is courageous," the brave said.

"Have you seen him in battle? Has he ever killed anyone while you watched?"

The Indian shook his head.

"What about scalps? Does Colorow brag about the scalps he has taken in battle?"

"No," the brave said. "He measures his worth by the number of horses he has."

"Does Colorow have many?"

"He gives them to his people," the brave said proudly. "He gets food for us and gives us many rifles and horses. He makes himself poor so his people can be rich."

"Chief Colorow does not look as if he's missed many meals," Cray said, smiling. "Does he have many wives?"

"Two."

"Colorow has been annoying settlers around Hayden and Hot Sulphur Springs asking for food. He simply barges into a settler's house, invites himself to dinner, and the settlers are afraid to shoo him out. He's stayed to eat more than one family out of house and home for a week or longer."

The brave shrugged. It made no difference to him whether Colorow ate well or not, as long as his chief took care of his tribe properly. In the brave's mind, Colorow did that well.

Cray heaved a sigh, passed the pipe back to the young warrior, and let his mind wander. Colorow might be a clever tactician, but he was no fighter. He let firebrands like Jack risk their necks in battle, but Major Thornburg's ambush and killing had been well planned. For that, Cray thought Colorow and Jack should have been brought to justice.

He stood and walked to the window, looked out on the fresh fall of snow, and shivered. Memories of an earlier winter with Towa crowded back. Since he had seen her with the brave in the agency barn, he had not heard from her. Word filtered down that she had gone to live with a Northern Ute band, but Cray had never heard the name of the brave she had chosen as her new husband. Cray wondered if his fascination with Colorow centered on the corpulent chief's begging abilities and possible role in slaughtering a hundred soldiers, or if he only wanted to find where Towa had gone. Colorow was a chief of a small group of Nupartka Ute to the north. Towa was there.

Cray held back asking the brave sitting behind him in the center of the room about Towa. The chances were good he did not know Towa, or if he did, Cray was not certain what he would ask. Was she happy? Would that make him any less miserable? Cray knew he would have heard if Towa had died. This winter was a cold one, but not as fierce as the one they had spent together at his mine.

He rubbed his hands against his pants. He had sold the mine for a tidy sum that allowed him to take poorly paying part-time but important jobs for Charles Adams. Coal was increasingly important to fuel the trains making their way through the parks from north to south, and even over the mountains from Denver. He had never realized the vast fortune in gold or silver he hankered for, but now such wealth seemed less important than the job he did working with the Ute.

"Over the Shining Mountains," he said, but he could not see the Rockies due to the low clouds and the flurries of snow building again to a full-fledged storm.

"I not go over the mountains," the brave said.

"No, nor will I. This land is too beautiful to ever leave." Cray stopped, turned, and stared at the young brave. "What do you mean that you won't go over the mountains?"

"You move us."

"The *Maricat'z?*" he asked.

"Yes. Meeker took the land of Canavish and Quinkent. The rest of the land will be stolen from us also."

"I don't know," Cray said. He had not heard anything about the Ute being relocated. Chief Ouray would argue against such a move, unless it was presented to him in such a fashion that his people would lose everything if he did not agree.

Cray looked back outside and saw a rider making his way along the frozen road. The horse slipped on an icy patch and almost fell before the rider jumped to the ground and walked the rest of the way to the agency headquarters. When the door opened, a gust of cold wind sneaked in, giving Cray a shiver. He wasn't sure if it was the frigid air or the expression on the courier's face that chilled him the most.

"You in charge?" the courier asked, pulling out a leather wallet thick with papers. "Got to deliver these right away."

"I can take them," Cray said. "Most of the bosses are snowed in or somewhere else."

"Like Washington?" asked the courier. "Most of these messages were wired in from there."

Cray signed to accept the telegrams, leafed through them, and saw they were mostly routine, all except one that seemed to leap out at him. He looked up and saw the courier staring at him.

"Why don't you get yourself some coffee over at the mess hall?" Cray said. "You might grab a bite to eat, too." Cray wanted to get rid of the courier without seeming too eager. He had to decide what to do with the flimsy yellow envelope he held in his hands. Curiosity killed the cat, the old saw went.

Cray felt like a fire had been lit in his belly as he stared at the telegram.

"Me go?" asked the brave.

"Show this gentleman to Mrs. Kincaid's kitchen, would you?" asked Cray. The brave jumped to his feet, eager to eat. He was a worthy member of Colorow's band.

"Much obliged. It's colder'n a witch's tit out there."

"Looks like a new storm might turn it even colder," Cray said, running his fingers over the telegram envelope.

When the door closed behind the two, he stared at the envelope, then opened it. He knew this was not for him. For some reason he could not fathom, he had to see what was in the communique.

"I'll be damned," Cray muttered as he read down the page with its terse message from Charles Adams. Ouray and the other principal chiefs had gone to Washington with Johnson, Douglass, and the others charged in the Meeker massacre.

Douglass had pled guilty and been sentenced to a prison term at Fort Leavenworth. Johnson and the others had been exonerated after lengthy Congressional hearings.

Jack, Colorow, Johnson, and all the others responsible for killing over a hundred soldiers and agency workers had received no punishment, and a single man had been assigned the blame for everything. Perhaps it was a proper solution. Cray didn't know. Soldiers expected to fight and die, but the agency employees had deserved more than a verdict dictated more by politics than justice.

They had certainly deserved better than Nathan Meeker and his wild-eyed vision of how to civilize the Ute. But they should not have been slaughtered because of their employer's zealotry.

Cray carefully folded the telegram and replaced it in the envelope. The glue had become so soaked from snow and rain on the way to the agency that the envelope would never be resealed.

That hardly mattered to Cray. The Indian Agent would have to know right away, because Cray read accurately between the lines. Douglass had taken the blame for a great number of crimes, but there would be a huge price for allowing the other Ute to go free. Ouray must have been in sessions with the Secretary of the Interior and other Washington politicians to draft the real cost.

Sending Jack, Colorow, and Johnson to the gallows might have been better for the Ute.

A quirk of the storm parted the clouds and gave Cray a momentary glimpse of the Rockies before hiding them again behind driving white snow. He hoped the Ute throughout western Colorado had also seen the soaring, majestic slopes, because it might be the last time they would look on their holy Shining Mountains.

A NEW TREATY

March 6, 1880
Los Pinos Agency

Cray Eachin stood to one side of the room, watching the reactions of the men in the room. Charles Adams looked as if he had swallowed a rock. General Hatch wasn't any more cheerful because he knew what it meant to both his command and the Ute Nation. For all his bluster and bluntness, Hatch had a true liking for the Ute that now would have to be directed in some other direction. And some of the businessmen from the area, including Otto Mears from Animas City, clustered together, whispering and pointing rudely at the Ute as if they were strange animals to be gawked at in a circus sideshow.

For his part, Chief Ouray was the most dignified in the room. He sat at the same table General Hatch had used during the hearings on the Meeker massacre, but seemed more involved than Hatch ever had. He greeted various Ute chiefs and spoke briefly to the handful of politicians who had come from Washington.

"Gentleman," said General Hatch. "Please come to order. We are here today to read the terms of a treaty between the Ute Nation and the United States of America."

Cray felt a sinking feeling. He had tried to get Adams to tell him the terms, but had been rebuffed, Adams saying the treaty deserved to be revealed to everyone by Ouray. That meant Cray's premonition, when he had seen that Douglass alone was to be sent to Fort Leavenworth, was accurate.

Cray listened with half an ear as one politician after another made his pointless speech. Then Cray perked up when it was Ouray's turn to speak.

"The great chief in Washington has given the *Nunt'z* land on the Unitah Reservation, in northeast Utah. When the Ute sign the treaty, we will leave Colorado and go immediately to these new lands to be ours forever." Ouray fell silent and stared straight ahead.

Cray felt sorry for Ouray, knowing he had been forced into agreeing to the terms of this treaty. Ouray had swapped leniency for most of the perpetrators of the Meeker massacre and the attack on Thornburg for this treaty, one dictated more by businessmen like Otto Mears than by anyone else.

Almost as if he had overheard Cray's thought about him, Mears jumped to his feet.

"Thanks, Chief. This will open up a new era of prosperity for the entire state of Colorado. I plan on building a toll road into Animas City, and several of you have plans that will bring settlers and ranchers to southern Colorado as soon as the former Ute land becomes available for sale."

"Please, Mr. Mears, you are jumping the gun," General Hatch said, obviously uneasy at the way the man was moving in on land that was not yet his. "The treaty must be approved."

"I know, General, I know," Mears said cheerfully. "But with good Indians like Ouray here backing the treaty, how can it fail to be approved by all the Ute?" He grinned as he turned toward the chief. "Everybody, give Chief Ouray a great big standing ovation. He deserves it for being such a good leader of the Ute!"

Cray left, the applause ringing in his ears. He wondered if it sounded like a death knell to Ouray as much as it did to him.

DEATH OF A CHIEF
AND A NATION

August 24, 1880
Los Pinos Agency

"They won't vote, not with Chief Ouray as sick as he is," moaned Otto Mears. The businessman tore his hair as he paced back and forth. Cray Eachin watched, not the least bit sympathetic. Mears cared nothing for Ouray. The old chief had taken ill ten days earlier, and had finally lapsed into a coma. Mears ignored how near death was for the only man able to hold the entire Ute Nation in line, and worried that his expansion throughout the former Ute reservation land was endangered.

If three-quarters of the Ute did not vote to approve the treaty moving them to Unitah, the treaty process had to begin anew. This time, without Ouray's strong hand on the tiller of compromise, the Ute might decide they liked it where they were. Cray almost wished that would happen, not that he wished Ouray any harm. Still, the chief's death might serve a higher purpose if it kept vultures like Mears from stealing the Ute land.

"You cannot do more than you've done," Charles Adams said sarcastically to the conniving businessman. The tone was lost on Mears.

"Nonsense, I must do more. There is a fortune to be made, and it is slipping away because one man is dying. That is unacceptable! The entire region can be properly developed, but only if the treaty is approved posthaste."

Cray started to say something, but he saw Saponowera coming across the yard in front of the agency headquarters. The chief walked slowly, head high and face impassive, but there was a look to him that warned Cray of the bad news.

"Saponowera, welcome," Adams said in greeting. Then he, too, saw the expression on the Ute's face. "Do you bring news of Ouray?"

"He has gone on," Saponowera said.

"Kidney failure," Adams said sadly. "I was afraid of this, but there was nothing that could be done. It's a pity he has been in a coma for so long. He could have shared his wisdom, if he had been capable of it."

"I think he leaves a great legacy, Mr. Adams," said Cray. "The Ute have been peaceable for years, except for the massacre." In spite of the sorrow he felt at a great man's passing, Cray experienced a buoyancy that he had not encountered for some time—not since he was with Towa.

Without Ouray guiding the treaty vote, it was likely to fail. None of the Ute much liked or trusted Mears or the others on the commission appointed by Washington, and Saponowera didn't have the stature to guarantee the needed three-quarters vote, even if he would have tried to do so in memory of Ouray. Saponowera had made no bones about his opposition to the treaty provisions moving the tribe to Unitah, but he knew the deal had been made and he would abide by it—while Ouray was alive.

"He was a great chief," Saponowera said softly, "and he was an even greater friend. I will miss him."

"We all will, we all will," said Adams.

"Are you pushing ahead with the treaty vote?" asked Mears. "I know this isn't the time to inquire of such matters, but you'll want your people to be settled as quickly as possible. It gets mighty cold over there in Utah."

"Mr. Mears," Cray said angrily, "even if they voted today for the treaty, they would not be able to go until spring at the earliest. You cannot expect the entire tribe to move during winter."

"There are a whale of a lot of them to move," Mears agreed. "Three bands of Southern Ute, the Uncompahgre, the Northern Ute. All the more reason to vote now instead of putting it off. Think of all the gifts the great chief in Washington will send when you get settled at Unitah, Saponowera."

"The greatest gift would be the return of my chief," Saponowera said. He turned and left. Cray started after him, but hesitated when he heard Mears muttering to himself.

"What's that?" Cray demanded. "What did you say?"

"I said now that the old chief is gone, I'm going to have to take matters into my own hands."

"How do you intend to do that?" asked Cray. He saw that Adams was also intent on the answer. "You can't force the Ute to vote. With Ouray gone, they might not want to put the treaty to a vote until next year, out of respect."

"There's a time for mourning and a time for action," Mears said, showing his enthusiasm for removing the Ute from their land. "Saponowera doesn't have it in him to be of any help, so I propose to ride a different road."

"What might that be?" Cray asked.

"The treaty has to be submitted by September eleventh," Mears said.

"That is correct. If it is not turned over to the government by then, the process must start over with someone other than Ouray elected to bargain for the Ute," said Adams. "I wish I had been there to help Ouray, but personal matters took me away from Washington immediately after Douglass's sentencing."

"Old Ouray did a good job, if you ask me. The politicians could have dumped him and his tribe over in Oklahoma. Who'd ever want to be stuck there in that hellhole? No, he got prime land up in Utah. I've seen it. Great place to live, great."

"But not as good as Colorado," Cray said acidly. Mears either did not catch his tone or ignored it.

"You got it, sonny boy, you got it. This is the finest land God put anywhere on earth, and I intend for it to be opened up."

"You intend to make a few bucks off it."

"Why not? If the land is up for grabs, why shouldn't I be the one grabbing? I'm not greedy. I want what's best for everyone, I do, even the Ute. I reckon they will make out just fine up on their own land. In Utah."

"They did well on their own land," Cray said, but he knew arguing with Mears was pointless. The man was blinded by the promise of gold as surely

as Cray had been when he had sneaked onto Ute
land to prospect for color. "What do you intend to
do?"

"The Ute are always going around with their
hands stuck out, waiting for 'gifts' to drop into
them. You ever see how rapacious that Nupartka
chief Colorow is? He's more open about his begging than the others, but they are all the same deep
down."

"Blankets? Rifles? Food? What do you propose to
offer them as inducement to give away their birth-
right and land promised by the Treaty of '68?"
asked Adams. He did not try to hide his horrified
expression at such a crass transaction.

What bothered Cray Eachin was not knowing if
he ought to blame Mears, or if any Ute would accept such a paltry offer.

"That's way too much. I don't see why I can't offer,
say, two dollars to every Ute who signs. I'll get three-
quarters and more to sign with no trouble."

By the September 11th deadline, Mears had all
the necessary signatures to ratify the treaty.

EPILOGUE

September 13, 1881
Unitah Reservation, Utah

"Mr. Eachin, whatever you want, you just ask," said the eager young agency clerk. "If you want an interpreter so's you can talk with 'em, we can—"

"That won't be necessary," Cray said. "I can understand them well enough." He smiled just a little. No one on the agency staff spoke the Old Language, and they thought any visiting bureaucrat was unable to also. He wondered who the clerk would have rousted to translate for him if he had asked. Cray wondered if he would know the translator.

"Most speak English pretty good, I reckon," the clerk said thoughtfully. The young man looked at Cray, weighing the possibilities for a visitor to the agency. "What're you here for now?"

"Washington wants a report on how the Ute are settling in, what supplies they might need for the winter, how best to serve them. Things like this."

"Serve them?" The clerk laughed out loud. "Sounds like you want to cook 'em up."

"Nothing like that. I know that their traditional hunting grounds have been denied to them all summer long, and now that they have settled in here, they might need meat or other foodstuffs to see them through the winter."

"Gets mighty cold up here, it does," the clerk said. "I been here eight years, in Utah, that is, and the winters are a whale of a lot worse than back in Ohio."

"Buildings?" Cray asked. "Do the Ute have sufficient quarters?"

"We built what we could. They done the rest. If they needed more, they would have asked, wouldn't they?"

Cray knew that the Ute might not have, thinking that whatever they saw was all that Washington had allowed them under the terms of the treaty they had signed. Mears's two-dollar bribe had not gone far for many of the Ute. It still rankled Cray that the head of the commission, a man named A.B. Meacham, supposedly a knowledgeable, caring soul fresh from dealing with the Modoc in California, had not been more outraged at the blatant attempt—the *successful attempt*—to buy passage of the treaty. Cray had put in a formal complaint, but his lowly status had worked against him. Even when Adams and other senior officials had protested, the commission had decided that Mears's meddling, while unfortunate and inappropriate, had not materially changed the treaty vote.

After all, Chief Ouray had been for it. That he had died and the treaty had been ratified only showed the Ute's love for their deceased leader.

Cray had gone off into the hills for a week after hearing that. Then he had returned and worked with Adams to get a permanent job with the Bureau of Indian Affairs. His position wasn't too lucrative, but he still got some royalty money from the coal mine in the hills above Powell's Valley, which was no longer on Ute land. He was comfortable, and wanted to do what he could to make sure the Ute were also.

"Mind if I look around? There's no need getting a guide for me. I can find my way."

"Well, go on, but you better report right back to the agent when you return. He'll want to know what you found."

"I will," Cray said, knowing what the clerk really meant. The agent wanted to know if trouble brewed over his handling—or mishandling—of funds destined for the Ute themselves. Each tribal member was supposed to receive a yearly stipend as payment for the land in Colorado they had deeded over to the United States. Cray wanted to ask to be sure they were getting the money rather than allowing the agent to collect and spend it for them. He remembered all too well how Nathan Meeker had treated the Ute and the unfortunate result, partly because he'd controlled their purse strings at the White River Agency.

But Cray saw as he rode out on the barren land that rebellion was not likely to happen again. With Douglass in prison, the fire of rebelliousness had gone from the braves remaining. Somehow, the heart and soul of the Ute Nation had died with Ouray.

All day Cray rode and spoke with the Ute he found. Their houses were like those any white man would have. He suspected most had been built by whites for the Ute. Here and there he saw a traditional tepee, but those living inside were newly relocated, mostly from the Uncompahgre band, who were the last to be moved.

Cray would have ridden past yet another cabin

indistinguishable from any of the others, but something made him turn his horse down the narrow path leading to the front door.

"Hello!" he called. *"Maiquas!"* From inside the cabin came small scurrying sounds, as if someone tried to hide and then thought better of it. The door opened a crack.

"How do you do?" Cray said. "I work for the Bureau of Indian Affairs and am out checking to be sure you've got ample supplies to get you through the winter." When he didn't get a reply, he repeated the request in the Old Language.

"Your tongue has improved," Towa said, opening the door. Cray's heart almost exploded in his chest. Then he sucked in a lungful of the cold Utah air and let it out slowly.

"Thanks, I had a good teacher," he said. "Are you, uh, where's your husband? I need to talk to him about the government gifts."

"I have received my blanket and a case of peaches."

"That's all? That won't do. Where's—? Cray let the question hang in the air. He had never found out the name of the brave who had claimed Towa for his *piwán.* He had never had the heart to ask.

"Tsit'z is gone," Towa said. "I threw his moccasins out."

"How's that?"

"I am no longer married to him."

"Oh," Cray said, not sure what to do. "Is Kanneatche here then?"

"My father is dead. He fell from his horse and broke his neck on the road to Unitah."

"I'm sorry," Cray said. "I didn't know."

"Do you still scratch at the earth to find gold?" Towa asked.

"No, I've given that up. The coal in the mine, well, I sold it. Not for anywhere near as much as if it had been gold or silver, but I got a little income from it. After that, I've worked for the Bureau since Ouray died."

"I was there, too, when Ouray died," Towa said.

This surprised Cray. He had not known she had been within a hundred miles.

"That's when I decided to help out however I could," he said. "I wish you'd let me know you were there."

"I was with Tsit'z," Towa said simply. She came from inside and closed the door behind her to hold in the heat. She had never looked lovelier to Cray.

"Oh," was all he could say.

Cray found himself at a loss for words again. He had thought what he felt for Towa was past, but he discovered that it wasn't.

"Do you need to go?" Towa asked.

"I've got to report to the Indian Agent," Cray said.

Towa looked crestfallen.

"Would you like me to come back?" he asked.

"If you want," she said. Towa went into the house, but she paused, turned, and looked at him from inside. A hint of a smile erased some of the sadness on her face. Then the door closed with a click.

Cray sat astride his horse for several minutes, wondering if he should go in. Later. He could write his report on the conditions he had found and get it sent to Washington. Then he could return. He didn't know if there would be anything between him and Towa as there had been before, but he wanted the chance to find out.

"Giddyup," Cray Eachin said, putting his heels into his horse's flanks. He didn't quite gallop back to the agency—not quite.

Western Adventures
From Pinnacle

__Requiem At Dawn
by Sheldon Russell   0-7860-1103-3 $5.99US/$7.99CAN

They called it Fort Supply, the last outpost of the U.S. Army on the boundary of Oklahoma Territory—home to the damned, the disgraced, and the dispirited. Now, Doc McReynolds has been ordered to establish a redoubt at Cimarron Crossing. But while McReynolds leads his company to Deep Hole Creek, a past he'd like to forget dogs his every step.

__Apache Ambush
by Austin Olsen   0-7860-1148-3 $5.99US/$7.99CAN

For a military man it was the farthest you could fall: the command of a troop of Buffalo Soldiers in the Ninth Colored Cavalry Regiment. For Lieutenant William Northey, managing misfits was all that he was good for. Amidst the dying and the valor, a bitter, defeated army man would find a woman to love, soldiers to be proud of, and the warrior that still lived in his heart. . . .
